The Light at Grace Hill

The Light at Grace Hill
THE TUNBRIDGE SERIES

ELLE CHRISTOPHER

VALOR PRESS

This is a work of fiction. Names, characters, places, and incidents are the product of the author's imagination. Any resemblance to actual events, locales, or persons, living or dead, is purely coincidental.

Published by Valor Press

THE LIGHT AT GRACE HILL. Copyright © 2025 by Elle Christopher.

All rights reserved.

www.ellechristopher.com

Designed by Elle Christopher

Identifiers: LCCN 2025912045 | ISBN 9781966386117 (hardcover)

ISBN 9781966386100 (paperback) | ISBN 9781966386131 (ebook)

No part of this book may be reproduced in any form or by any electronic or mechanical means, including information storage and retrieval systems, without written permission from the author, except for the use of brief quotations in a book review.

Also by Elle Christopher

THE TUNBRIDGE SERIES
WHERE LOYALTY LIES
UNTIL YOU FOUND US
THE LIGHT AT GRACE HILL
A HISTORY OF ALMOST
THE EDGE OF GOOD THINGS

Standalone love stories set in the same unforgettable small town.

THE TUNBRIDGE HOLIDAY COLLECTION
CHRISTMAS AT TOLLIVER'S BOOKSHOP

*For the women who chose themselves
before anyone else did.*

"Longing is the deepest instinct in us.
It leads us back to where we belong."

— DAVID WHYTE

CHAPTER 1

Twelve Fifty-Two

They say accidents happen fast.

This one started slow.

The kind of slow that sneaks up on you, so quiet you don't realize how close the edge is until you've already crossed it.

The white lines blurred.

I blinked hard—one of those heavy, dragging blinks that lasted a little too long. My eyes burned. The headlights stretched ahead in a narrow tunnel of light, slicing through a low mist that rolled off the fields. Beyond it, the night was empty. Quiet. Wide open.

The dashboard clock glowed 12:52.

Ten minutes to go.

The road hummed under the tires, hypnotic. My fingers flexed on the steering wheel. My body ached with the kind of tiredness that sinks into your bones—the kind that doesn't come from work but from life itself.

I cracked the window. Cold air rushed in, sharp and dry. It stung my cheeks and filled the SUV with the scent of dirt and hay and the faint metallic tang of early frost. Somewhere in the distance, a coyote howled—one long, low note that disappeared into the hills.

The wind helped for a while. Until it didn't.

I turned the music up. Static crackled, then a song filled the air—something slow and familiar that should've kept me company. My eyes felt like they'd been sanded raw. Every blink scraped. Every mile dragged longer.

Just ten more minutes.

I'd driven these roads a thousand times. Back and forth between one life and another. I could do it half-asleep, and maybe I was. The blacktop curved through the low country hills. Nothing but open fields on both sides. A sky swollen with stars.

Then—

Brake lights.

Red. Sudden. Blinding.

The car ahead of me stopped short. My heart seized. I slammed the brake pedal with both feet, but I already knew it was too late.

"God—"

The tires screamed. I yanked the wheel right, hard.

The SUV veered off the road, the world tilting hard to the right. My stomach dropped as the passenger-side tires caught the edge of the asphalt, lifting just enough to send the whole vehicle into a roll.

For a heartbeat, everything went weightless.

Then gravity hit back.

The car rolled.

Once.

Twice.

Three times.

Four.

Each rotation was violent—metal shrieking, glass exploding, air whipping through broken windows. My phone flew from the console and cracked against my cheekbone before vanishing into the dark. My knee slammed into the underside of the dash. My head snapped sideways and hit the side window. My scream never made it out.

Then everything stopped.

Silence, thick and impossible.

The only sound left was my heartbeat, hammering against the seatbelt.

I was upside down. Hanging.

The belt bit into my collarbone, the only thing keeping me suspended above the shattered roof, the world flipped and unrecognizable beneath me. My hair dangled down. Glass dust glittered under the sweep of the headlights, still blazing across the hills like they couldn't accept what had happened.

For a moment, I couldn't think. Couldn't move. It was as if my mind had been left behind somewhere in the spin, still tumbling while my body hung there—silent, weightless, suspended between the before and after.

The air was thick. Metallic. It smelled of gasoline and scorched rubber and something else—something warm and coppery. My blood. It slipped from my head in slow, deliberate drops, falling onto the fabric of the ceiling beneath me.

My hands wouldn't obey me. They trembled as if they belonged to someone else. I tried to lift one—slow, careful—and the motion sent glass raining down in a soft patter. My fingertips brushed the seatbelt buckle, but my mind wasn't there yet. The thought of escape hadn't landed. All I could do was stare at the faint glow outside the cracked windshield, the headlights cutting through a fog that looked too calm for what had just happened.

A shape flickered through it. Movement. Then—footsteps.

My pulse surged.

A man's voice, rough and breathless.

"Oh my God... are you alive?"

I blinked, trying to see him through the fog of blood and shock.

I turned my head. The movement shot pain through my skull. A shadow crouched by the shattered passenger window, backlit by his headlights. His eyes went wide.

"I... I saw the whole thing—you rolled four times. I can't

believe... I can't believe you survived that." He said in a shaky voice.

I wanted to answer. Nothing came out.

He ducked lower, flashlight trembling in his grip. "Don't move. Just breathe. You're bleeding real bad."

My hand twitched toward my scalp. He froze.

"No, no—don't touch it!" His voice cracked. "There's glass in your head."

That's when I felt it—the sharp sting, the trickle of warmth running down my temple tickled. I gasped, and the sound seemed to startle us both.

"Deep breaths," he said, more to himself than to me. "You're okay. You're okay."

The fog brightened again—headlights cutting through the wreckage, white and unreal. Tires hissed as other cars slowed. Someone shouted to call 911. Then his voice was closer, breathless with urgency.

"Stay still. I'm coming in."

Glass splintered as he shoved his way through the shattered back window. The crunch echoed in the small space, raining fragments across the roof that used to be the floor. The frame groaned under his weight as he ducked inside, twisting past broken glass and hanging fabric. His breathing was fast, uneven, but his hands were steady when they found me.

"This thing's jammed," he muttered, tugging at the seatbelt. His shoulder brushed mine, close enough that I could feel the heat of him through the cold air. "Don't move. I've got you."

He wedged himself awkwardly under me, one arm braced behind my back, the other fumbling for the buckle. Metal clicked. Nothing gave. He cursed softly, shifting closer until I could feel his heartbeat against my side.

"Come on," he whispered, yanking once, twice—then the latch gave way with a loud snap.

For a split second, gravity claimed me—but he caught me before I dropped, his arms wrapping around me, bearing my full weight. My body folded against his, the air driven from my lungs. Shards of glass pressed into my arm, but his grip stayed firm.

"I've got you," he said again, his voice rough and shaking now. "You're alright."

He adjusted his stance, crouched low beneath the crumpled frame, and began to pull us both toward the window. Each movement was careful, deliberate. I could feel his strength in every inch of it—his body taking the brunt of every scrape, his breath ragged against my hair.

Then, suddenly, cold air hit my face. The night opened up. He maneuvered us through the gap, his hand shielding my head from the jagged glass, and carried me clear of the wreckage before lowering me onto the wet grass.

The earth felt unsteady beneath me, still spinning, still upside down. But his hand stayed at my shoulder, solid and grounding, while the sound of sirens began to rise in the distance.

"Can you hear me?"

I nodded, barely.

"Good. Stay awake, okay? Don't close your eyes."

Another voice cut through the dark. "Ambulance is coming!"

He yelled back, then turned to me again. "You're gonna be fine. Just don't move."

The sirens grew louder, closer. The first flash of red lit the fog.

He exhaled like he hadn't breathed since the crash.

When the EMTs arrived, their faces told me everything. One whistled under his breath when he saw the SUV. Another muttered, "How the hell did she crawl out of that?"

"She didn't," the man said. "I pulled her."

They strapped me onto a board, checked my vitals, asked me questions I couldn't process. I caught flashes—their gloved hands, the crunch of glass under boots, the stranger's silhouette watching from behind the flashing lights.

When they loaded me into the ambulance, he was still there. Arms folded. Eyes following.

"Sir, you can't ride with her," one paramedic said.

The ambulance lights strobed red across the fog, flashing through the open doors. Voices blurred together—urgent, low, overlapping.

"She's losing too much blood."

"Pressure's dropping."

"Let's move—now."

The doors slammed shut. The siren wailed, and everything became motion and light. The ceiling above me hummed. A paramedic's face came in and out of view—young, tense, eyes flicking between monitors.

"Stay with me, ma'am. Can you hear me?"

I tried to nod, but my neck felt too heavy.

The siren blurred into a steady drone, a heartbeat I couldn't sync to. Every bump in the road sent pain radiating through my skull. My fingers were cold, slick with blood. Someone pressed gauze against my head, and the sting pulled me back just long enough to hear, "BP's stabilizing. Hang on, sweetheart."

Then darkness again.

When I opened my eyes next, there were lights—bright, relentless lights above me. The world tilted as hands guided the stretcher down a hallway. The ceiling tiles moved past in a rhythmic blur—white, white, white. Voices echoed around me.

"She's got glass embedded into the scalp."

"Lacerations to the forehead, neck, and arm."

"Get a transfusion ready—type and crossmatch now."

I tried to speak, to ask what was happening, but my mouth wouldn't form the words. A hand brushed my hair back—gentle, practiced.

"You're at Northside Hospital, honey. We're taking care of you."

I wanted to believe her, but the words slipped through me like water. The light above turned to a halo. The hum of machines grew louder, steadier, until it was all I could hear.

Then pain. Sharp. Unforgiving.

"You're going to feel some pressure. We have to get the glass out."

The pressure came—and then fire. My scalp burned as tweezers scraped against skin. I bit my lip until I tasted more blood. Tears slid down my cheeks, and someone dabbed them away before they reached my jaw.

"Lucky," the nurse murmured, almost to herself, as another shard clinked into a metal tray. "You hit that window hard. You... shouldn't be here."

The words barely registered. My body was trembling, my vision tunneling in and out. I caught flashes—the gleam of instruments, the sterile brightness of the room, the red streak on the glove of someone trying to save me.

Then warmth spread through my arm. A voice said something about saline, then another mentioned blood type. I drifted again, half-hearing:

"She's still bleeding."

"Clamp that."

"Start the transfusion."

The world narrowed to a pulse that wasn't mine. Time dissolved somewhere between pain and peace, life and whatever waited on the other side of it.

And then, slowly, the edges softened. The lights dimmed. Voices turned into whispers.

When I woke up again, the air was still. The steady beep of a monitor marked proof of life—mine.

A nurse's voice floated near my shoulder. "You're okay now, sweetheart. Rest."

CHAPTER 2
The Sound of Survival

I woke to a room that smelled like bleach and stillness.

A soft hum vibrated through the air—the low, mechanical kind that belongs to places where people cling to life. For a few seconds, I didn't know if I was one of them. My body felt heavy and foreign, as if I was trying to live inside someone else's skin.

Light seeped around the blinds, gray and uncommitted, the kind that could belong to dawn or dusk. I tried to swallow, but my throat was dry sandpaper. I had the taste of metal in my mouth. When I shifted, the sheet brushed my leg, and pain answered everywhere.

A monitor beeped beside me—steady, patient, as though it had nowhere else to be.

"Good morning, Rose."

The voice came from a woman stepping out of the glow—blonde hair in a tight bun, calm eyes that had seen too many kinds of hurt. Her badge read *Laney*. She smiled softly, as if she knew smiles were rationed here.

"How's your pain, one to ten?"

"Seven."

"Let's fix that." She pressed a button on the IV line. Warmth crept through my arm, softening everything until I could breathe again.

"You scared us last night," she said, half teasing, half scolding. "Don't do that again."

"Did I?" My voice barely belonged to me.

"Head lacerations, a mild concussion, no fractures." She tapped the chart, efficient but kind. "You're lucky."

Lucky. The word hit wrong. It didn't feel like luck—it felt like borrowed time.

Laney adjusted the blinds, dimming the light that made my head throb. "Your mom's here. Tunbridge, right? She's been pacing the hallway for hours. We convinced her to go get coffee."

I blinked hard. "She's here?"

"Couldn't keep her away."

The door eased open. Mom stepped through, hair undone, sweater thrown over pajamas. Her face was pale from worry.

"Mom."

She crossed the space in two steps and took my face in her trembling hands. "Rose. Oh, thank God."

"I'm okay," I said automatically.

She traced the edge of the bandage at my temple, eyes filling. "They said you rolled four times." Her voice cracked. "Do you have any idea how long that drive was, not knowing if you were alive?"

"I'm sorry."

She shook her head, swallowing hard. "Don't apologize for surviving."

Laney smiled faintly, quietly leaving us to the hum of machines. Mom dragged the chair closer, her hand wrapping around mine. I could feel her pulse racing under her skin.

"Do you remember what happened?" Laney asked gently.

"Some of it."

Memory returned like shards of glass—red brake lights, a snap of motion, the sound of glass raining down. The rest was just sky and noise.

"Small sips of water," Laney said, handing me a cup. "And no heroic acts or big decisions today. We'll discharge you this afternoon if you can walk and eat."

Mom sat at my bedside with fuzzy socks covered in pink stripes. "I brought these."

I tried to smile. "Of course you did." She crouched and slipped them on like I was still her little girl.

She took my hand, rubbing warmth into it. "Your father called. He's somewhere over the Atlantic, wanted to get on a plane. I told him to wait. He said to tell you he's proud you're strong."

"That's his way of saying he's scared." I assured her.

She smiled. "I think he said it through tears."

"And Grant?"

"Your brother texted from Austin. Said he's sorry he missed my birthday, meetings stacked all day. He said he loves you and he's so glad you're okay."

"That's sweet."

We sat in easy quiet until a knock broke it.

A uniformed officer appeared, hat in hand, eyes still too young for scenes like mine. "Ms. Bennett? I'm Officer Jacobs. I have the preliminary report."

Mom's shoulders tensed beside me.

"You were behind a pickup," he began. "It braked for a deer. Seems like you lost control. You swerved right, caught the shoulder, rolled four times. Landed upside down. A bystander pulled you out before paramedics arrived."

My stomach turned at the words *upside down*. I could almost feel the seatbelt again, biting across my collarbone.

"Do you remember any of it?" he asked.

"No," I said, though that wasn't entirely true. I remembered flashes—light, motion, the sound of my own breath catching—but memory was slippery, mercifully incomplete.

He placed a card on my tray. "If you recall anything else, call me. The first twenty-four hours are fuzzy for most people. Glad you're alright."

When he left, the silence filled with something fragile.

Mom brushed her thumb along my knuckles. "You don't have to remember it all."

"I remember enough." I stared at the window. Morning sunlight striped the curtain, golden and ordinary. It didn't feel right that the world looked so normal. "I shouldn't have been driving. I was sleepy."

"What were you doing out that late?"

I hesitated. "Work ran long. Then the dinner meeting kept dragging, and I didn't want to drive all the way back to Atlanta just to turn around in the morning." I swallowed. "You always leave the porch light on. I figured I'd just let myself in, sleep in the guest room, and take you to breakfast for your birthday."

Her mouth twitched between a laugh and a sob. "You could've just called."

"It's your birthday. And Dad and Grant are gone."

Her grip tightened. "You're always thinking of me. You owe yourself rest."

That word sounded foreign. I'd built my life around motion—deadlines, clients, expectations stacked higher than sleep. I didn't know what to do with stillness.

In the mirror above the sink, I saw the version of me that almost didn't make it—bandaged temple, bruised cheek, eyes too wide. A cold ripple moved through me. Seeing it made the whole thing feel real in a way it hadn't yet.

Mom stood behind me, her reflection calm and unbroken. "Still beautiful," she said softly.

"Define beautiful."

"Alive."

She smiled and I tried to believe her.

. . .

By afternoon, I was discharged. Laney hugged me before I left. "Go live your lucky life," she said.

Lucky. The word kept following me like a stray.

The elevator ride down felt longer than the crash. A volunteer pushed me in a wheelchair I didn't need. Mom walked behind, tote on her shoulder, eyes locked on me as if she could will me to stay upright.

We got in the car and drove in silence for miles. The wipers squeaked against a drizzle that couldn't decide if it wanted to fall.

A mile past the county line, something in my chest tightened. Up ahead, the shoulder on the right was torn up—grass flattened, dirt scraped raw—but what hit me hardest was on the pavement itself. A long dark skid mark slashed across the lane, the kind of mark you leave when instinct slams your foot down before your brain catches up. My stomach dropped. That was the spot. I blinked hard, but the tears still came, quiet and fast. One moment I'd been fine. The next had been metal, air, nothing. Mom didn't speak. She just eased off the gas as we passed, like she understood that some places bruise you even after you leave them behind.

A few minutes later, she finally spoke. "You sure you're okay?"

"I'm fine."

"You always say that."

"It's easier than saying I don't know."

Her hand left the wheel long enough to squeeze mine. "Then I don't know. Let that be enough for now."

My parents' house sat low on the ridge, cedar siding worn by years of weather and memory. The watering can still waited by the steps, half full, like someone had meant to come right back.

Inside, the air held the faint echo of the life we'd lived here. The hum of meals shared. The quiet warmth of a home that never stopped believing we'd return. I could almost hear Grant's voice in the doorway, light and sure as he set the table. And if I let myself pause, I could still picture Dad between assignments, uniform jacket slung over a chair, his laughter filling every corner like it had never left.

Mom led me into her studio. Light pooled across the floor, catching on canvases stacked along the walls and jars of brushes worn soft from years of use. Through the tall windows, the lake shifted in quiet silver.

She handed me a mug of tea and returned to her easel, touching her brush to blue and letting it bloom across the page.

"What are you making?" I asked.

"Nothing yet. Just settling the air."

I watched the color drift, slow and gentle. Something in me eased with it.

"Do you ever stop working?" she asked.

I hesitated. "If I stop, everything stops."

She turned slightly, her voice softer. "Maybe it's time to let something stop."

The words carried more weight than the brush in her hand. I wasn't sure how to hold them.

Dinner was simple. Soup and grilled cheese, the same cure she made every time someone in our family needed comfort. Afterward she walked me to my old room, smoothed the quilt, and kissed my forehead.

"Sleep. Let yourself be here, fully in this moment."

When she left, the house settled around me. Wood shifting. Crickets chirping. My pulse tapping at the bruise on my temple. I should have felt grateful. Instead I felt hollow, like the crash had shaken everything loose except the instinct to keep moving.

Work. Prove. Achieve. Repeat.

The rhythm I knew. The rhythm I couldn't seem to let go.

CHAPTER 3
Seven Days of Stillness

Mom's voice drifted from the kitchen. Humming. The clink of a mug. The rhythm of someone determined to make the morning gentle.

The world was too loud again. Refrigerator buzzing. Footsteps. Even my own pulse felt like a crowd. The headache pulsed behind my eyes like a second heartbeat.

The mirror said lucky. The bruise at my temple said something else. I felt suspended between two lives. The one that had nearly ended and the one I still wasn't sure I wanted.

Mist curled over the lake outside, thinning into ribbons that caught the first gold of the sun. A blue heron skimmed the water, wings brushing the surface like it was smoothing out the day.

"Morning," Mom said as I walked in. She stood barefoot in her painting apron, hair in a loose knot. "How's your head?"

"Still attached."

A beat of awkward silence stretched between us.

"You're staying here. No arguments. The concussion is serious." She poured coffee before I could reply. "No driving for a week. You can sit. You can walk to the dock. You can breathe. That's it."

"Mom." I groaned dramatically.

Her brown eyes softened.

Seven days felt like being wrapped in cotton. I nodded because fighting would take more energy than I had.

When I mentioned needing things from home, she already had her keys in hand.

Driving back into Buckhead felt like stepping into a life I no longer fit. Traffic pressed close. Buildings rose like glass cliffs. Noise everywhere. My chest tightened the closer we got to my condo.

A message pinged from insurance. My SUV was a total loss.

"I'll need a rental car," I said.

Saying the words out loud made everything feel real again. The impact. The damage. The fact that any breath after that night was borrowed.

We parked along the curb, heat wrapped around us, heavy and unmoving. Inside the lobby, the doorman's smile faltered when he saw the bandage.

Eugene had worked here since my first week in Buckhead ten years ago. He'd watched half the building grow up, move out, break up, start over. He knew everyone's dogs by name.

Which was why the shift in his smile hit harder than I wanted it to.

"Miss Rose. You alright?"

"Mostly."

I kept walking, pretending I didn't see the worry in his eyes. Connection felt too heavy to hold today.

In the elevator, a woman stood beside us, perfume sharp. She didn't look at me. I watched our reflections instead. Mom in a paint-smeared sweater. I looked washed out and worn.

Inside my condo, everything was perfect in a way that felt hollow. Spotless counters. Plants surviving only because timers told them when to drink. The skyline stared back through the glass, a view I used to chase.

Mom opened the blinds wider. It only made the emptiness clearer.

She checked the fridge and frowned. "You live like a college student. This is not a home. It's a storage unit with a view."

"I worked late a lot."

She found fortune cookies in a drawer. Her message read *You will soon take a trip.* Mine read *Love arrives when you least expect it.*

She arched an eyebrow. "Mine is clearly about me visiting you more."

I smiled. "Then mine must be about you, too."

For the first time that day, the room warmed.

Still, the space did not feel like mine.

I packed a bag for the week and we drove back to Tunbridge. I slept the whole way.

The days settled into a rhythm that felt forced but safe.

Mom painted by the window every morning. Greens and blues spread across the canvas. I sat nearby with tea instead of coffee. No screens. Doctor's orders. My phone buzzed with reminders until I shut it off to get some peace.

Work was already pulling at me. Meetings. Deadlines. An inbox that grew louder each day. The weight of everything I had left behind pressed against my chest.

Late morning, a delivery arrived from Beloved Blooms. Madonna lilies. White and soft and steady. The card said: *You are the apple of my eye. Love, Dad.*

He still remembered. I held the card for a long moment. Lilies had always been my favorite. They opened like they were reaching. They made me feel like I mattered to him, even when he couldn't prove it in other ways.

My phone buzzed on the counter. Dad. FaceTime.

I hesitated, suddenly aware of the bruise on my temple, the shadows under my eyes.

His face appeared, lit by the thin, gray light of some foreign morning. A cot and metal locker stood behind him. Another rotation overseas. Another month of living out of a duffel. His hair was whiter than before, but his blue eyes were the same steady ones I grew up with.

I used to wait on the top stair when I heard his boots after months away, pretending I wasn't waiting at all.

"Hey, Peach," he said, voice low, soft, already frayed with concern. "You look hurt."

Peach. He'd called me that since I was little, ever since I fell out of the backyard tree and insisted I was "fine as a peach." The name softened something in me that had been locked tight since the crash.

"I'm okay," I said. "Really."

He leaned closer to the screen. "When your mom told me you rolled your SUV." His jaw tightened. "I thought about getting on a flight home."

"You can't just leave a job site in another country," I said.

"I wish I could." He rubbed a hand over his face. "God, Rose. I hate being across the world when you need me."

Something inside me pinched at that. He had said those words my entire life. "I know."

He looked at me the way he did when I was little, like he was memorizing me just in case the world tried to take something from us. "How's your head?"

"Sore. Bruised. Still attached."

A ghost of a smile pulled at his mouth. "Good. I like it where it is."

Warmth slid through me, unexpected and sharp.

Behind him, a distant hum of generators throbbed through the screen. His life overseas was always this—bare rooms, long hours, odd meals, no windows. He worked as a civilian contractor on bases around the world, keeping whatever facility he was assigned to standing, patched, running. When I was a kid, I'd imagined him fixing giant machines in deserts and forests and cities with names I couldn't pronounce.

"Mom said she's making you rest," he said.

"She's enforcing it like a federal law."

He laughed, and something in his face softened. "That tracks."

A pause hung between us. It wasn't awkward. Just honest.

"You scared me," he said finally. "Hearing her voice shake like that... it took me right back."

"To what?"

He shifted, settling on the edge of the cot. "You were eight. Broke your arm. I'd flown to Germany for work. Your mom called from ER. Cried on the freezing floor of Frankfurt airport."

My breath stilled. I remembered the fall, the pain, Mom's panic. But not that.

"You never told me that."

He shrugged. "Parents don't need medals. We want our kids safe." His tone didn't change, but something in his eyes did. "We stay steady so you don't see us panic." He nodded at me. "You were the brave one. Wouldn't even let them cut your coat."

I blinked, my throat tightening. I had forgotten that. Or maybe just buried it.

He watched me for a long moment, gaze softening. "You've always been tough. Tougher than you realize. But toughness doesn't mean you have to snap back instantly."

"I know," I said, though part of me didn't.

He leaned closer to the screen. "You don't have to prove anything to anyone right now. Not to work. Not to the world. Not to me."

The words hit deeper than I expected.

"Oh—and the lilies," he added, rubbing the back of his neck. "Had them set to auto-ship before I flew out. Didn't know they'd arrive in the middle of all this."

"They're beautiful."

"So are you," he said quietly. "I wish I was there. I hate that I'm not."

"Listen," he said, leaning closer, voice low. "I'm glad you're home. With your mom. With the lake. That place has a way of telling the truth."

I felt something warm slip under my ribs.

He looked at me then like he could see every bruise, visible and not. "You'll be okay. You've always been stronger than you think."

A boarding alarm blared in the background. He winced.

"They've got me on another run," he said. "A supply convoy this time. We'll talk soon."

"Okay."

"Peach?" He said.

"Yeah?"

"You really are the apple of my eye."

My breath caught. "I know, Dad."

When the call ended, the kitchen felt softer. The lilies seemed brighter. And for the first time since the crash, something in me loosened.

In the afternoons, I walked to the dock. Heat clung to the air. Honeysuckle drifted across the yard. Cicadas buzzed. The lake held its own kind of silence, nothing like the condo. Here, I could hear my own mind again.

By the third night, a storm rolled over the water. Rain hammered the roof. Lightning flashed across the trees. I sat awake, pulse quickening with every crack. I hated how easily fear rewired me.

Mom joined me with cocoa.

"You're afraid of stopping," she said.

"I'm not."

"You are. Stillness feels like failure to you."

I didn't answer. She touched my shoulder before she left. "Try to rest. You don't have to earn this breath."

But part of me believed I did.

By day five, the bruises faded but the restlessness grew stronger. I sat at the dock with my laptop despite the doctor's orders. Three marked urgent. One from Dieter—my boss, of course—demanding a project update like I hadn't almost died.

I turned my phone face-down until it stopped vibrating.

The guilt came first. Then relief.

Mom called from the porch. "Everything okay?"

"Perfect."

It wasn't.

When she went out for groceries, I walked the property barefoot. The air smelled like wet pine. Halfway down the hill, my pulse kicked hard and fast. I sat until my breathing steadied.

The lake path curved along the far edge of the yard, just beyond the pines. A few early walkers moved through the haze—someone with a golden retriever, a kid on a bike too small for him, and a man jogging at an easy pace.

He didn't look my way. None of them did.

For a moment, I let myself watch them move. Ordinary people in an ordinary morning. A life I still wasn't sure how to rejoin. As he came closer along the curve of the path, the shape of his eyes caught the light in a way that tugged at something half-buried inside me.

A breeze lifted, colder than before, and that was all it took to bring the crash back. The slam of metal. The drop. The voice that pulled me through it. Calm. Certain. I hadn't thanked him. I didn't even know his name.

The memory didn't feel like trauma anymore.

It felt like a tether.

Proof that someone had been there when everything else gave way.

. . .

On the seventh morning, I woke before dawn. The lake mirrored the sky. Pale pink. Soft gold. Mist drifted low over the water.

I sat with a blanket around my shoulders and watched the sun rise. It felt like something inside me finally stopped running.

Stillness wasn't failure. It was the moment when your life caught up to you.

Later, Dr. Glodner came by. He checked my pupils and cleared me to drive again. "Ease back into normal," he said.

The pill bottle stayed unopened on the counter.

"I need to get back," I told Mom as I packed my bag.

She nodded, though I saw the worry in her eyes. "Just try not to disappear again."

"I won't."

We both knew healing is never that simple.

The drive to the rental lot was short. Mom handled the wheel while I watched the lake shrink behind us until it felt like a memory. When she hugged me goodbye, she whispered, "Drive carefully."

I didn't tell her how nervous I was to drive again.

Once I slid into the rental car, the city pulled at me again. Billboards. Brake lights. The old rhythm of urgency. But something in me resisted it. The speed felt wrong. Like trying on clothes that no longer fit.

Seven days of stillness had done something I couldn't name yet.

Tunbridge wasn't done with me.

And deep down, I didn't want it to be.

CHAPTER 4
Return to the Machine

From a distance, the skyline looked merciful—glass softened by morning haze. But mercy didn't last long here.

The closer I drove, the more it became itself again—fast, loud, unbothered. Buckhead had a way of reminding you that you were replaceable.

My pulse started counting miles instead of minutes. Every green light felt too fast. My hands were damp on the wheel, but I didn't dare let go.

The air vents hummed, pumping cold air over the faint throb in my temple. My old route came back like muscle memory. Same traffic lights. Same billboards preaching hustle as a religion. A city built for people who never stopped.

I had stopped for a week. Long enough for everything in me to question why I was coming back.

The memory flashed—taillights bleeding red across an empty road. I'd left this same skyline behind that night. Choosing work over myself, over everything that mattered.

A horn blared somewhere behind me, sharp enough to pull me back.

The plan had been simple—drive home and maybe ease into

the week tomorrow. But the closer I got, the more the pull of routine took over.

I told myself I'd just stop by the condo, grab a blazer, feel normal for an hour. Normal was eyeliner and coffee in a travel mug. Normal was motion.

By the time I'd changed and locked the door behind me, my body had already decided where to go.

I told myself I was just driving in to check messages, grab a few files, ease back in like the doctor said. But deep down I knew the truth—I didn't know how to stop showing up, even when it cost me everything.

The parking garage opened beneath the building like a mouth, swallowing me whole. Third level, same corner space—my name stamped on a small metal plate. The blue sedan looked out of place among the Teslas and black SUVs. I cut the engine and sat there for a moment, staring at my reflection in the rearview mirror.

No blood. No glass. No reason I should still be here, except that I was.

I'd always thought survival would feel triumphant. It didn't. It just made the ordinary sharper.

The elevator doors opened with their usual whisper. Thirty-four floors up, the air changed—chilly, filtered, humming with caffeine and fluorescent ambition. The place I'd spent four years building marketing campaigns big enough that the executives finally stopped calling me "the girl from Branding" and started using my actual title. Elaren Engineering: where everything was polished, fast, and replaceable.

"Rose!"

Kevin from analytics waved, coffee in hand. Tall, thin, always a little hunched from too many hours over spreadsheets. His voice was too cheerful, like he was congratulating me on a promotion instead of surviving a rollover crash.

"Hey, glad you're back. Heard about the accident. Scary stuff, huh?"

"Yeah," I answered.

"You doing okay?"

"I'm here," I said.

He nodded, satisfied with the only answer he wanted. People liked survival stories better when you didn't make them feel anything.

I walked through the open office. Glass walls, chrome desks, quiet keyboards. Screens lit faces in blue light. The city stretched out below us, full of strangers doing exactly what we were doing—pretending this was life.

My office was just as I'd left it. The cleaning crew had probably dusted around the small things—succulent, notepad, coffee mug with a chip in the rim. A note from HR was taped on my monitor: *Welcome back, Rose! Don't hesitate to reach out if you need support during this transition.*

I laughed quietly. HR never called it what it was. Trauma didn't fit in a dropdown menu.

I opened my inbox.

287 unread emails.

Project updates. Deadlines moved up, never back. Meeting invites stacked like falling dominoes.

One caught my eye—Richard's name: *Team meeting at 1 p.m. to review Project Helios product launch and next sprint planning.*

I froze.

That was *my* presentation. *My* project. I'd been building the Helios campaign for nine months with the engineering team—late nights, drafts, test launches.

Richard hadn't been a part of a single piece of it.

I stopped by his office. He looked up, surprised, mid-sip of his protein shake.

Richard Evans, Director of Strategy. Late thirties. Golden hair, golden-boy reputation, golden everything. The kind of man who wore confidence like cologne and carried himself as if the whole floor should be grateful he showed up. His wire-rim glasses gave him that clever-clogs look he leaned on whenever he wanted to sound authoritative.

"Hey. Didn't expect to see you back yet," he said.

"Hey," I managed. "I'm not really ready to present today. Still catching up. Maybe we can postpone—"

"Don't even worry about it," he cut in. "I've got it covered."

Before I could say another word, he was out the door with his laptop.

The team filed into the conference room. Bright lights. The air sharp with espresso and ambition. I sat halfway down the table, trying to breathe evenly. Richard stood at the head, sleeves rolled, looking every bit the company's next golden boy.

"Before we start," he said easily, "I want to walk you through the campaign strategy to get Helios maximum visibility in the market."

My breath caught.

My slide deck glowed on the screen. My numbers. My plan. My work.

When I tried to speak, Dieter shot me a sharp warning look—finger to his lips, the universal sign to *hush* someone. The air thickened, my vision narrowing to the edge of the screen. It felt like falling again. Not fast, just endless. The humiliation burned hotter than my pulse. My throat locked around words I couldn't afford to say.

Richard talked for twenty minutes. He read my plan and my notes. I heard nothing but the blood in my ears. Every sentence landed like a bruise. My name didn't leave his mouth once.

My pulse thundered. For a second, I thought the room was tilting again—like it had that night on the road.

When the final slide appeared—Campaign Timeline and Rollout—Richard smiled like he'd just saved the company.

"And that's how we'll get the greatest ROI in our history."

Applause.

Actual applause.

Kevin whistled. Someone said, "Brilliant work, man."

Richard gave a modest shrug. "Team effort," he said, locking eyes with Dieter. He didn't look at me.

My throat burned. I sat there stunned, hands in my lap, pulse hammering. The floor had fallen out, and I was still trying to pretend it hadn't.

After the meeting, people drifted toward the break room, laughter echoing down the hall. Compliments floated like confetti. I stayed behind, watching my reflection in the glass—pale, detached, like I was watching someone else's humiliation play out.

Richard reappeared, holding two coffee mugs. He set one beside me.

"Didn't know if you were ready to jump in yet," he said, casually. "You've been through a lot."

"So you presented my work for me?"

He blinked, smiled like it was no big deal. "Hey, we're all on the same team, right?"

"Right," I bit out. "Some of us just forget who's on it."

He gave a short laugh, unsure if it was a joke, and walked off.

The cup trembled in my hand. My throat was tight, the type of anger that shakes your bones.

I almost threw it—just to hear something break.

"Rose," Dieter's voice came from behind me.

I turned. He stood with his hands in his pockets, an expression carved from ice.

"I hope you're not upset," he said evenly. "It's an important project. We couldn't risk delays. I didn't know how long you'd be out, and Richard was happy to step in."

Oh, of course he was.

I stared at him. "I was gone for a week, Dieter. Everything was done. Richard didn't step in—he presented nine months of work that *I* did."

Dieter's jaw flexed. "You've been here ten years, Rose. You know this company values collaboration. I'd hate to think you're not being a team player."

"Not a team player?" I repeated, disbelief scraping my throat raw. "After everything I've done for this place?"

He sighed, disappointment thick as smoke. "You've always been one of our strongest marketers. Don't ruin that reputation now."

Then he turned and left me standing there, shaking, the taste of bitterness at the back of my tongue.

I wanted to scream. Or cry. Or both. But nothing came out—just the raw silence of disbelief. My body couldn't keep up with my fury; it just stood there, trembling, as if the shock itself was holding me upright.

Suddenly, the walls felt too close. The hum of printers and keyboard clicks pressed in until it felt like a swarm.

Ten minutes later, I was sitting in my car, parked four levels below the sun. My hands trembled on the steering wheel. I didn't start the engine.

The air inside the car felt thick. I pressed my forehead to the wheel and let out one ragged sound that wasn't quite a sob, more like air escaping a crack in something that had finally split.

My throat locked. For a second, I couldn't tell if I wanted to scream or disappear.

I could walk away. Drive home. Never come back.

The thought flickered—then died.

Then the silence settled again, heavy and absolute. I wiped my eyes, straightened my blazer, and stared at my reflection in the rearview mirror until I looked like someone who could walk back inside.

Every choice I'd made to get here replayed in reverse. The all-nighters. The weekends traded for deadlines. The dinners I'd cancelled. The relationships I'd outgrown because ambition didn't leave room for them.

And for what?

A paycheck. A title.

A life that looked steady from the outside but felt hollow.

My phone buzzed with a calendar alert: *Sprint review—3:30 p.m.*

Of course.

I went back upstairs. My badge beeped like a judge at the gate.

The rest of the afternoon passed in fragments. Slack pings. Deadlines moved up. Tasks reassigned. No one asked if I was okay. I wasn't sure I was.

At four-thirty, Dieter came by, "Rose, can you update the status report before morning?"

"Already done."

He grinned. "Knew I could count on you."

I looked at him and said nothing.

When the lights dimmed automatically at six, I was still staring at my monitor. The reflection on the black screen looked foreign.

I grabbed my things, stood, and walked toward the elevators. My heels echoed off the marble like small gunshots.

I got in the car and drove out of the garage. The city stretched in front of me—glittering, indifferent. The sun hung heavy behind the skyline, turning every window gold. I rolled down my window, breathing in exhaust, heat, and the faint sweetness of roasted nuts from a street cart.

This was the view I'd fought for. And somehow, I couldn't remember why it had ever felt worth it.

At the crosswalk, a man laughed into his phone. A woman balanced a latte, a laptop bag, and her exhaustion with practiced grace. Nobody looked up.

A truck screamed by, and my body flinched before I could stop it. The echo faded. I still felt it in my ribs.

When I finally drove home, the streetlights blurred in the windshield, long streaks of white that looked like motion without direction.

At a red light, I whispered to no one, "I can't keep doing this."

The car behind me honked.

I pressed the gas.

Back at the condo, everything waited exactly where I'd left it—shiny floors, perfect stillness, city view polished to glass. I set my bag down and leaned against the counter, dizzy with the weight of pretending.

I opened my laptop again.

Emails waited like an open wound.

Reminder: deliverables due EOD tomorrow.
Revised timeline for new branding campaign—see attached.
Dieter: Great job in today's meeting, team. Proud of everyone.

My cursor hovered over *Reply All* on that one.

My heart pounded. I could expose them both. I could burn it all down.

Instead, I shut the laptop. Slowly.

I made some tea and stood at the window. The skyline glittered, cold and bright, as if it had never known dark.

Was this success?

Exhaustion dressed up as purpose?

I touched the bandage near my temple. The ache had dulled, but it was still there. A reminder that life could end in seconds.

And here I was, back in the machine, pretending I didn't hear the gears grinding.

I turned off the lights and let the city shine through the glass instead.

Somewhere below, a siren wailed. It didn't sound like a warning anymore—it sounded like a truth. The kind you can't un-hear once you've survived it.

The faintest scent of rain lingered through the cracked window—or maybe it was just metal and memory, the smell of what almost took me.

CHAPTER 5
The Breaking Point

Two weeks later, the city pretended to be kind.
Morning light softened the glass, making the skyline look less like a blade and more like a promise. My coffee steamed against the kitchen window. The mug warmed my hands, but the heat never reached my chest.

By seven, the sidewalks had shaken off the quiet. Delivery trucks hissed, a bus sighed at the corner, an engine revving threaded the distance and then disappeared. I put on the navy blouse I kept for important days and the black heels that made me two inches taller. The bandage was gone. The bruise at my temple had faded to the color of old straw. I looked almost the same. It was a lie, and the mirror knew it.

The lobby downstairs smelled like wax and cologne. Eugene tipped his chin.

"Looking sharp, Miss Rose."

"Trying," I said.

He glanced at the elevator numbers. "Big day?"

"Something like that."

. . .

The drive to work was routine again. Thirty-four floors up, the doors parted on cold air and bright light. Offices opened into glass corridors, everything polished enough to reflect you back at yourself. People looked up when I passed. The smiles were careful. The tone in their voices had that shape grief gives to small talk.

"You doing better?"

"You look great."

"Scary accident, huh?"

I said I was fine. I said thank you. I said it like a person who had practiced.

The invite on my phone read *Promotion Announcement—11 a.m.* Three rounds, ten years, every late night I had to give.

Room 4A was already half full. The projector hummed. A bowl of chocolate mints sat by the water pitcher. Dieter stood nearest the screen, tie too tight. Richard leaned on the edge of the table, sleeves rolled, fancy wristwatch catching the light.

"Morning," Dieter said. "Let's keep this brief. Full sprint this afternoon."

He clicked to a slide that read *Leadership Update*. The font was corporate and harmless.

He smiled.

"I want to congratulate our new marketing director."

The pause was long enough to notice I had stopped breathing.

"Richard Langley."

A few people clapped. Someone knocked their knuckles on the table. Kevin whistled softly, then swallowed the sound when he caught my eye.

Richard lifted a hand, modest, practiced.

"Team effort," he said. "I couldn't have done this without the support of the people in this room."

He didn't look at me when he said it.

My hands had gone cold. The ringing started in my right ear the way it did when the memory came back without asking. I stared at the slide, at the bullet points that meant nothing and everything, and counted my breaths. One. Two. Three.

Dieter's gaze found me.

"Rose, you have been a steady force through transition," he said. "Your dedication has been invaluable."

That was the word for nine months of work stolen in broad daylight.

My throat burned. Every clap sounded like static.

When the congratulations simmered down, Richard touched my shoulder like it was a kindness.

"You okay? You look a little pale." He smirked.

"I'm fine."

"Dieter said it was neck and neck till the end. Could have gone either way."

"Right," I said. "Either way."

I left before my face betrayed me. The hallway stretched wide and white. The floor trembled under someone rolling a cart. My heart picked up to match the rhythm.

At my desk, I sat. The monitor woke up to a low blue. New messages stacked on top of older ones. Meeting requests multiplied like cells. A Slack ping opened with a confetti emoji.

Congrats, Richard! Well deserved.

Well deserved. The phrase scraped.

I stood up so fast my chair hit the wall. My pulse pounded in my throat.

Dieter's office door was half-closed. He was on the phone, smiling, voice low and polished—the kind of voice that smoothed over every betrayal.

I pushed the door open.

He looked up, startled. "Rose—"

"We need to talk."

He covered the receiver, muttered something about calling back, and hung up. "Everything alright?"

"No," I said. "Everything isn't alright."

I closed the door behind me. The sound was sharp, final.

He leaned back in his chair, hands folded. "If this is about the promotion—"

"It's about everything," I said. "It's about you giving my work to Richard. It's about being told to 'be a team player' when you mean 'stay quiet.' It's about ten years of staying late, missing holidays, taking on every project no one else wanted—so you could pat the next guy on the back for it."

His expression didn't change. "Rose, this isn't the place—"

"This is exactly the place," I said. "You taught me that, remember? Always show up. Always deliver. Even when it costs you everything. Well, I showed up. I delivered. And you let him take it."

"Richard's leadership—"

"Richard's leadership?" I laughed, sharp and shaking. "Richard's leadership is my work with his name on it. You knew it. You let it happen."

He sighed, heavy and performative. "You're emotional. Maybe you should take the rest of the day off."

I stared at him. "You think this is emotion? No. This is clarity."

He opened his mouth to respond, but I didn't let him. "I'm done, Dieter. Done giving this place everything I have so you can hand it off to the next man who smiles right."

"Rose—"

"I quit."

His face flickered—shock, then something colder. "You're making a mistake."

"No," I said quietly. "I've been making the same one for ten years."

For a second, I thought I might cry—not for them, but for the years I'd given to something that would never love me back. Then even that feeling passed, like smoke leaving a room.

I turned, opened the door, and walked out.

The hallway lights buzzed overhead. I heard my own footsteps on the polished floor—steady and sure.

At my desk, I grabbed my phone and keys. I left the mug, the plant, the cracked pen cup. Let them keep it.

As the elevator doors closed, I caught Dieter's reflection in the glass. A man who'd already forgotten me.

I pressed the button for the lobby. My hands were shaking, but it wasn't fear anymore. It was freedom finally finding a pulse.

In the lobby, the security guard clipped the corner of his newspaper without looking up. My badge felt heavy at the end of its lanyard. I set it on the desk. The plastic clicked against the surface. A small, precise sound. The kind that means something has ended.

I got to my car and sat with the door open for a minute.

I drove home without music.

The condo blinked awake when I opened the door. Lights rising by degrees. Air cleaner kicking on. The smell of lemon and a faint trace of burned toast that had lived too long in a heating element. It was spotless, the way it always was. The couch had never sagged. The dining table had never held a meal longer than twenty minutes.

My purse slipped from my shoulder and thudded on the floor. I laughed. It startled me. The sound had edges.

"For what?" I asked. "For who?"

No one answered. The silence answered instead.

I walked the perimeter like a realtor. I looked at the couch, the art, the stack of unread magazines that arrived every month because I paid for a life that was supposed to be full. I opened the fridge. Condiments. Sparkling water. A lemon that had gone hard.

I dialed my best friend, Abby. We'd been glued together for years, even after she moved a few towns over and built the kind of warm, settled life I never quite figured out. She was a stay-at-home mom now, happily married, settled in all the places I wasn't. The person I could call at any hour and know she'd pick up. The voice of reason. The shoulder that had carried more of my tears than anyone else's.

I pressed her name and waited, hoping she was free.

It rang only once.

I almost hung up. Saying it out loud would make it real, and I wasn't sure I was ready for real yet.

"You never call in the middle of the day," she said. "What's wrong?"

"I quit my job."

A beat, then a soft, delighted swear. "Finally."

"I thought I would feel sick," I said. "I don't. Not yet."

"You will. Then it will pass."

"I lost the promotion. They gave it to Richard."

"Of course they did."

"Dieter thanked the *team*."

"Of course he did." Her voice softened. "Where are you."

"Home," I said. "If that's what this is."

I walked into the bedroom. The closet light came on as if it had been waiting. Dresses in a neat row. Blouses sorted by color. The suitcase stood in the corner, upright, like a student. I pulled it out and set it on the bed.

"I'm finally going to use that luggage I bought."

"Are you packing?" Abby asked.

"I think I am."

"For where?"

"*Home*. Tunbridge."

"Good."

"Abby."

"Yeah?"

"I want another life." The words came out quiet. Once they existed, I felt lighter and worse.

"You deserve it," she said.

I sat on the edge of the mattress. The coverlet was white and textured, one that shows every crease. I smoothed it with my palm, then gave up.

"I wasted ten years."

"No," she said. "You spent them. You didn't get what you bought. That's different."

I swallowed. My head felt clear and raw, the way the air feels after lightning.

"I could have had a family," I choked.

"You still can," she asserted. "But you won't find it in that circle."

I picked up the first thing my hand could reach. Jeans. Then the soft sweatshirt I had been sleeping in at Mom's. I pulled down my duffle bag and stuffed them in without care. I pulled the charger from the socket by the bed, the book from the nightstand, my brush, the small jar of night cream that always felt like trying too hard.

"I don't know what I'm doing," I shrugged.

"You do," Abby said. "You're leaving."

I laughed. It hurt the way a stretch hurts when you have not moved in weeks.

"Come with me," I pleaded.

"I have a five year old and a dog with separation anxiety," she said. "I'll come on Friday. With muffins. And tell you that you're brave until you believe it."

We were quiet for a moment. The quiet didn't scare me the way it had before. It felt like a place I could put something down.

"Text me when you get there," she said.

"I will."

"And Rose?"

"Yeah."

"Everything is going to turn out okay."

"We'll see," I murmured.

We hung up. The condo resumed its hum, patient and indifferent. I zipped the suitcase after filling it. The sound carried like a line drawn with a ruler.

In the kitchen, I filled the kettle and set it on the stove. The flame clicked to life and found its shape. I reached for the mug I always used. The one from a conference five summers ago with a logo that promised to optimize something.

The handle was smooth from a thousand mornings.

I poured the water and watched the steam rise. My hands shook. Not fear. Something like relief. Something like grief settling.

I carried the tea to the window and leaned my forehead against the glass. The city glittered at noon, bright and sure of itself. A man ran with a backpack bouncing against his spine. A woman shouldered a bouquet in tissue paper. The wind blew the newspaper out of the hands of an old man sitting on a bench.

Somewhere below, a siren wound up, then slipped out of earshot. My body flinched, then steadied. The echo stayed only a moment. It left room for another sound. My own breath.

I texted my mom.

> Me: Coming home for a while.

> Mom: Good! I'll put fresh sheets on your bed. Drive careful.

I walked to the bathroom and opened the cabinet. I took the toothpaste, the small bottle of ibuprofen, and the face wash I never finished. I looked at the lipstick I wore for important events and left it where it was.

Before I locked the door, I turned once in the entryway and looked at the life arranged inside the frame. The couch that never knew a family. The table that never held a birthday cake. The kitchen that learned my patterns but not my people.

"Thank you," I said. It felt right to say goodbye to a space that had kept me warm and alone.

The elevator took a breath and opened. Eugene looked up when I crossed the lobby with my bag.

"Heading out?" he asked.

"For a bit," I said.

He smiled the way kind people do when they don't need the story. "You take care now."

"I will. You too."

Outside the garage, heat lifted off the sidewalk. A delivery truck beeped in reverse. A cyclist threaded a gap between taxis and raised a hand without looking back. I loaded the suitcase into the trunk and stood for one last second with the car door open, the city tipping toward afternoon.

I took a deep breath. Then I got in, turned the key, and let the air blow cold at my face until my jaw unclenched.

The light changed, I pressed the gas, and the buildings disappeared in the mirror, one by one. Ahead, the road unrolled like something waiting to begin.

I didn't know what was waiting in Tunbridge. I only knew that wanting another life had just turned into driving toward it.

CHAPTER 6
The Road Home

By the time I hit I-75 north, the city was behind me—glass and skyline fading into the gray. It started raining, streaking the windshield and softening everything to a blur.

An hour later, I turned off onto the county road toward Tunbridge. The world quieted there—no traffic, no billboards, just wet asphalt winding through open fields. My wipers kept time, the hum of the tires the only sound left.

When I reached mile marker 212, I slowed. The shoulder dipped gently toward a shallow ditch, grass slick and bent from the rain.

I eased the car onto the shoulder and let the wipers thump in time with my pulse and I replayed what the accident must have looked like.

For a long time, I couldn't move. I just watched the rain slide down the glass. The memory was too clear. The slam of my foot against the brake, the jolt snapping up my leg, the wheel wrenching under my hands as I cut hard right. The tires screamed. The world tilted. Metal lifted. My stomach dropped. The first roll hit like being punched from the inside out. Then another, and another, and another. Each one slower than it should've been, louder than I could stand. Glass shattered. The air turned white. And when everything stopped, I didn't know which way was up.

"Thank you, God," I whispered. My voice shook. "For letting me stay."

The relief hit hard, then the guilt right behind it.

If I hadn't made it... if that had been it...

Mom would never celebrate another birthday without tasting that day in it. She would've blamed herself. She'd think I wouldn't have been on that road if I hadn't been coming to see her.

Grant would have flown in from Austin, furious at the universe and then at himself for not being here. And Dad... I couldn't even let myself picture that. He'd already stopped knowing what to do with the pieces life handed him. Losing me might have snapped something in him for good.

Abby would have shown up at Mom's door before anyone asked. She'd organize, comfort, take over every necessary thing, then cry later in her car where no one could hear her.

The thought of all of them living inside that kind of pain made my chest tighten.

I hadn't just survived for me.

I drove the rest of the way in silence, watching the familiar turns appear one by one—the exit for Brittle Road, the billboard for peach cider at Drucker's General Store, the first glimpse of the old Tunbridge water tower rising pale against the fog.

By the time I reached town, the rain had softened to a mist. The streets were wet and the sidewalks scattered with leaves. October had come quietly here, just enough chill to make the air smell clean.

My parents' house sat on the edge of the lake road, shutters a fresh coat of green. Light spilled through the windows. I could see Mom's shape moving inside.

She opened the door before I could knock. "You made it."

Her hair was pulled back with a paint-stained headband, her

hands still streaked with color. She pulled me in and held on longer than she usually did.

"You look like you've seen a ghost," she said into my shoulder.

"I stopped," I said. "At the crash site."

Her hand tightened on my back. "Good. It's time to leave that piece of road behind."

I nodded. The air inside the house was warm and filled with something cooking—garlic, rosemary, a hint of lemon.

"Granny's here," Mom said. "And Abby's coming over. She wanted to surprise you, but you know I can't keep a secret." She smiled.

"Abby's driving down from Dahlonega?"

"She said she knew you needed her."

Something in my chest loosened. Abby always did that. She showed up before I even admitted I wanted her to.

I laughed, the sound small but real. "She totally faked me out. She said she couldn't come."

Of course she did. That was her way. Let me pretend I was fine until she could get here and prove I wasn't alone.

Mom smiled and turned back to the stove. "Go sit. You look like you need rest."

My grandmother was already in the living room, knitting something in a color that didn't exist in nature. She looked up when I entered. "Well," she said, "don't you look lovely today, dear."

"Oh, Granny," I said.

She waved a needle and smiled with her eyes. "I'm so happy you're here."

I sat beside her, sinking into the couch that smelled faintly of cedar and old stories. She patted my knee. "You did the right thing by leaving. Sometimes courage looks like walking away from what's killing you slowly."

I leaned back, letting her words settle in the quiet between us. Outside, rain tapped softly against the porch roof.

By the time Abby arrived, the house felt full. She came

through the door with a container of muffins in one hand and a bottle of wine in the other.

"There she is!" she shouted, kicking off her shoes. "The woman who finally told her boss to go to hel—."

"Language," Granny wagged her finger.

"Sorry, Granny," Abby said, grinning. "To heck."

"You came! I thought you couldn't make it until Friday?" I asked.

"Well, this is a big day for you and I wasn't going to miss it. Shawn can hold down the fort for one night." She laughed.

We laughed, too. All three generations at once, and the sound filled the kitchen like sunlight.

Dinner was amazing—roasted vegetables, crusty bread, Mom's chicken piccata—and comforting. We sat around the table for hours, talking about everything and nothing: the art fair coming up, the renovation on Main Street, the adorable couple that owned The Oasis.

When Mom mentioned it, Abby's eyes lit up. "Oh, we're going," she said. "No arguing. You're back in town, and it's Thursday. That means live music and peach sangria. Remember?"

"I'm not exactly in a going-out mood," I said.

"That's why we're going out," she said. "To remind you the world didn't end."

The rain had stopped by the time we parked.

From the road, it looked almost ethereal—the restaurant perched high above the lake, its terraces carved into the cliff like a secret kept too long. The building seemed to breathe with the landscape, every pane of glass catching the last blush of sunset. The mountains in the distance were draped in mist, softening into blues and golds.

We followed a curved path toward the entrance, our shoes brushing against flagstone still damp from the storm. The air was cool, heavy with petrichor and the faint sweetness of something blooming. Along the walkway, the gardens spilled over with October color—goldenrod, marigolds, and late-blooming dahlias glowing beneath the lantern light. Ivy curled up the stone walls, and clusters of purple asters trembled in the breeze. A few white roses lingered in bloom, their petals touched with rain.

The sound of water came from somewhere—a hidden fountain tucked between hedges, its gentle trickle rising and falling beneath the murmur of voices and the low hum of music drifting from the open doors. As we climbed the last few steps, the lake came into view far below, spread wide and endless, its surface catching the reflections of string lights and the first stars breaking through the clouds. Boats looked small as birds from this height, their wakes thin and fleeting against the glassy water.

For a moment, I just stood there, taking it all in—the elevation, the stillness, the way the world felt paused. The Oasis had always been beautiful, but this was something else entirely. Like the place itself had grown up while I was gone.

Inside, the air was warm and fragrant, layered with the scent of roasted vegetables, and wood smoke. A grand stone fireplace anchored the far wall, its flames casting soft light across the polished floors. The old, familiar bones of the restaurant were still there—arched doorways, wooden beams, and the wide windows overlooking the lake—but everything felt more open now. More alive.

The dining room buzzed with quiet energy. Couples leaned close at tables lit by flickering candles. A jazz trio played near the bar, soft and slow, filling the space with the type of music that made people linger. Along one wall, framed photographs of Tunbridge through the years hung between shelves of potted herbs and bottles of local wine.

Near the host stand, a voice stopped me cold. Emerson Sterling moved through the dining room with the same quiet grace I'd admired since elementary school. Her hair was swept into a loose twist, a few strands falling free to frame her face. When she turned her head, the sconces lit the gold in it like something celestial. She leaned toward a server and murmured something encouraging, and just like that, I was ten again—shaking before a chorus recital, clutching sheet music with sweaty hands. She'd said something similar back then. Worn the same calm smile. And somehow, made me believe I could do it.

Her husband, Sam, appeared beside her, the kind of man who made space just by standing still. He brushed his hand against her arm as he leaned in, and the small, unthinking gesture said more than any grand display ever could. She looked up at him and smiled—one of those smiles that had a story behind it, the kind you only give someone who's seen every side of you.

"Heading home to relieve the sitter," he said, his voice easy, familiar. He pressed a quick kiss to her cheek, and she caught his wrist as if she might not let him go just yet.

"Be careful," she said softly.

"Always."

He grinned at her, then at the bar staff, lifting a hand in farewell before he disappeared through the door. She watched him until it closed, her expression a mixture of love and knowing.

For a second, I forgot to breathe. That kind of love—the quiet, steady kind—wasn't loud, but it filled the room.

My parents had loved each other like that. Never dramatic, never performative. Just two people who kept choosing each other in the ordinary moments—coffee cups, porch lights, Sunday drives. But Emerson and Sam... they had something almost cinematic. A spark you could feel even across a room. The kind of electricity that made you believe in destiny for a second.

I wanted that. Someday. Even if I didn't know what it would look like for me—or whether it would ever really exist outside the stories I wrote in my head.

Emerson turned and her face lit up. "Rose?"

I laughed. "Hey, stranger."

"Oh my gosh." She stepped in for a quick hug. "How long are you in town?"

I hesitated. "I don't know. For a while."

"Then we're catching up. I'll text you."

"Deal."

She smiled and walked to a far table, Sam's laughter echoing faintly as he disappeared through the front door. It felt like no time had passed yet also like a lifetime had.

The host stand was surrounded by tall vases of autumn branches—russet oak leaves, dried hydrangeas, and golden wheat. A couple laughed from a nearby table, and the sound mixed with the clinking of glasses, the distant low of conversation, the pulse of a place that had found its rhythm.

Strings of lights glowed over the patio, reflecting off puddles in soft halos. The air smelled like grilled corn and lake air. A small band played near the bar—an old country song I half-remembered from childhood.

Mom waved to someone inside. "Half the town's here," she said.

"Exactly," Abby said. "We're reintegrating Rose into society."

I laughed, though part of me wanted to bolt. It had been years since I'd felt small in a crowd, but here, it wasn't the bad kind.

We were taken to a table near the back, the wood worn smooth by time and elbows. The waitress brought menus and water with lemon.

"You should see your face," Abby said. "You're glowing."

"That's sweat," I said. "Or panic."

"Same difference." She raised her glass. "To new chapters."

I clinked mine against hers. "And surviving the last one."

As the night settled in, music rose through the chatter. Someone at the next table started a round of laughter that caught half the room. A man at the bar. Tall, broad-shouldered, dark hair silvering at the temples. He was talking to the bartender, smiling with the type of ease I wanted to be around.

Abby followed my gaze. "See something interesting?"

"No," I said too quickly.

She smirked. "You're a terrible liar."

I shook my head, embarrassed. "I'm not ready for something interesting."

"Then don't be ready," she said. "Just notice it."

The band shifted to something slower. The lights dimmed. For the first time in months, I felt my pulse slow to match the rhythm instead of fighting it.

Mom leaned over. "You okay?"

"Yeah," I said softly. "I think I might be."

The next few hours were a blur of drinks, appetizers, and that divine apple cobbler. And a lot of laughter. I forgot about my problems for a while.

We left The Oasis under a sky that smelled of wet earth and woodsmoke. The streetlights cast pale circles on the pavers. Leaves stuck to the soles of my shoes.

When we reached Mom's car, she turned to me. "You know, your old art teacher's husband rents that loft on Main Street. The one overlooking the square."

"Short-term?" I asked.

"He mentioned it at the market last week. Said it's available through winter."

"I'll call him tomorrow."

She smiled. "You don't have to rush."

"I do," I said, but gently this time.

Somewhere down the ridge, a frog croaked once and stopped. The lake was still that night. I stood on the back porch wrapped in one of Mom's quilts. The reflection of the moon wavered in the dark water.

I breathed in the clean, damp scent of October pine and for the first time since the crash, my lungs didn't fight it.

Inside, I could hear Mom humming again, the same tune she always hummed when she painted. I thought about the condo—

its sterile silence, the hum of machines, the emptiness pretending to be order.

The quiet pressed close around me, but it wasn't heavy anymore. It felt like grace. Like the world had paused just long enough for me to exhale. I realized I wasn't mourning the life I'd left—I was finally making room for the one I'd been meant to live.

I pulled out my phone and opened the real estate app. My thumb hovered for a second before I hit "List Property."

Fully furnished. Immediate availability.

When the confirmation screen appeared, something loosened in my chest.

The porch light flickered once in the wind.

I whispered into the dark, "I'm home."

But I didn't go inside right away. The screen still glowed in my hand, the app suggesting "similar listings nearby." I scrolled absently though cottages, farmhouses, lake rentals and then paused.

A thumbnail photo filled the screen: *The Old Mill Lofts of Tunbridge*—historic building, lake access, exposed brick, available now.

My breath caught.

That building. The old cotton mill.

When I was little, I used to press my hands against its cool brick walls and imagine what it must've been like a hundred years ago—machines humming, denim dyed blue as the lake. I remembered the smell of dust and oil, the way the sunlight used to pour through the broken windows in wide, golden slants. It had sat empty for years, this quiet giant at the edge of town.

And now...

The photo showed it alive again—string lights strung across weathered brick, window boxes spilling with ivy, a sliver of lake glowing gold behind it. The beams, the arched windows, the bones of something that had survived. It looked nothing like the modern condo I'd just left behind. This place was old, imperfect, *real*.

A smile crept up before I could stop it. I didn't even check the price. I just stared, heart beating faster than it should.

I'd always loved that building.

And somehow, it felt like it had been waiting for me.

Something in me stilled. The sort of stillness that comes right before you move.

CHAPTER 7
Built Twice

Lease in one hand, key to my new loft in the other, I stood two weeks later in front of the old Tunbridge Mill. The air was warm for October, filled with sunlight and the smell of pine and baked earth. Gold leaves drifted across the cobblestone drive, catching on the steps before tumbling away.

I'd signed the lease the same day I saw it, without hesitation. Ten years of saving every spare dollar had finally bought me something worth keeping: freedom.

Now, standing in the doorway of my new place—a short-term rental, for now—I wondered if maybe this was what starting over was supposed to feel like: terrifying and holy in equal measure.

I looked inside—exposed brick, black-framed windows, lake views that caught light like glass.

So different from the floor-to-ceiling panes in the Buckhead high-rise where I used to work. Those windows showed the city but never let me feel it. They reflected pressure, expectation, ambition. These windows held something else entirely—quiet, breath, the sense that my life might finally belong to me.

My unit sat at the end, just above the waterline, with a deck that looked out toward the trees. You could still see the faint lettering of *Tunbridge Cotton Mill Exchange* ghosted across the old brick. Someone had left one of the factory pulleys hanging from a beam, like a relic refusing to leave. I loved it immediately. It reminded me that things could be built twice and still be beautiful.

I closed the door. The space smelled like lemon cleaner and sawdust. Two bedrooms, one bath, wood floors that creaked like they remembered every life that had come before mine. The ceilings were high, the light soft and golden. I told myself it was perfect.

The silence disagreed.

I'd lived with so much noise for so long. Traffic, construction, conversations stacked on top of each other in stifling rooms—that the quiet of Tunbridge felt almost defiant. Every creak of the floorboard, every hum of the fridge seemed louder here, like the house was learning my heartbeat. I cracked a window just to remind myself the world was still moving. Outside, laughter drifted up from the square. Someone walked a dog past the bakery, its collar jingling in time with distant music. A screen door shut somewhere, soft and final. The town had its own kind of noise. Gentler, human, alive. I just had to learn its rhythm again.

Boxes were stacked in the main room, some labeled in my handwriting from the condo, others fresh from delivery—dishes, clothes, the last pieces of my old life mixed with new things I wasn't sure I needed yet. It smelled faintly of cardboard and clean wood, the scent of starting over.

The essentials were already here. A new mattress, still crisp from delivery. Clean sheets. A coffee maker on the counter. Enough to live, if not to feel settled.

The first box I opened was full of furniture parts and bad decisions. "Assembly required," it warned, as if I didn't already know. I stared at the manual, some cruel joke of black-and-white drawings that clearly assumed I had a background in engineering. "Right," I muttered. "Sure."

By midafternoon, I'd built part of a chair and stripped every screw on the coffee table. My hair was a knot, my hands a battlefield of tiny splinters. I gave up, laughed at myself, and decided the only thing I was qualified to assemble was caffeine.

Drucker's General Store was only a block away and it looked just like it did many years ago, happy in its original rustic state. That was part of its charm. The bell above the door jingled as I stepped into a world that smelled like cedar and fresh bread.

Arnold, the manager, looked up from the register and sang, "Goooood morning!" like he was auditioning for a musical.

Inside, narrow aisles wound between bins of apples and potatoes, shelves of canned goods and hand-labeled jars of local honey. Wooden crates held warm loaves from the town bakery, their paper wrappers fogged from heat. A galvanized tub near the entrance overflowed with small pumpkins and white gourds. Two straw bales flanked the produce section, each propped with a tiny scarecrow that had probably been pulled from storage every October for the past twenty years.

One aisle offered work gloves and seed packets. Another stocked coffee, soap, and pie filling. Everything carried a gentle slant. Crates a little askew, chalkboard labels angled from years of being handled—but it all felt intentional, like the owners knew exactly what the town needed and kept it ready. It wasn't just a store. It was a little piece of Tunbridge that had stayed steady while the rest of the world sped up.

A woman about my age stood near the front, arranging buckets of flowers. Her blonde hair was tied back with a ribbon, her apron dusted with flower petals. She looked up when I entered, eyes bright with instant recognition.

"Rose?"

I blinked, caught off guard. "Alice?"

She turned, a bundle of dahlias in hand, and her whole face lit up. "Rose? No way." She wiped her palms on her apron and pulled me into a quick hug that smelled faintly of cloves and eucalyptus.

When she stepped back, she gestured to the buckets of flowers around her. "Drucker's started carrying a few of my arrangements on weekends. Locals kept asking, so now I restock twice a week. Keeps me on my toes."

"That's amazing," I said.

She laughed. "Busy is an understatement. Fall weddings, homecoming, tourists pretending they're locals... plus the twins' Halloween parade yesterday. Jack went as a dragon. Lucy refused to be anything but a pumpkin princess. And Johnny swears he didn't almost cry when they walked out, but he's a terrible liar."

Warmth rushed through me. "They sound perfect."

"They're wild," she said, eyes soft. "But perfect."

She leaned against the counter. "So... how's big-city life? Still working at that big-city marketing job?"

"I'm kind of between jobs," I said. "Decided to slow down for a bit. Recalibrate."

Alice nodded knowingly. "Good for you. This town has a way of doing that. Forcing you to recalibrate."

"I could use that," I said.

She reached behind the cart, pulled out a small bouquet, and tucked it into my bag—dahlias, eucalyptus, and something wild that smelled like cloves and cinnamon. "Welcome back to Tunbridge," she said softly. "First bouquet's on me."

"That's really kind."

"Not kindness," she teased. "Marketing. You'll learn."

I walked home through the chill, the bouquet brushing my wrist. When I set it on the counter, it changed the whole place. Just a few stems in a mason jar—and suddenly, the loft didn't look like a holding space for uncertainty. It looked like possibility.

By Friday, I'd befriended the delivery drivers, learned which light switch hummed, and given up on the coffee table. Abby texted around five.

> Abby: How's the glamorous new life?

> Me: Unorganized. Slightly crazy.

> Abby: Sending reinforcements.

Two hours later, she arrived with Emerson and Alice in tow, plus tuna melts from Sundancer—courtesy of Emerson herself.

"Perks of knowing the owner," she said with a wink.

Alice carried a cordless drill that looked more powerful than my rental car. "We came prepared."

Within minutes, the loft turned into a construction zone. Emerson knelt over the disassembled chair like she was solving a mystery. Alice sorted screws into tidy piles. Abby played DJ, queuing up the songs we used to listen to in high school.

"Remember when the old gym ceiling leaked every time it rained?" Abby said as she unpacked the food.

"And they pretended buckets were part of the décor," Alice added.

"They finally remodeled last year," Emerson said. "New floors, new lights, no more 1960s beige everywhere. Kids these days don't know the trauma of learning algebra with rainwater dripping on the whiteboard."

I laughed. "Or eating those square pizzas on plastic trays that smelled like crayons."

"Still the best pizza of my childhood," Abby said. "I stand by that."

We kept building and talking—about homecoming parades, teachers we loved, teachers who definitely didn't love us, and the rumor that the eighth-grade hallway was still haunted.

Emerson tightened the final screw on the chair and stood with a proud flourish. "You've got good bones here," she said, glancing around. "And the kind of light you can't buy."

Alice nudged me gently. "Start settling in. And next weekend? Cocktails at Sundancer. No excuses."

"I'll think about it."

When they left, the loft felt different. Still raw. Still unfinished. But warmer. Their laughter clung to the brick and the air, filling the empty spaces. For the first time since the accident, the place felt like somewhere I might actually belong.

A call came from the impound lot a few days later.

"Your vehicle's been released," the man said. "You can come by anytime to collect your belongings."

Belongings. The word felt strange. What could possibly be left worth keeping?

The lot was on the edge of the industrial district, where everything looked temporary—chain-link fences, gravel crunching under tires, the metallic smell of rain and rust. When the man led me down the row, I spotted it before he pointed.

My SUV.

Or what was left of it.

It didn't look like something that had rolled, it looked like something that had been *folded*. The roof caved in and the frame was twisted. My breath caught. It was one thing to remember the sound of metal, another to see what it had become.

He stopped beside me, hands in his jacket pockets. "I'm sorry for your loss," he said quietly.

I almost told him no one had died. Then I realized maybe, in some way, someone had.

I stepped closer, fingers brushing the door handle that used to fit my palm like second nature. The metal was cold. The windows were gone, blown out by the roll. Inside, the airbags hung deflated, gray against twisted metal. Dark stains covered the roof —the part that hit the ground when it flipped. My blood. I hadn't realized how much there was until now.

It looked like a tomb. And yet, somehow, it saved me.

For a second, I hated myself for thanking it. Then I realized it wasn't gratitude for survival. It was for the chance to start again.

I leaned in, took the registration and insurance from the glove box, a pen from the console, the tiny ceramic charm Abby had given me years ago that somehow hadn't broken. When I straightened, the wind caught my hair and pushed it across my face.

"Thank you," I whispered.

Back in the rental car, I sat for a long time before turning the key. I couldn't stop staring at the wreck in the mirror—silent proof that I shouldn't be here and yet was.

That night, I searched online for the same model. Same year, same everything. It wasn't sentimentality. It was respect. That SUV had done its job. It saved my life. Two days later, I drove off the dealership lot in a pearl-white one. The color felt deliberate. My old car had been charcoal, the kind of shade that swallowed light. This one seemed to reflect it back. Clean. Bright. New. It made me think of fresh starts and blank pages and the strange relief of still being here to turn them.

The engine sounded the same. The seat fit like memory. For the first time since the accident, the silence inside didn't scare me.

A few days later, three women from my Buckhead circle came to "see the new place." They arrived in perfume clouds and designer boots that hated gravel—the type of women who never stood anywhere without marble beneath them.

Vanessa, my old agency partner, immediately started filming a Story for her followers. "Wait—you *live* here now?" she asked, panning toward the exposed brick.

"Why would you ever leave that condo?" murmured Claire, an old co-worker from Elaren.

"It's rented now," I said lightly. "Someone else can have the skyline. I like waking up to trees."

They blinked at me, unimpressed.

Mallory, who once threw launch parties that made magazine

spreads, ran a manicured finger over the railing. "So rustic," she said, like she ate a bad word.

Within minutes, they were checking their phones, asking if Tunbridge had Uber Black and where they could get oat milk lattes "that don't taste like barn." They didn't mean to be cruel, but they were. I could feel it in every glance—the quiet horror at my downgrade, the pity disguised as politeness.

They stayed barely an hour, long enough to confirm that the air here was too still, the floors too old, and the view too real. When they finally left, the silence that returned wasn't lonely. It was peaceful.

When the door shut behind them, the silence that returned felt different from every other quiet moment I'd had here. It wasn't loneliness. It was a relief. I stood for a long time in the stillness, trying to remember if I had really been that woman—the one who measured her worth by skyline views and job titles and how fast she could climb a ladder no one actually cared about. Maybe I had been. Maybe I'd just been pretending. Watching the three of them walk back to their perfect cars felt like looking at an old photograph of myself taken from too far away. Whatever life they lived now, it wasn't mine. And for the first time, that didn't feel like a loss. It felt like liberation.

Rose Bennett Consulting.
    The words came before I could second-guess them.
    I said it out loud. It filled the room.
    It sounded like permission.
    The morning had felt restless.
    I had brewed strong coffee and opened my laptop at the kitchen table. One of the flowers from Alice's bouquet had wilted, but it still smelled alive. I had stared at the blinking cursor. Then the idea materialized.
    I started writing—not a full plan, just fragments of the life I

wanted. Notes scribbled in margins: *clarity that connects, no jargon, no noise, just meaning.*

Names of old clients came next, each one like a spark. I wrote them down and imagined the calls I could make, the freedom of choosing who I worked for and what I believed in.

The sun climbed. Coffee went cold. My fingers cramped, but I couldn't stop. By noon, I had outlined services, drafted packages, even sketched a logo in the corner of a napkin—clean serif font, black ink, honest. For once, I wasn't hiding behind someone else's company.

A pulse of fear broke through the rush—sharp, bright. I typed, "How to start an LLC in Georgia." My heart thudded as the state portal loaded.

I didn't click "submit." Not yet. I clicked "save."

Maybe courage wasn't jumping. Maybe it was the pause before.

A knock broke the quiet.

Alice stood outside with a pastry box.

"Emergency sugar delivery," she said. "Florist code for 'you look like you haven't eaten in a while.'"

"Accurate."

Her eyes flicked to the laptop. "Are you working?"

"Plotting," I said. "Thinking of starting something of my own."

Her grin widened. "That's how all the best Tunbridge stories start—someone who's got a passion they can't put down."

"You sound like my Granny."

"Your Granny is a smart woman," she said. "If you need a logo or sign, I know a guy."

When she left, I stood in the doorway holding the pastry box and realized my face hurt from smiling.

I worked until dusk. Registered a domain name. Chose a color palette that felt like confidence—warm ivory, slate, and the faintest blush of copper. I uploaded my first header image: sunlight over the lake. *Clarity that connects.*

By midnight, I had a rough website, a candle burning low beside me, and a kind of exhaustion that felt clean.

I leaned back and looked around the loft. It wasn't perfect, but it was mine. The air smelled like pastry sugar and cedar. Outside, the lake was still except for one ripple that caught the moonlight.

For the first time in months, I didn't want to go to sleep just to escape my thoughts. I wanted to stay awake and see what came next.

I closed the laptop and went to the window. The glass was cool under my fingertips. My reflection looked different—barefaced, unarmored, alive. The woman staring back wasn't waiting for permission anymore.

Somewhere across the water, a train sounded its low, mournful whistle. The note stretched long and clear, like a thread pulled through time.

I thought of Richard, of glass towers and clipped smiles and the endless climb that never led anywhere. I thought of the road outside town—the roll, the crash, the man whose voice pulled me back. How maybe that night hadn't been punishment, but an intervention.

The world hadn't tried to break me. It had tried to stop me.

To make me look.

To make me choose.

Maybe this was what it had been saying all along: Start over. But this time, start with yourself.

I whispered it to the window, to the water, to whatever had been listening all this time. "This time, it's mine."

Not a vow. Not a performance. Just the quiet certainty of a woman who finally understood her own worth.

My job had been taken. My project had been handed off. My life had spun out on a wet Georgia road. But this?

This was the one thing no one could take from me.

Built by my hands. Defined by my voice. Answering only to me.

Behind me, the laptop screen dimmed, leaving the faint outline of my new logo glowing in the dark:

Rose Bennett Consulting.

Building what matters.

The words glowed soft and certain. A beginning.

Outside, the wind stirred the leaves on the trees. They caught the moonlight and lifted, like something learning how to rise.

CHAPTER 8
A Voice I Already Knew

The morning opened slowly and bright over the lake. Sunlight pushed through the mill windows and warmed the old brick. I stood at the sink with my coffee and watched a small boat cut a neat seam across the water. The whirring of its motor drifted up the hill, then faded. My loft had settled overnight. Wood planks relaxed. A loose window screen ticked in a breeze that tasted like pine and cold.

I had work to do and nowhere to be. That freedom felt like a gift and a dare. The website draft waited on the table with a handful of names scrawled beside the laptop. I stared at them until the letters blurred. The quiet stretched and could tip either way, into peace or into nerves. I grabbed my bag.

The Rusty Skillet was already busy when I walked over. The air carried that thin edge of October, all woodsmoke and quiet endings. Trucks lined the side fence. The scent of bacon and syrup spilled into the chill like a promise. I stepped inside and the bell over the door gave its tired little ring. Warmth rolled over me, a mix of coffee steam, maple, and old wood. People talked in the voices of a town that had known itself for years. Dixie waved me toward a booth by the window.

"Back again, sugar?" she said, setting down a mug before I asked. "It's so wonderful seeing your face here again."

"Hi Dixie. You know me, I'm easy to please. Coffee and a corner," I said.

"Kitchen is behind, life is ahead, and the ass-kicking happens in between," she replied with a wink, then moved on, refilling a farmer's cup in one smooth swing. The old diner ran on that kind of rhythm. It felt like music you only hear if you sit still a minute.

I set my notebook on the table and tried to focus. Words came in fits, little sparks that fizzled as soon as I chased them. The room was half chatter and half clink. A baby squealed. A fork scraped a plate. Someone laughed at the counter with a sound that made other people smile.

The bell over the door rang again, sharper this time, and a cold draft sliced through the warmth. I didn't look up at first. I was trying to coax a sentence to behave.

Then I heard it.

That voice.

Low. Steady. The same calm that broke through the crush of metal and dust that night.

"Morning, Dixie. Can I get a coffee to go?" he said.

Everything in me stilled.

I looked up and there he was. Not ten steps away. A navy flight jacket, crew bag at his feet, sunglasses hooked into the collar like he'd just come off a long-haul. His hair slightly pushed back. Tired in the way people look when they've seen too many time zones before sunrise.

A pilot.

Of course he was.

Some part of him already carried the sky.

Dixie lit up. "Charlie, you're early. Headed out again?"

Charlie.

The name hit me low and steady, two syllables that landed like a heartbeat.

Char-lie.

It suited him in a way I couldn't explain. Solid. Rooted. Yet with something restless pulsing underneath. The kind of name you didn't just hear. You felt.

I didn't know him. I shouldn't have reacted at all. But something in me tightened, not fear, not attraction, just awareness. A small tug, like the moment before a compass needle swings north.

He gave a small nod. "Connection in Atlanta. An hour to spare."

That explained everything. Why he had been on the road that night. Why he'd vanished before I could speak. Why he was here now and already half gone.

She handed him a to-go cup. He wrapped his hand around it, testing the heat like someone who'd burned themselves on too many airport coffees to trust a lid.

He looked up.

Straight at me.

Recognition hit like a tide. His expression didn't change much—just a softening around the eyes, a faint pull at the corner of his mouth, like he was relieved I was upright and breathing.

I felt my hand tighten around my mug.

He took a step toward the exit. Then paused. Turned back.

"Hey," he said quietly.

My throat worked before the sound came. "Hi."

He had the kind of green eyes that made silence feel like conversation.

"You're alright?" he asked.

Not casual. Not obligatory. A check-in from someone who'd seen me bleeding and still.

"I am," I said, softer than I meant to. "Thanks to you."

Something flickered across his face—embarrassment maybe, or something gentler. "Good."

We held there, suspended by a thread that neither of us tugged.

He shifted his bag higher on his shoulder. Someone at the counter called his name. Charlie. He lifted two fingers in acknowledgment.

He hesitated—just long enough to make my pulse do something strange—and then tipped an invisible cap in my direction, with the same piercing eyes that lived in my memory since the wreck.

He pushed through the door. The bell rang. The cold swept in. And then he was gone.

Dixie set a plate in front of me. Pancakes that looked like clouds. Butter melting in a slow slide. I thanked her, then didn't touch them. Every inch of me felt lit from the inside. Gratitude pushed up through my chest so fast it hurt. Also something else. Not attraction yet. Something older than that. Safety maybe. A memory of being seen when it mattered and not claimed for it.

The sound of the door shutting echoed through me longer than it should have. For a second, I hated how quickly life resumed—plates clattering, laughter rising again—like the world hadn't just folded back on itself.

I exhaled without meaning to. Dixie leaned against the next booth with a coffee pot in her hand and a look that could read a mile.

"You alright there, Rose?" she asked.

"Fine," I said, and heard the way the word shook. "Just a long week."

She topped my cup with gentleness as if coffee could be laid down like a blanket.

"Feels shorter with pancakes," she said. "Eat before the butter runs away."

I took a bite because she was right and because the act of chewing returned the earth to its axis. Syrup pooled on the plate in a slow amber lake. My hands steadied. My body knew how to do normal things again, like swallow and breathe.

I watched the door as if it might open and turn the moment into something else. It didn't. That was alright. The room warmed around the edges and a baby squealed again. Life snapped back into place.

The bell rang a few minutes later. Emerson slipped in wearing an apron and a smile that was already apologizing for being late. She spotted me and came over, her cheeks bright from the wind.

"I told you the pie was dangerous," she said, dropping into the seat across from me without asking. "I'm here to bear witness."

"You'll have to fight Dixie for the last piece," I said.

Emerson leaned over the table, lowered her voice.

"How's the loft?"

"Starting to feel like a place a person could live," I said. "Not just a storage unit someone put windows on."

"And the business?" Her eyes flicked to my notebook. "I was so happy to see your text about it. You've got the skills."

"I'm working on it," I said. "Scared, but pushing through the fear of failure."

She grinned and squeezed my hand once. "Tell me when you are ready to tell the town. We gossip kindly."

I laughed, the kind that felt easy again.

"And I want to be your first client," she added, tapping the table for emphasis.

We ordered pie to share. Emerson told me about a delivery mix-up at The Oasis that left her with fifty extra packages of burger buns and how, for two straight weeks, her house had smelled like burgers and her kids were one meal away from rebellion. I told her I owned three hammers and still hadn't built a shelf.

Somewhere between the laughter and the crumbs, it hit me—we'd grown up. But somehow, this felt the same. Two girls trading dreams at a diner table, only now the dirt under our nails was replaced by plans we might actually keep. Maybe that's what growing up in Tunbridge meant. You come back to who you were—just cleaner shoes, better pie.

While we ate, I thumbed the edge of my notebook and tried to coax my pulse back down. The door opened twice. Neither time was him. The second time a man in a cap brought in a box of paper cups and shouted hello toward the kitchen. The ordinary pressed in again, steady and welcome.

When Emerson left, I stayed with my coffee. Dixie cleared a table and refilled creamers and kept an eye on me without hovering. I could have gotten up then and found the rest of my day. The thought of the laptop waiting on the kitchen table tugged like an invitation and a test. I was about to slide out of the booth when I saw it.

Dixie appeared with the check and offered, "We keep extra pie in the back if you need to think it over."

"I might take you up on that," I said.

Cups clicked against saucers. A boy in a hoodie carried a box of donuts past the window and tilted his head back to laugh at something his friend said. Sunlight traveled a slow diagonal across the floor.

I paid and stepped out into the cold that had sharpened while I sat. The sky was hard blue and high. The wind smelled like leaves and the lake. A car door thumped somewhere up the block. I stood for a moment with my hand on the diner's railing and looked at the storefronts as if they might answer a question I hadn't asked yet.

A rack of rakes and brooms stood outside Drucker's, with a chalkboard sign leaned against the window that read CIDER TODAY. The door to Alice's flower shop, Beloved Blooms, wore a wreath of dried grasses with a silk ribbon that lifted and fell as the door opened and closed. Someone propped the door open with a brick. A small girl in a pink coat ran to catch a leaf with her hands and missed, then laughed at her own attempt.

I crossed to the bakery and bought a loaf of bread still hot from the oven. The bag warmed my hands and fogged a little in the air. On my way back to the loft, I paused at the edge of the mill's yard and looked out over the water. The bones of the trees on the far side were starting to show between leaves. The surface had that old pewter color it takes on in October. A pair of ducks cut a clean V across it, indifferent to everything else.

At home I put the bread on the counter and the receipt on the table. I didn't look at it. I wrote an email to one of the names on my list instead. Then another. *Thank you for your note last spring. I'm consulting independently now. If you are taking proposals, I would love to talk.* I read each message three times and cut every word that sounded like an apology.

The lake shifted color as clouds drifted over the sun. A shadow moved across the far bank and set the water shivering. I sent the emails one by one and felt the small click of each decision as it left my outbox. Courage rarely arrived as a speech in my life. It showed up as a series of small choices that looked almost ordinary.

And somewhere in all that quiet movement, Charlie drifted through my mind—not loud, not demanding, just present, like a thought you don't fully examine because you're not ready for what it might mean.

Maybe tomorrow I would walk into The Rusty Skillet at lunch and there he'd be, bent over the coffee machine again, saving the morning a second time by fixing something everyone else had given up on. Maybe I would say hello and his face would react the way it had before, with recognition that didn't reach for ownership. Maybe we would exchange names and nothing else. Maybe that would be plenty.

The mill creaked once like an old man settling his joints. I could feel the town moving through its day. Someone at the orchard would be shaking apples into a bin. Someone at The Oasis would be whisking dressing in a metal bowl. Someone would be backing a truck down a narrow driveway and cursing a little under their breath. Life continued. I had a part in it now that didn't require me to prove anything but that I was here.

I poured myself some coffee and stood at the window.

When I sat back down, I tucked a single sheet of paper into the front of my notebook. The top line read *Rose Bennett Consulting*. The second line read *Clarity that connects*. The third line said *Clients to call,* and the list waited for ink. I looked at the receipt beneath the stone dish and thought of a country road and a steady voice in smoke.

Thank you, I thought, finally finishing the sentence my body had started weeks ago. *Thank you for opening the door. Thank you for staying. Thank you for leaving a town small enough that I could find you again without needing to chase.*

Outside, the late light caught the lake and held there in a bright band. It looked like a path. It looked like a sign. It looked like the kind of beauty that doesn't demand you choose it, only that you notice.

I picked up my pen. I wrote the first name on my list. Then I wrote the next.

CHAPTER 9
When the Wind Shifted

The Tunbridge Market stretched across the old square like a living mural—tents in every color, strings of lights zigzagging between oak trees, the air alive with chatter and cinnamon. The pavement shimmered faintly from a morning drizzle, and the scent of roasted nuts drifted from a nearby cart.

I followed Mom and Granny through the crowd, half-listening as they debated whether to buy peach jam or honey butter. Booths lined the street in a patchwork of local pride—hand-thrown pottery, stitched quilts, stacks of mason jars catching the light like amber glass.

It wasn't a holiday, just Tunbridge being Tunbridge—everyone showing up to remind each other they still belonged somewhere.

"Half of the county's here," Mom said, weaving through a line for coffee.

"Exactly why I love it," Granny answered. "You can't get lost in a place that remembers your name."

I smiled, distracted by a sign near the fountain: *Buy Local, Build Together*. The words hit deeper than they should've. That's what I was here for today—connections.

Not for fun, not yet. I'd come to hand out cards for *Rose*

Bennett Consulting, testing whether this new life could have roots in old ground.

A gust of wind rattled one of the tents, sending paper flyers tumbling across the cobblestones. I caught one on reflex, straightened it, and froze at the logo printed across the bottom—*Warren Tutoring and SAT Prep.*

My stomach fluttered.

"Helen Warren!" Mom called suddenly, waving at a woman across the way.

I turned. A petite woman with silver hair tucked behind her ears looked up from arranging cupcakes on a table. Her face sparked instant recognition—time having softened but not erased the familiar warmth in her eyes.

"Rose Bennett?" she said, beaming as I approached and hugged her. "I was just telling your mother I still have your third-grade poem on my bulletin board. Something about hearts and strawberry ice cream, wasn't it?"

I laughed, cheeks warm. "Oh no, you remember that?"

"I remember all my dreamers," she said. "Do you know my daughter? Elizabeth—she's the baker in the family. Elizabeth looked up from arranging her display, brushing flour from her hands. Her eyes widened a little, like she was flipping through old yearbooks in her head.

"Rose Bennett? No way," she said, stepping around the table. "I thought that was you. Didn't we have algebra together? Freshman year? Mr. Haber's class?"

I laughed, caught off guard. "Oh my gosh. Yes. He had that giant Georgia Bulldogs flag above the whiteboard."

Elizabeth groaned. "And the matching tie. And the coffee mug. And the socks. I swear he owned more Bulldog merch than actual lesson plans."

"That man loved that team more than oxygen," I said.

"He still does! He's still teaching." She leaned in for a quick hug that somehow felt warm and familiar, like picking up a friendship that had been paused instead of lost. "It's so good to see you back in town."

"And that's my son, Charlie—when he's actually in town." Mrs. Warren added.

Charlie straightened from where he was tightening the tent pole behind her booth. He wore a faded blue thermal, dust on his hands that somehow belonged there. When he turned, recognition slid across his face like sunlight breaking through clouds.

For a second, neither of us said anything. The world narrowed to the sound of a guitar tuning somewhere nearby and the slow flap of the market banner overhead.

"You two know each other?" Mrs. Warren asked, glancing between us.

Charlie's mouth tilted. "Not *officially*."

I cleared my throat. "But we've met. Sort of."

"Ah." Mrs. Warren gave a knowing smile that mothers seem born with. "Well then, *officially*, Rose—this is my son, the elusive pilot who refuses to stay grounded."

He wiped his palms on his jeans and offered his hand. "Nice to meet you, Rose."

"You too," I said, taking it. His grip was warm, firm. The kind of steady that had once anchored me in chaos.

Elizabeth laughed lightly. "Charlie's home for a few days, then off again. We never know where he's going next. Some people collect postcards—he collects runways."

"Occupational hazard," he said. "And you're back in town, too?"

"For now," I said. "Testing what it feels like to stay still."

His eyes flicked with something like recognition. "That's a good experiment."

"Speaking of," Elizabeth said, leaning over her table, "you're officially hired to taste-test whatever's left. I over-baked again."

Mom was already halfway to her purse. "Over-baked means perfect in this family."

Granny nudged me. "Help them, Rose. That tent looks like it's about to fly off."

I stepped forward, catching the corner just as the wind pushed through. Charlie reached at the same time. His hand landed over mine on the canvas tie.

"Got it," he said quietly.

"Seems that way," I replied, though I hadn't meant to sound breathless.

He secured the rope, then glanced sideways at me. "You always pick fights with the weather, or just on Saturdays?"

"Only when it starts first."

His laugh was low, unhurried. "You're not as city-soft as I expected."

"Don't test me," I cautioned, but I was smiling.

He studied me for a beat longer than polite before turning back to check the stakes.

"You know," he said, "That was a scary night."

The noise of the market dimmed.

He nodded, almost like he had to steady himself before going on. "I was behind you on 212. You braked hard and swerved—at least that's what it looked like. Everything went quick. I pulled over the second your SUV went over." A slow breath left him. "It rolled more times than I could count. I didn't think anyone would climb out of that."

For a moment I couldn't breathe. Words felt too small for what he'd done, but anything bigger would've broken the fragile normalcy between us. I wanted to ask where he went after, if he thought about it the way I did—but his mother's voice saved us both from the question.

"I was scared you were seriously hurt," he said simply.

Something in me slipped. The truth rose before I could cage it.

"If you hadn't been there…"

I couldn't finish. My throat refused to let the rest out.

His eyes softened, the kind of softness that reached deeper than comfort.

"I'm just glad you're here," he said quietly.

Something shifted in my chest—gratitude, grief, awe—all tangled and raw. I opened my mouth, but the words tangled, too.

Mrs. Warren's voice floated over. "Charlie, honey, can you bring another box from the truck?"

"On it," he called back. Then, softer to me, "I'll be right back."

When he walked away, I let out the breath I'd been holding.

Mom came up behind me with a cupcake. "He's kind, isn't he?"

"Very," I said carefully.

"You know, his mother still brags about him flying into hurricane zones with supplies. Every time I see her, I feel like I need to apologize for not raising a superhero."

I smiled faintly, eyes still following him through the crowd. "He seems grounded for someone who practically lives in the air."

Granny appeared beside us, balancing a cup of cider. "Don't analyze, just notice," she said, echoing Abby's advice from weeks earlier. "Life's easier when you let it surprise you."

My phone buzzed in my pocket. I stepped aside from the booth, excited to see Grant's name glowing on the screen.

"Hey stranger," I answered.

"Rose?" His voice had that distracted warmth I'd known my whole life, the kind of tone that meant he was talking while typing, probably hunched over a laptop with three monitors glowing around him. "You alive?"

"Last I checked." I swallowed, still feeling the tremor of the past few minutes. "How's Silicon Valley?"

"Exhausting. Lucrative. Loud." A soft sigh. "You good? Mom texted me. Something about you being out at the market today."

"I am. It's... a lot. Good, though." I hesitated, glancing back toward the Warrens' tent where Charlie was lifting a box like it weighed nothing. "You'll never guess who lives here."

"If you say one of my exes, I'm hanging up."

Despite everything, I smiled. "Well, that, too. But no, remember Mrs. Warren? My third-grade teacher? Strawberries and poems and the stickers you used to steal?"

"Oh wow. Yeah, I remember her." A beat. "Why?"

"She has a daughter my age and a son, I think around yours. Charlie." I wasn't sure why my heart kicked at the word *Charlie*.

Grant hummed thoughtfully. "Name sounds familiar. Didn't he play football? Or was that someone else?"

"You might be right." I watched Charlie laugh at something his sister said. "He, um... he helped me the night of the accident."

Grant's voice dropped, steady and older-brother serious. "Then he's someone I like already."

My throat tightened. "It was fast. I didn't get to thank him. Not properly."

"Then maybe you get to now," he said. "Life's weird like that." Papers shifted on his end. "Listen, I have a call with a client in two minutes, but... I'm proud of you, Sis. Really."

I closed my eyes. The wind moved the tent canvas beside me, soft and sure.

"Call me later," he added.

"I will."

We hung up, and the world pressed back in—music, laughter, the cinnamon-sweet air. But something inside me felt steadier. Like the day had anchored itself in more than one place.

By afternoon, the square was humming with music. A local band played from the gazebo, kids danced barefoot near the fountain, and sun spilled over everything in lazy gold.

Charlie returned with the box, set it down near his sister's stand, and dusted off his hands. "You should try the gingerbread muffins before they sell out," he said.

"Is that professional advice or local hospitality?"

"Both," he said, offering one wrapped in parchment.

Elizabeth called him over again, handing him a box of pastries. "Delivery for the music tent."

He rolled his eyes. "The glamorous life of an unpaid assistant."

When he was gone, Mrs. Warren leaned over her table with a conspiratorial smile.

"He pretends to complain, but he loves being home. Flew cargo for years, now he contracts out of Atlanta. I think he uses work as an excuse to keep from landing anywhere too long."

"Sounds familiar," I murmured.

She patted my hand. "That kind of restlessness burns out eventually. Then you realize roots don't trap you—they hold you steady when the wind blows."

I nodded, her words sticking deeper than I expected.

As the market began to wind down, I helped Elizabeth pack up the leftover pastries.

She offered me a loaf for the road, wrapped in brown paper and twine.

"Call it a bribe," she said. "To make you come back next week."

"I just might," I said.

Charlie reappeared, arms crossed, watching me with an expression somewhere between curiosity and quiet recognition.

"So," he said. "We're both from here. How'd we never meet?"

"Bad timing, maybe," I said. "Or maybe we weren't supposed to until now."

He tilted his head, amused. "You believe in that kind of thing?"

"I believe in fate," I said. "And interruptions that save your life."

His eyes softened, but he didn't push it. "I leave again Tuesday," he said. "Flight to Denver. Then probably Portland. It changes every week." He paused. "But this place... it's the only place that ever feels like home."

Before I could answer, the band struck up one last song, and the crowd began to sway. A child's sparkler lit nearby, tiny bursts of light flaring in the dusk. The smoke curled between us, carrying the scent of cinnamon and cedar.

The air had that late-October sharpness, the kind that hints at cold but still carries the comfort of firewood and cider.

"See you around, Rose," he said quietly, and something about the way he said my name—gentle, unhurried—felt like a promise wrapped in maybe.

"See you," I said.

He walked off toward the edge of the square, the crowd folding around him like he'd always been part of it.

That night, I sat on the deck of the loft, laptop open beside a cup of cocoa gone cold. The market sounds still lingered in my head—the laughter, the music, the murmur of belonging. I'd gone there to sell myself, but what I found was something steadier—a reminder that maybe I didn't have to rebuild my life alone.

The loaf of banana bread sat beside me, still warm through the paper. I should've been exhausted, but my mind felt alive in a way it hadn't in years.

I opened my email again. Three responses out of ten proposals. One tentative yes. It wasn't much, but it was a start.

Outside, the wind shifted, carrying the faint sound of a departing plane overhead. I watched the lights fade across the lake until they disappeared into the clouds.

The world was moving again.

And this time, I wasn't afraid to follow.

CHAPTER 10
Something Like Peace

As I settled into life in Tunbridge, the quiet stopped feeling like a dare and started feeling like a rhythm. Morning light poured through the mill windows and turned the steam from my mug into a pale ribbon. The lake held still, a mirror edged with russet trees. Somewhere on the trail, a dog barked. Someone laughed. The town woke the way people do when they aren't late to anything.

I opened my laptop. *Rose Bennett Consulting* blinked back at me—clean serif, white space, a tagline I wasn't sure I believed yet: *Clarity that connects.* Good enough for now. I posted last night in the Tunbridge Business Network group: Local marketing consultant accepting small-business clients—branding, digital, strategy. One like. Emerson.

"Onward," I told the empty loft.

I packed a stack of flyers and pushed into the early-November air. On Main, I pinned a flyer to the cork board at Drucker's between Hay delivery—call Stubbs and a missing-cat note with a Polaroid of a suspiciously grumpy Clementine. Clementine belonged to Mrs. Porter over on Sycamore, and that cat went missing often enough that half the town kept an eye out. I hoped she'd turn up again.

When I stepped back out of Beloved Blooms, a silver SUV rolled through the intersection. The sun flashed off its hood, bright enough to throw my reflection at me in the shop window. For a second, the world narrowed to white.

Brake lights. The jerk of a wheel. The feeling of falling without moving.

My vision tunneled for half a second, the sound around me flattening until even my own heartbeat felt far away. A bird startled from the wire above, its wings sharp against the silence.

I pressed my palm to the cool glass and counted—four slow breaths. The reflection dissolved into a street scene: a kid in a red raincoat, an old man lifting his hat to a friend, a woman tugging a dog who didn't agree with her route. The sound of someone hammering. A radio from the hardware store. The small, specific music of a town being itself.

Not that road. Not that night. I was upright, breathing, and alive. I lowered my hand and kept walking.

By early afternoon I was back at The Rusty Skillet with coffee and a corner booth, answering emails until one subject line rooted me to the vinyl: *Website help?—Elizabeth Warren.*

Hey! I saw your post in the Networking Group. I've been meaning to redo the bakery's site—maybe we could meet to discuss? -Elizabeth

I smiled at the screen, typed yes, and meant it.

Oak & Oven smelled like cinnamon and warm butter and the good kind of trouble.

Elizabeth had her mother's eyes and flour on her sleeve. "Mom has been talking about you," she said, tucking a strand of hair behind her ear. "Said she's so happy you're back."

"It's so sweet to see her," I said. "And you."

We sat at a table.

"How old are you?" She asked.

"Thirty-one. You?" I said, opening my laptop.

"Thirty-six. That explains why we missed each other in school."

"I was wondering that, too."

We looked at the bakery's site across my screen: charming, chaotic, twelve tabs that led nowhere good. She talked flavors while I talked function.

"I want people to feel like they can smell the bread," she said.

"We'll make a homepage that breathes," I told her. "Big photos, fewer words. Let the images do the talking."

She smiled. "That's what Granddad always said—that good bread doesn't need a speech."

I glanced up. "He started Oak & Oven, didn't he?"

"Yeah. Built it from a side porch and a hand-me-down oven. He retired last spring and finally let me take over." She brushed flour from her arm. "He still drops by every morning to 'check the yeast,' which is code for stealing muffins."

"That sounds like something worth keeping," I said.

"I think so," she replied softly. "He built this place on smell and stubbornness. I'm just trying not to mess it up."

The back door creaked; footsteps came down the hall. A voice slid ahead of them—low, rough around the edges in a way that made it sound like it had already been useful somewhere else.

"I fixed the pilot light. Reset the timer before morning."

I didn't have to turn to know. My body did it anyway.

Charlie stepped around the corner with sleeves shoved to his elbows and a smudge of soot on his shirt, like the building had put a claim on him. He looked past Elizabeth first, then at me, and stopped like he'd reached a ledge he hadn't expected.

"Hey," Elizabeth said, bright. "Remember Rose Bennett? She's saving our website from 2010."

He nodded once. "I remember. Hi Rose."

I tried not to blush, "Hey."

"Anything else?" he asked Elizabeth.

"Go home," she said. "You've already fixed three things that weren't yours."

"Occupational hazard."

"Pilot hazard?" I asked, because apparently my mouth had taken over for my brain.

The corner of his mouth tilted. "Something like that."

He looked back at me, and the room thinned to air and heartbeat. "Good to see you," he said.

"You too," I answered.

Elizabeth clapped like the referee of a sport she enjoyed too much. "No flirting over dough. Cinnamon rolls rising."

He kissed her temple, promised to see her before he flew out Sunday—"weather willing"—then gave me the smallest, old-fashioned nod. When he left, the air warmed a degree, like the room remembered a sun.

"You two okay?" Elizabeth asked, after the door closed.

"I owe him a thank-you I haven't found words for yet," I said.

"You'll get your chance."

Over the next few hours, we mocked up a new website. We argued about fonts like people argue about football and landed on one that felt like breath and flour in equal measure.

"Is your brother really always gone?" I asked, clicking a button that erased an entire row of clutter. Satisfaction swooped through me.

"He lands and leaves," Elizabeth said. "He's good at both. I'm never sure he believes in the part in between."

"I recognize the type." I took a bite of something fried and perfect. "My dad consults overseas—logistics. He's been in and out my whole life. My brother's in sales; the man chases a quota the way some people chase addiction. We Bennett kids were raised on flight plans and calendar invites." I shrugged. "I thought grinding made me safe. Turns out it just makes you tired."

Elizabeth's smile was knowing. "You're good at this. Not just the site—the naming of what things really are. People in this town will want that."

"Do me a favor and tell them."

"Come to the small-business fair next week," she said. "Set up a table, hand out cards. It's not fancy, but it works."

"I'll be there." It felt like saying yes to a door.

She hugged me on my way out. "He'll probably be back by then," she added, like it wasn't loaded with anything at all.

"Maybe I can find the words by then," I said.

When I got home, the loft returned to its own heartbeat: a tick in the ductwork, the hum of the fridge, the distant, comforting wail of a train.

My inbox still looked like a dare—twelve website visits, nine bounces, two spammy SEO offers, one real lead from a gift shop I liked. I answered with a pitch that sounded like me, not like a brochure: *You don't need noise. You need meaning. Let's make people feel your shop before they walk in the door.*

I hit send and stood at the window. The lake shifted from pewter to black ink. Somewhere high, a plane threaded two white beads through the dark—blink, blink—like a pulse you can't find until you look for it.

I stepped onto the deck. The boards were cool; the night smelled like oak leaves and the last of summer's water. A breeze moved across the lake, and the surface shivered so slightly I might have made it up.

"I'm figuring it out," I said into the dark, testing the sentence against the air.

Inside, I poured coffee I wouldn't finish and sat back down at the table. A car drove down the road—one clean sweep of headlights along the far bank—and for a flicker of a second the glass reflected white like the night I turned over and over and lived. The flash went, and I was still. The chair under me. The pen in my hand. The names on my list waiting for ink.

I wrote to six more potential clients—short, clear, and direct. I drafted a one-page rate sheet and hated it and tried again. I set a reminder to order a simple standing banner for the fair: *ROSE BENNETT CONSULTING—clarity that connects*. I added *websites + brand voice + launch strategy* beneath it and felt the click of something finding its place.

My phone lit—a text.

> Elizabeth: Sending a photo of cinnamon rolls under a towel like newborns. I'll save you one if you promise to post about it.

> Me: Deal! But you have to tag my site in your stories.

> Elizabeth: Done.

On the table, my business cards sat in their little cardboard cradle, white on white. My name looked like it belonged to me again.

Tomorrow I'd print a banner. I'd call the gift shop. I'd meet Elizabeth at dawn for coffee, sugar and a picture that made the internet hungry. And if I walked into The Rusty Skillet and found a certain jacket slung over a stool, I'd ask, "Hi. How can I ever thank you?" And if I didn't, I'd say it anyway—to the air that had carried a voice the night the world turned over and put me back.

I turned off the lamp. The loft went soft and blue. The faint scent of cinnamon still lingered on my hands from the bakery, a reminder of warmth that had nothing to do with fear.

Outside, the lake held the moon like it had practiced, and the mill's old bones felt like a hand at my back.

CHAPTER 11
Almost Was the Bravest Word

A knock, soft as the morning itself. The scent of coffee still hung in the air, edged with the damp chill that slipped through the old mill windows.

"The door's open," I called.

Mom stepped inside with something long and flat tucked under her arm, wrapped in brown paper. No bag, no ribbon, just the neat folds she always made when she wanted to show care without making a show of it.

"I brought you something," she said, laying it on the counter.

The pencil marks caught my eye first—my name, in her careful handwriting, the same way she used to label my lunch sacks for school trips. It made my throat tighten. The paper crinkled like the lunch sacks she used to pack—peanut butter sandwich, carrot sticks, and a note she never signed but always slipped inside.

"Go on," she said.

I peeled the paper back. The scent of watercolor drifted up before the image fully appeared—trees, endless trees, standing tall in quiet rows. The kind that breathes peace into a room just by existing. Light filtered through a break in the canopy, not harsh but soft, golden, choosing one narrow path to touch.

"It's beautiful," I whispered.

She nodded, brushing an invisible wrinkle from her sleeve. "For your new chapter," she said, and I could tell it was a blessing disguised as a sentence.

I crossed the room and hugged her. She went still for half a heartbeat before relaxing into it, her chin resting on my shoulder.

"Thank you," I said against her hair.

"You don't have to thank me. Just hang it where you'll see it."

After she left, the loft held her warmth like sunlight that takes its time leaving a room. I hung the painting above the desk I'd built with Macey and Anna, Allen wrench blisters and all. The wall looked different instantly—less like a wall, more like a window.

When I sat down, it felt like I was facing a clearing.

The laptop screen glowed to life.

My inbox pulsed with three new messages—all from Tunbridge contacts.

The glow from the screen reflected against the watercolor frame above the desk, the light and paint overlapping like old and new pieces of my life trying to blend.

The first was from The Stationer on Main, an older shop with heavy paper and writing accessories. The owner wanted a simple web refresh and help with product photos. The second was from the woman who ran the yoga studio above The Rusty Skillet. She wanted better class sign-ups and was tired of wrestling her calendar. The third made me sit a little straighter.

Dixie at The Rusty Skillet. *Subject: coffee, logos, mercy*

I smiled before I clicked. The message was short.

Rose,
Everyone says you are the kind of woman who gets things done without making a mess. My menus and logo are both a mess. Come by this afternoon and tell me what you see. I'll feed you while you say it.
– D.

I checked the time. If I worked two hours I could make it by two. I wrote back yes and added a smile she could hear.

Outside, the lake was a dull silver. A heron stood near the reeds like a guard. I could hear someone hammering two units over. The mill always carried other people's lives in small sounds. I liked it. It made solitude feel less empty.

I spent the morning building out The Stationer's product grid and fixing a signup flow that sent every yoga student the same confirmation email, regardless of class. The sort of chaos people get used to until someone says they don't have to be. Fixing it felt like sweeping a floor no one had seen in years. Satisfying, simple, and mine.

At one, my phone lit with an Atlanta number I still knew. I let it ring, then went back to the yoga calendar. The voicemail icon popped up a minute later. I hovered, then tapped.

"Hey, Rose. It's Mark from Folsom Tech. We heard you left Elaren. I'm sorry they let that happen. If you're open to short-term work in the city, we'd love to talk. You were always the brain behind the campaigns. Call me."

I tasted metal. My pulse went shallow, the way it used to in glass rooms when someone said my name too loud. Campaigns. Brain behind. Compliments that forgot to say my name when it mattered. I saved the number and put the phone face down like it might burn the table if I kept looking. The painting hung steady above me. Light through trees. One path brighter.

At two, The Rusty Skillet smelled like butter and heat from the ovens fogged the front windows. A handful of leaves skittered across the sidewalk like they were chasing warmth.

The lunch crowd had gone soft and chatty. Dixie waved me behind the counter without ceremony and shoved a plate of hot cornbread into my hands. She wore a fresh, new shade of red lipstick.

"Honey, we're keeping up by habit and prayer," she said, flipping a ticket onto a spike. "I want menus that look like you aren't gambling on heartburn. And a logo that says home without looking like we found it in a box labeled 1998."

I laughed. "Show me what you have."

She spread everything out on a back table. Menus stapled until the staples gave up. A logo with a skillet so clipart it made me wince. Specials scrawled in a handwriting only the cooks could love. It was all honest, but tired.

"What do you see," she asked.

"I see heritage left to limp," I said, and she slapped the table and grinned.

"That's exactly it," she said. "We're better than our fonts."

I laughed, surprised at how right it felt.

We walked the space while I talked, and she listened like owners do when they are ready to change. The windows were generous, the booths lived-in, and the light forgiving. I heard myself suggesting small things first. A word bank that belonged to this room: skillet, sunlight, steam, pie, whistle, easy morning. A typeface with weight but not fuss. Colors pulled from the place itself. The bright red of the booths. The butter gold of the cornbread. The sienna where the floor wore thin.

"And the logo?" she said.

"No skillet," I said. "Everyone knows where they are. A mark that carries your name, not your tools." I sketched a rough idea on a napkin. R and S linked by a curved line that hinted at steam. Nothing clever, just right.

Dixie looked at it and got quiet in that way people get when a thing finally looks like itself. "Lord help me, that might be handsome."

A cook shouted "order up" and she snapped back to motion. "I have twenty minutes before the school crowd, sit with me." We took a corner booth and I asked questions while she refilled my cup without asking. Hours. Mornings. Peak traffic. Who orders what and when. Where the light hits at five. The details that sell without anyone feeling sold.

"I can pay you," she said. "But not like the city probably did."

"I'm not in the city," I said. "And I want the kind of work I can point to and say I helped. Pay me fairly. We'll call it good."

We set a price that respected us both. When I left, the bell on the door felt like applause.

Back at the loft, the inbox had two replies from the client emails I'd sent earlier. One said *let's talk*. The other said *we loved your work on Helios and would love your eye on a smaller project*. I stared at that sentence. *Loved your work on Helios*. I closed the laptop and walked to the window. The heron had moved to the other side of the reeds and looked exactly the same.

My phone chimed.

> Abby: You need to see what he just posted.

I clicked. Instagram. Richard, grinning in a suit that made him look like he knew the answer before anyone asked the question. Behind him, a slide filled the frame.

Helios: Record ROI in Q3

His caption read like a victory lap. *So proud of the team. So honored to lead. Sometimes leadership means stepping in when it matters most.*

I sat down because if I didn't I would put my fist through the wall. The photo swung a door open in my chest I had been trying to keep shut. My name was nowhere. The comments were full of praise from people who had never stayed in that building past six or eaten stale almonds from a drawer because leaving meant you'd miss the impossible deadlines.

My vision narrowed. My pulse skidded like tires on wet asphalt, that same helpless slide of control I hadn't felt since the accident. The urge was like an old reflex. Grab keys. Get on I-75. Find the glass building and let the fury lead. Tell him in front of everyone what he was made of. Tell him what I was.

I stood before I knew I had moved. The keys were in the bowl by the door. My hand hit the bowl and stopped. The painting hung where I could see it from the entryway. Light through trees. One path brighter because someone had chosen it twice.

I didn't grab the keys. I grabbed my shoes and sat on the floor. I put them on slowly to make the impulse pass. I counted eight breaths. Eight in. Eight out. By the time I stood, the urge had changed shape. Not gone. Just new. Not rage that burns everything. Heat I could use.

I texted Abby.

> Me: Why did you send me that? I almost drove back.

> Abby: I'm sorry! I thought you'd want to know. Almost is the bravest word in that sentence.

I set the phone down and made tea and grabbed a handful of wasabi almonds. While the kettle hummed, I opened a new document and wrote a list called *What I Build Now*. The first line was my prices. The second was a policy I should have written years ago. The third was a sentence I wanted to send to anyone who pretended my work was theirs.

I sent two proposals. I sent Dixie a mood board with three type options and a rough color palette pulled from her booths. I sent The Stationer a product shot I had taken on the window ledge with the afternoon light and Granny's quilt.

The phone rang again. A Buckhead number. I let it go. The voicemail came. I listened. Elaren's HR, rehearsed and careful. They were opening a new contractor path for brand leads in Q4.

They would love to keep me close. If I wanted to return even in a limited capacity, they could make space.

I laughed once. It sounded like the start of a cry that had missed its cue.

I moved the message to a folder named Later and took the trash out because movement was the only thing that made sense. On my way back from the trash bins, I saw Alice carrying a box of eucalyptus and a tray of muffins.

"You look like you just wrestled a bear," she yelled as she walked closer.

"I wanted to," I said.

"Then you did, because you didn't," she said, not unkind. "Are you free tonight? I have to make a dozen boutonnieres and avoid my own thoughts. I could use some company who knows how to tie satin ribbon and not panic."

I smiled because she wasn't asking for my story, just offering a place to put my hands. "I'll be there."

Beloved Blooms at sunset was like an enchanted garden—eucalyptus, mint, and rain in the air, the kind of freshness that wakes you without warning. Stems lined the counter. Music low. We worked side by side without talking much. I tied ribbon and she wired eucalyptus and the room filled with small sounds. Snips. Paper rustle. The soft thud of stems in a bucket. Eventually she asked if I had seen Charlie again.

"At the market, and at the bakery," I said. "He helps his sister a lot. And that weathered voice."

"Ah, yes." She laughed. "Elizabeth says he glances at the sky like a person taking attendance."

"He leaves and returns," I said. "I'm not sure which scares me more."

Alice's hands went still for a moment. "It's better than someone who leaves and never comes back." Her voice was soft but sure, the kind that came from living through something and walking out the other side. "At least Charlie circles home. Some people don't."

I glanced at her and she gave me a small smile, one that didn't hide the truth but carried it gently.

"Johnny left once too," she said. "When his life was falling apart. But he found his way back and stayed for good. Sometimes the leaving is just part of the story. What matters is where they choose to land."

Something in my chest eased at that.

"Good," she added. "If it's already easy, it's probably not real."

When we finished, she packed the boutonnieres in a small box and looked at my hands. "You are good at fixing delicate things."

"So are you," I said.

On the walk home, I stopped by Drucker's for apples and came out with a box of brownies I hadn't meant to buy. The bell over the door gave its usual half-hearted ring, and Arnold looked up from the counter, flour dusted on his shirt pocket.

"Picked up the new peach jam yet?" he asked.

"Not yet," I said, eyeing the rows of glass jars catching the afternoon light.

He nodded toward them like they were an old secret. "It's worth finding toast for."

I smiled. In Tunbridge, that counted as a sales pitch—less persuasion, more invitation.

Back at the loft, the lake had gone dark except for the house lights across the water. The painting glowed pale in the lamplight. I sat at the desk and adjusted the frame so it hung a little straighter. My phone buzzed.

> Emerson: When are we meeting? I was supposed to be your first client, remember? I'm waiting.

> Me: Maybe not the first, but the favorite. Call you tomorrow.

Another message slid in on top of that one. A number I didn't recognize—Atlanta area code.

> (404) 555-7829: Hey, it's Charlie. I hope it's okay that I asked Elizabeth for your number. Saw your mood board on Dixie's counter. She looked proud. Nice eye.

I stared at the letters until the smile surprised me. I typed and erased twice and then kept it simple.

> Me: Thanks. Her cornbread did most of the work.

> Charlie: True. Try the pie when you have a win to mark.

> Me: I'll do that, thanks.

> Charlie: I'm headed to Edinburgh. Have a good week.

> Me: Sounds amazing. You too.

I set the phone down and pressed both palms to the desk, grounding myself in the wood. The hollow that had followed me all day loosened its hold. I had chosen what the painting kept telling me—a path brighter because someone keeps walking it.

I worked for another hour. Then another because I was finally in that place where the work made time pass without cost. I built The Rusty Skillet's landing page, mocked up a new menu block and wrote three lines of copy that sounded like Dixie talking to regulars she liked.

At ten, I stood and stretched and caught my reflection in the window glass. Bare face. Hair up. No armor. A woman who was beginning to look like she could trust herself.

Before bed I opened a small box I hadn't touched yet. A framed photo of my dad in uniform sat on top. He isn't deployed anymore. He retired from the military years ago and works stateside for a defense contractor, but he still lives like he's on duty somewhere far away. His days are measured and precise and his calls short and steady, like he is saving his voice for something important.

I smiled at Grant's corporate headshot, all image and polish in a custom suit and a Rolex. He sells enterprise software like it could save a soul. Under all that shine he is still the steady older brother who taught me how to work, how to aim higher, how to keep going. We don't talk the way we used to, but our bond has never thinned. Most days it shows up in quick texts or late-night check-ins, reminding me that I'm not moving through the world alone.

I lined both frames under Mom's painting. Father. Brother. Light through trees. It felt like a small place of keeping, a corner for the parts of me I had carried too hard for too long.

I turned off every light except the one over the sink and stood on the deck with the night pressed close. An owl hooted in the distance. I breathed in until the air felt like it could reach all the way to the places that still burned.

I closed the computer and looked up at the painting. The path glowed like it had its own small engine.

I went to bed with the windows cracked and dreamed of trees. Not the kind that block the road but ones that make a tunnel so the light can show you where to go. In the morning I would print the proposals, meet Dixie, photograph paper at The Stationer, and call the yoga owner about her calendar sync. The work wouldn't fix what had been stolen. It would build something in its place.

My phone buzzed once on the nightstand. I didn't reach for it.

The hollow ache didn't vanish. It softened. It left room.

In the dark, I could feel the town sleeping around me. The

mill creaked like it remembered a thousand mornings when the first bell rang and people stood up and went to work.

Cold air pressed through the cracked window, carrying a faint mix of earth and rain that settled over the room like memory.

I would stand up, too. On purpose. On my own terms. And when the light came through the windows, the painting would catch it and lend it back, generous as a morning.

CHAPTER 12
A Table above the Lake

The road to The Oasis climbed in slow curves through pine and oak. Sunlight flashed off the lake between the trees, bright enough that I had to lower the visor. November brought air that was both crisp and cool. I rolled the window down and let it in.

My phone vibrated.

> Emerson: Lunch? My treat.

> Me: Absolutely! I'll be there at noon.

Emerson used to spend summers with her grandmother, just down the street from our house. We ran barefoot over the docks and built forts out of fallen limbs. Eventually, she stopped coming and then I moved to Buckhead. I wasn't sure if the old closeness would still be there, or if we'd have to build something new from scratch.

The Oasis crowned the ridge above Emerald Ridge Lake, as if the earth itself had lifted it toward the light. Stone paths curved like ribbons down the hill, spilling into patios that seemed to grow straight from the rock. Gardens surrounded everything—

lavender and thyme brushing the air, rosemary spilling over low walls, ivy climbing toward strings of golden lights that swayed in the breeze. The building was part glass, part stone, all reflection and sky, so that standing there felt like stepping into the space between water and heaven. It was the kind of place that quieted you without asking, beauty so complete it rearranged your breath.

I parked under a sycamore and hesitated before getting out, trying to take a mental photo. The breeze carried roasted garlic from the kitchen vents and the clean mineral smell of the lake. A hostess held the door open with a hip and flashed a grin like we were already friends. I stepped inside.

Emerson was waiting near the host stand in a slate dress and white sneakers. Her hair was pulled into a low knot. She looked like the place itself, polished but easy. For a second I saw the girl who could climb a tree faster than any of the boys and still make it home without a grass stain.

"Look at you," she said, arms already open. "You came home and got prettier."

I laughed into her shoulder. "You built heaven and pretend it's just a restaurant."

We held on a breath longer than politeness required, then stepped back, smiling the way people do when they've both survived something.

"I can't take any credit," she said, tipping her chin toward the patio. "That was all him."

Sam moved between the tables, a dish towel over his shoulder, sleeves rolled, the late light brushing gold across his arms. When he looked up at her, the room seemed to pause—music, clatter, air—all of it waiting. His grin was quiet but full. She didn't wave; she didn't need to. He winked, and the world exhaled again.

"Wow," I murmured. "If I ever find love like that, I hope I still look that calm."

Emerson smiled, soft and certain. "Find your person," she said. "Don't settle. That's my cracker-jack advice."

The sight of it—a love that sure—hit a place I didn't know was still hollow.

The host led us to a corner table on the upper patio where the lake spread out in a long silver fan. A band was loading gear down on the lower terrace for the dinner set. The sound of a guitar case latch clicking traveled up the steps and then disappeared.

"Are you hungry?" Emerson asked.

"I've been hungry for about three weeks," I said.

She laughed. "Good. Sam keeps trying to feed the whole town. I might let him."

We ordered huckleberry lemonade, flatbreads and a salad with roasted pears. The food came fast, as if the kitchen understood we didn't want to lose the thread of catching up. We talked through the first bites—childhood summers, how Mom still hums when she paints like she's keeping time with her own thoughts, how Emerson's Gran once taught us that a perfect pie starts with cold butter and that books are the quickest way to grow a wiser heart. I told her why I left Buckhead, how much I loved living at the mill.

When I mentioned the crash, she didn't flinch. She just rested her hand over mine for a moment and said, "I'm glad you stayed." We ate in companionable silence for a moment. The lake moved in a slow sheet under the light breeze down below. A pigeon found crumbs on the patio. Emerson watched me more than she watched the view.

"You look different," she said. "Better. Lighter."

"Some days," I said. "Other days I feel like I stepped off a moving walkway and my legs don't know how to slow down."

"That sounds right," she said. "You will find your pace."

Sam came up the steps with the kind of energy that gets things done. He kissed Emerson on the cheek, then offered me a hand, as Emerson introduced us.

"How's it going?" He asked.

"This place is incredible," I said. "I feel like I'm on vacation in Europe."

"Nothing here is ordinary," he said, pleased. He glanced over his shoulder toward the bar. "Great to meet you. You ladies enjoy, I have my own lunch date with an old friend." He tipped his head. "Holler if you need anything."

He squeezed Emerson's shoulder and headed down toward the bar. She looked at me, eyebrows lifting just a touch, but she didn't ask. She didn't need to.

We ate, talked and let years fold into each other. I told her about the consulting work starting to come in. She told me about the ads she ran that flopped.

"Want a refill?" she asked, nodding toward my glass.

"Please."

She stood, then paused. "Be right back. Sam just waved me down."

I followed her gaze. He stood at the far end of the bar with a man whose back was to us. Oh my—it was Charlie. Even from behind, calm radiated from him. Something inside me settled and woke at the same time.

Emerson headed down the steps. They spoke for a minute. Sam pointed up toward me. Charlie turned.

He didn't smile. He just nodded once, like he had seen weather he expected. Emerson said something that made both men laugh. Then she and Sam started up the steps with him a step behind.

"Rose," Emerson said as they reached the table. "This is Charlie—."

"I know Rose." Charlie interrupted. His eyes were a deeper green than I remembered.

"You do?" Emerson seemed shocked.

"Yes." The rough edge of it traced a line down my spine and settled there. The mischievous smile on his face gave me goosebumps.

A server appeared at Emerson's shoulder and whispered something that made her wince.

"Kitchen delivery mix up," she said to Sam.

Sam glanced at his watch. "Of course."

He smiled at us. "Give us five minutes. Don't let him talk you into climbing the old bridge truss. He is persuasive and it's a terrible idea."

"Noted," I said.

They walked towards the kitchen. The table felt bigger without them. The lake felt closer. A gull circled once above the water and vanished behind the roofline.

Charlie sat across from me—not too close, not too far. He rested one forearm along the table's edge, fingers tracing a slow half-circle on the wood. The other hand stayed in his lap. There was a steadiness about him, the kind people earn from learning how to move through crowded rooms without colliding with anything.

"So," he said, his voice calm but weighted with interest, "how are you?"

I smiled faintly. "I'm here."

He nodded. "That's a good place to start."

"How was Scotland?" I asked, grateful for a safer direction.

His eyes lit up. "Edinburgh might be the most beautiful place I've ever seen. I take every route to Scotland I can, just to steal a weekend there." His voice shifted, softening. "You'd love it. The way autumn turns Princes Street Gardens into a sweep of orange and gold. The colored houses on Victoria Street. The quiet climb up the Vennel where the castle sits right over you like it's guarding the whole city."

He paused, thumb brushing the table. "And Calton Hill... the view looks impossible. Like the city was built in layers just so the light could find its way through."

Then he looked at me again, focus steady as a hand on the yoke. "It feels like a place you've already been, even when you haven't."

We let the quiet stretch. It didn't feel empty.

A server with a pitcher of water was passing, Charlie asked for some.

"You flew in last night?" I asked.

"This morning. Red-eye."

"That sounds brutal."

He smiled. "Used to feel like freedom. Now it feels like a trick I played on myself."

He turned his glass slowly, watching the ice spin. "I heard you've got a place at the mill."

"I do," I said. "It's everything I hoped it would be. The floors creak. The light's best in the morning. I can hear the train at night."

"That building's got soul," he said. "You can't fake that kind of history."

I smiled. "That's exactly why I love it. It feels like a place with memory."

He nodded toward my bag. "Your mood board at The Rusty Skillet was great. Dixie was showing it off to half the diner like it was a newborn. That's why I had to text you."

I laughed. "That sounds like her."

"She's proud," he said, leaning back slightly. "You're designing her new logo, right? You're a graphic designer?"

"Not exactly," I said. "I worked in corporate marketing for ten years—climbed the ladder, or at least tried to. Then someone removed the next rung." I shrugged lightly. "So I quit. Moved here. Started over."

He smiled, slow and a little impressed. "That's brave."

"Or desperate," I said, though I smiled too. "I started freelancing. Built a small marketing business—just me and a laptop. I reached out to old clients from Atlanta and got nothing but silence. Then out of nowhere, the people here—Elizabeth, Dixie, Emerson—they started saying yes. Real yeses that come with pie and hugs. It's been…amazing. Better than I could've planned."

He studied me, that quiet focus of his turning everything into meaning. "Sounds like you built something that matters."

"I hope so," I said. "It feels like it."

He lifted his glass. "Then I'd call that a landing." He paused, eyes lingering a second too long. "You staying for good, or just... catching your breath?"

"I don't know," I said. "But the not knowing doesn't scare me anymore."

"That's rare," he said quietly. "Most people chase certainty until it outruns them."

A kayak skimmed across the far bank. The sound of paddles and wind filled the silence.

"Do you remember much?" he asked softly. "From the accident?"

The question landed gently, but it still found its mark.

"Too much," I said. "And not enough. I remember the sound most—metal, glass, everything going white. Then your voice." I swallowed. "It gave me something to hold."

He exhaled, slow. "I was afraid you only remembered the worst parts."

"I don't remember hitting my head. Just... being held."

"I didn't want you to be alone," he said. His voice dropped, almost rough. "I know that feeling."

He didn't explain, and I didn't ask. His gaze lingered like he wanted to, though.

"Thank you," I said.

"You don't need to."

"I do," I said, smiling. "And I'll probably say it again."

"Stubborn," he murmured, but there was a hint of warmth in it, the kind that softens a guarded face.

The server came by with more bread. We both reached at the same time. Our fingers brushed—barely a second, but enough. He didn't pull away right away. When he did, the air felt charged, like something invisible had shifted just out of sight.

"How long are you in town?" I asked.

"A week," he said. "Maybe two. Rome, then Rio. Depends where they need me."

"That sounds... complicated."

"Unsettled," he said. "Hard to keep roots like that."

I smiled. "Maybe roots aren't the goal."

He studied me, head tilted, eyes steady. "Maybe not. But you strike me as someone who could grow anywhere."

I looked away, trying not to smile too hard. "You miss it, though—routine?"

He nodded. "The small things. A mug that's only yours. A window with the same view. People who say your name because they mean it, not because they need something."

"Tunbridge can give you that."

He smiled faintly. "Can it?"

Before I could answer, Emerson's laugh drifted up from the lower terrace. The band tested a chord, the sound hanging in the warm air. Charlie glanced toward the steps.

"You and Sam grew up together?" I asked.

"Since elementary. We used to dare each other to jump off the boathouse roof." He smiled. "He was always the better jumper."

"I was the better climber," I said, remembering summer trees and scraped knees with Emerson.

"Me too," he said, smiling like he was picturing it. "Guess that's why we both survived the falls."

Emerson and Sam reappeared at the top of the steps, both flushed from moving fast. Emerson mouthed sorry and slid into her seat. Sam checked his watch again and then pointed two fingers toward the kitchen.

"Crisis averted," Emerson said. "For now. How are we doing over here?"

"Great," Charlie said, standing. "Hungry."

Sam clapped him on the shoulder. "Dinner. Let's eat at the bar," he said, as he nodded at me. "It was good to see you."

"You too," I said.

Charlie looked at me like he was memorizing something. Not the surface. Something under it. He tipped his head in a small goodbye and followed Sam.

As he turned, sunlight caught the back of his collar and stayed there, a thin line of gold until the door closed behind him. The space he'd filled didn't empty—it hummed.

Emerson watched me watch him go.

"You okay?" she asked.

"Yep," I said. "For the first time in a while, I think I am."

CHAPTER 13
After the Light Shifted

Emerson and I lingered over the last bites, conversation softening into the kind of quiet talk that fills a table after laughter has done its work. Emerson stirred her drink, watching the huckleberries swirl up from the bottom, and told me about the family who'd moved in next door—how the mother always wore gardening gloves and the toddler refused to nap. I told her about Elizabeth and the chaos of rebuilding a bakery website that had multiple "home" buttons, and about The Rusty Skillet's new menus that looked almost too good to hand to anyone with syrup on their fingers.

She laughed, that low, easy sound that always made people turn their heads. "You sound like you're settling in," she said. "I love hearing you talk about this stuff. You light up."

I shrugged, but it was true. "It feels good to build something from the ground up. Not for a cut-throat corporation. For good people."

Her eyes flicked toward Sam. "Speaking of people," she said, "we've been meaning to ask if you'd take a look at our marketing for The Oasis. We have all these incredible wedding photos from last year and no idea what to do with them. Sam keeps saying we should start social media, but I can barely keep up with our reservations list, let alone hashtags."

I smiled. "You should. You've already got a brand—it just needs a voice."

"That's what Sam keeps saying. A voice." She rolled her straw between her fingers. "Maybe it's time we make this place a destination. Brides from neighboring towns, we've never leaned into that."

"I could help," I said. "Maybe start with storytelling instead of selling. People don't want a venue. They want a memory waiting to happen."

"That's exactly it," she said, smiling. "You just said in one sentence what I've been trying to explain to Sam for months."

We both laughed, and the conversation slipped into that warm, effortless space where ideas felt like possibilities instead of plans.

After a while, she grew quiet and watched the lake shift below us, light sliding over the surface like mercury. "You're right where you're supposed to be, Rose."

She reached across the table, squeezed my hand once.

We hugged in the gravel lot, the sun warm on our backs, and promised not to wait another decade before we remembered how easy this felt.

Back at the loft, the rooms still smelled like lemon oil and sun-warmed wood. I set my keys in the bowl by the door and stood for a second to listen to the quiet. It felt like a person I trusted now, not a stranger I had to make small talk with.

I went to my desk and opened my laptop. Emails. A logo that still needed one line weight adjustment. A draft proposal for Emerson. I made coffee and worked until the light slid off the floor and the edges of the room softened.

When my phone buzzed, I didn't reach for it right away. I let it buzz a second time. Then I picked it up.

> Charlie: That view from your table today. I've seen it many times. It never looked the same until now.

I didn't know what he meant exactly. But I knew how it felt—to have the world look different because someone was in it. I read it, then read it again, slower.

For a second, I wondered if I'd imagined the look in his eyes—that maybe it was just kindness and nothing else.

The loft creaked in a familiar place as the air cooled outside. I typed three words and erased them. I typed four different words and erased those too. I finally wrote what I meant.

> Me: Glad you were there.

I set the phone down and didn't wait for a response. I blew on my coffee and watched the steam rise and disappear. The lake out the window turned from silver to ink. Somewhere across the water, a train spoke once and then went quiet.

I went to the desk and stood in front of the watercolor mom had given me, the one with the light through trees. It looked different at night. Deeper. Braver. I ran a finger along the simple wood frame and felt something in me match its steadiness.

CHAPTER 14
The Weight of Almost

The days had started to fall into a rhythm.

Morning light slid across the mill's old brick walls, catching on the dust that shimmered like gold. I'd sit by the window with my coffee and watch the lake move through shades of pewter and blue, never the same twice. The quiet here was alive. The kind that made you listen harder—to wind through pine, to the far-off hum of a boat engine, to your own thoughts settling in their bones.

Most mornings, I worked from the kitchen table. Local clients were coming in steadily. Small businesses that had been running on word-of-mouth and wanted something new. A pottery studio. A boutique near the square. I'd open my laptop, design some things, build webpages, and watch ideas bloom into beautiful things.

Sometimes, I'd see Charlie. Not often. Just enough to feel it. He texted me a few times a week. Nothing earth-shattering, mostly just saying hi, asking how my day was going. Sometimes he'd send me a picture of the exotic food he was eating or an amazing sight somewhere.

He'd be in town running errands for his mother or helping Elizabeth at the bakery, always with that easy grin. Once, I passed him outside the post office, his hands full of boxes, head tipped back in laughter at something someone said. Another time, across Main Street, when I was stapling a flyer to the bulletin board by the hardware store. He nodded when he saw me. I nodded back. That was all. But it felt like a conversation anyway.

He was still flying. Elizabeth mentioned it one afternoon when she stopped by to drop off scones. Said he had a short run of flights lined up, a few weeks in Asia, then back through Atlanta. "He says the sky feels smaller lately," she'd added, like it meant something. I smiled and changed the subject.

The truth was, he lingered in my thoughts more than I wanted to admit. Not in the restless way of wanting something I couldn't have, but in the quiet awareness of being seen once—and remembered.

It was a Tuesday when my phone rang. Atlanta number.

I shouldn't have answered.

"Rose! Hey, how's Tunbridge treating you?"

Richard. Of course. The same voice that used to flatten me into politeness. I pressed my palm against the counter to steady myself. "Fine," I said. "Busy."

"Good, good." His pause stretched too long, rehearsed. "Listen, I'll cut to it. I could really use your help."

"With what?"

"You heard about the Helios launch, right?"

"I saw your post," I said flatly. "Looked like a big success."

He laughed, low and slippery. "Yeah, about that. It's not going as planned."

I didn't give him anything. Silence does more damage than words ever could.

He filled it like he always did. "The campaign's great—your campaign, obviously—but execution's been rough. Dieter's making noise, budgets are bleeding, and honestly, it's all landing on me. I just thought maybe—"

"Maybe I could fix it for you," I said.

"That's not what I said."

"It's exactly what you mean."

"Come on, Rose. Don't be like that. We were a team."

"No," I said quietly. "I was your cover."

That stopped him for half a breath. I heard paper shuffle, the old tell when he was flustered.

"You're still angry," he said.

"I'm not angry at all. I'm just not a doormat."

He tried another tactic, voice softening. "I was just hoping you'd consult—remotely, a few weeks. I'll make it worth your time."

"You already did," I said. "Nine months of unpaid overtime while you took the credit."

"That's unfair."

"You're right. It was."

He exhaled sharply, control slipping. "This isn't personal."

"It always was," I said. "You just called it strategy."

For a second, the line went quiet. I could almost hear him deciding whether to apologize or manipulate me again. He chose the familiar road.

"You know, I'm trying to help you. You don't want to burn bridges."

I smiled, but it didn't reach anything soft. "I didn't burn it, Richard. I built it. And then I walked off it."

Before he could recover, I hung up.

The words felt strong coming out of my mouth. They didn't feel strong after.

For a second, I hated how fast my pulse was still racing. How even from here, 50 miles away, he could still make me feel like the smallest version of myself.

I pressed my hand to the counter until it stopped shaking.

The silence that followed didn't feel like victory. It felt like withdrawal. I kept thinking about the girl I'd been in that office—staying late, saying thank you for crumbs. She'd have called him back and apologized for sounding strong.

The kettle clicked off behind me. I poured the water over a tea bag and watched the steam rise like forgiveness I didn't owe anyone.

A text from Abby buzzed on my screen.

> Abby: You okay? Need backup? I'm ten minutes away with brownies.

> Me: I'm fine. Promise.

> Abby: Lies. Fine, then I'll find you later.

Her timing was freakishly good. Abby had a way of sensing cracks before they formed.

That evening, I needed air.

By nightfall, I was still angry—just not at him anymore. At myself, maybe. For how small I used to make my world to fit inside other people's.

The square was glowing by dusk. Paper lanterns were strung between lampposts, the faint hum of a guitar drifting from the pavilion. The town was hosting its November Harvest Fair. Booths lined the street with cider, honey, woven blankets, and the kind of smiles that came from knowing everyone's story. Kids darted through the crowd with caramel apples, and somewhere someone was frying dough, the scent warm and sweet.

Alice was there too, tucked behind a little floral booth strung with eucalyptus and tiny copper lights. Her bouquets looked like they'd been gathered straight from a storybook—soft, wild, perfectly her.

It made sense that she and Emerson were side by side. The fair always drew the town's creators out of their corners, and these two were practically Tunbridge traditions at this point. If something beautiful was happening, they were usually right in the middle of it.

Emerson spotted me first and waved. "There you are!" She

stood behind a booth stacked with candles in mason jars, labels hand-stamped *The Oasis Home*. "You missed the pie-eating contest."

"Tragic," I said.

"Sam's over by the grill," she said. "He's in his element—talking and eating at the same time."

I laughed.

She waved me over behind a booth stacked with mason-jar candles. "Smell this one. Sam swears it smells like November in a jar."

She shoved a candle under my nose, and she wasn't wrong—warm vanilla, cedar, a hint of clove. Before I could say anything, a golden retriever slipped its collar and tore across the square, dragging a laughing teenager behind it. People clapped and stepped aside as the dog made a wide arc around the pie tent.

I smiled without meaning to. The whole place felt alive.

Then something caught my eye.

Near the ring-toss booth, a burst of laughter rose—Johnny, Alice's husband, stood with a handful of guys, heckling whoever was up next. A man stepped forward, wound his arm, and threw. The ring bounced off the post and smacked one of the guys in the chest. More laughter.

He straightened, rubbing his neck, sleeves rolled, cider in hand.

Charlie.

The soft glow from the string lights brushed against his jaw. He was talking to Sam, listening more than he spoke, that quiet confidence wrapped in calm.

Emerson followed my gaze and smiled, like she knew.

"A birdie told me he's staying awhile," she said. "Helping Elizabeth with some deliveries. Fixing the roof at Grace Hill. I think the sky can spare him for a bit."

Before I could answer, Sam called out for her, waving her over to help with a tray of sliders. She grinned and grabbed my arm. "Come with me."

"Emerson—"

But she was already leading the way.

Charlie turned as we approached. His eyes met mine like he'd been expecting it. Not surprise. Just quiet recognition.

Emerson nudged Sam and winked. "We'll leave you two to talk. The grill's calling."

When they drifted off, the noise of the fair filled the space between us—music, laughter, the rustle of leaves underfoot.

We leaned against the railing, side by side, watching the last orange streaks fade from the water.

"You grew up here, right?" I asked.

He nodded. "Born and raised. Couldn't wait to leave. Now I can't seem to stay gone."

"Do you fly different routes all the time?"

"I mostly pick up random flights. I always loved the adventure of not knowing where I'll be next week. It's exciting." He smiled. "The downside is, I spend most of my time in hotel rooms and airport terminals."

"That sounds lonely."

"It can be." His voice softened. "Freedom was fun for a long time."

I looked at him then, really looked. The lines near his eyes, the calm strength in his voice, the quiet grief of someone who'd seen too much sky.

"What?" he asked.

"Is it still fun?"

His brow lifted, like he already knew there was more behind that. "You'd think so. But not so much anymore. At some point... you realize you're not working towards anything. Just sort of floating through life, not stopping long enough to live it."

His voice dropped low at the end, and I felt it—right in the place I'd been keeping calm. It scared me, how easy it was to want to stay in that stillness with him.

"I get it," I said. "Corporate life felt like that. It stopped feeling like living."

He leaned closer, elbows on the railing, studying me like he was trying to line up the truth behind my words.

"You don't strike me as someone who stops," he said.

"Well, I never would have, if the circumstances didn't push me to," I said. "It was a blessing in disguise."

"Good." He smiled. "You've got that look, you know. The one people get when they've been through something and came out better, not bitter."

"Is that a compliment or a diagnosis?"

"Both."

The space between us was still small but full. His hand brushed the railing near mine, not touching, just *there*.

"So what about you?" I asked. "If you stopped flying tomorrow, what would you do?"

He tilted his head, thinking. "Maybe fix something with my hands. Build instead of escape. I used to think I was chasing freedom. Lately I think I'm just tired of airports."

"Then land somewhere," I said before I could stop myself.

His eyes flicked to mine. "Maybe I should."

He smiled, but there was something else behind it—hesitation, maybe guilt. The kind of look that said there was a story he wasn't telling yet.

The words hung between us. Neither of us looked away for a beat too long—the kind of pause that makes you aware of everything: air, distance, heartbeat.

Someone nearby dropped a glass, the spell broke, and he stepped back first.

"I should find Elizabeth before she sends out a search party," he said softly. "But... save me a dance next time."

"You dance?"

"Not with everyone." He smiled, then disappeared into the crowd—and the moment with him felt like a secret I didn't mean to keep.

I stayed there after the music faded, until the last lantern flickered out and the night folded soft around the lake. When I finally headed home, the mill lights glowed warm in the distance, a pulse in the dark.

Inside, I set my keys on the counter, kicked off my shoes, and poured a glass of water. Then I caught it—the low rumble above, faint but certain. I stepped onto the deck and looked up. A single plane crossed the night sky, its lights steady, moving east. I watched until it disappeared behind the clouds.

The quiet after felt heavier than it should have.

Maybe because for the first time, I wished he'd stop flying.

But the truth was, maybe he never would.

CHAPTER 15
Firelight Between Us

The air smelled like woodsmoke and sugar.

By the time I reached the marina, the sun had already dropped behind the ridge, leaving the lake glazed in a faint bronze light. Strings of Edison bulbs looped between poles, their reflections trembling across the water. The sound of laughter carried from the docks, mixed with the low strum of a guitar and the clatter of folding chairs being set out.

It was the last Saturday of November—cold and crisp, the kind that made breath visible and coffee taste better. Bonfire night. Tunbridge's unofficial way of saying the year had turned.

I walked under the sycamores, close enough to smell the lake. The air smelled clean. From where I stood, I could see the marina lit up like a postcard. Tables lined the dock, each one covered in crockpots and pies. Blankets draped over benches. Kids chased each other through the crowd with sparklers while dogs barked and tangled leashes.

Home, in all its loud, imperfect glory.

"Rose!"

I turned to see Mom waving from near the food tables, her brown scarf glowing against the dusk. She had that same steady brightness she always carried into a crowd—talking to everyone like they'd been waiting all week just to see her.

Beside her stood my dad.

For a second, I couldn't move. I hadn't seen him in person in a year

"Didn't think I'd miss the first Tunbridge bonfire you were back for, did you?" he said as I reached him.

"You didn't even tell me you were coming," I said, hugging him tight.

"Your mom wanted me to surprise you," he said, chuckling. "Plus, you know I'd never skip a free meal."

He smelled like cedar and aftershave. I hadn't realized how much I missed that until now.

Right on cue, Willie Dawson popped out from behind the dessert table like mischief given human form. His hair was more gray, his belly a little rounder, but he still moved with that same restless energy I remembered from childhood. Willie had been Tunbridge's unofficial ringleader since before I could spell my own name—retired fireman, professional spoon-stirrer of harmless chaos, the man who once let me "drive" the fire engine during the Fourth of July parade and swore me to secrecy about it.

"Still got it!" he crowed, throwing me a wink before immediately dropping an entire bag of marshmallows into the fire pit.

Granny sighed. "Lord help us."

But she was smiling. And so was everyone else.

The crowd roared. He was harmless chaos. The kind Tunbridge didn't know how to live without.

"Come on," Mom said, pulling me toward the edge of the dock. "Emerson and Sam just got here."

They were hard to miss. Emerson glowed—she always had that sort of soft radiance that didn't come from lights. Sam was right behind her, balancing one of their twins on his shoulders while the other clung to his leg. They looked exhausted and happy in the same breath.

"Hey, stranger," Emerson said when she saw me. "You remember sleep, right? We've forgotten what that is."

"I'd give everything to have what you have, Em. Your family is perfect."

She laughed, the sound carrying over the crackle of the fire. "I wouldn't trade it."

Sam grinned. "She says that now." He bent to kiss her nose, and even in the middle of noise and chatter, it felt like watching something sacred.

Ute, Sam's mom, appeared behind them in a swirl of perfume and cashmere. Every piece of jewelry she wore caught the firelight like she planned it. "If anyone needs me," she said, "I'll be over there pretending not to eat an entire funnel cake by myself."

"Save me some," I called.

"You can have an edge if you earn it," she said, already walking away.

Arnold was arguing cheerfully with Hutch, the fire chief, about whose chili was better. Alice and her husband, Johnny, were nearby with hands tangled together and her head on his shoulder. Their twins, Jack and Lucy, were darting between the tables with cups of cocoa so full they sloshed onto their mittens.

Everyone looked content. Whole. Like the world had stopped spinning just for tonight.

And then I saw Charlie.

My eyes were drawn to the far dock, carrying two crates of cider to the drink station. He wore a dark henley under a flannel jacket, like he was fresh off the cover of a *J. Crew* catalog.

My pulse shifted gears.

"Go say hi," Emerson murmured.

"I'm fine here," I said, pretending to focus on the fire.

"Sure you are," she said, smiling like she'd seen right through me. "Just don't let someone else get to him first."

I rolled my eyes, but my stomach did that same flutter it had at The Oasis.

As I moved closer, I caught pieces of his conversation with

Elizabeth. Something about the weather over Denver, and a canceled flight. He must have just come back. He spotted me before I reached them.

"Rose," he said, like he'd been expecting me.

"Charlie," I said. "You found the best job in town—free cider."

He smiled, a small lift at the corner of his mouth. "I'm only here for quality control."

Elizabeth elbowed him. "He's the entertainment tonight."

"The what?"

She pointed toward the small wooden stage near the dock. A stool, a mic, a couple of fairy lights strung overhead. "He brought his guitar."

I looked back at him. "You play?"

"Used to," he said, almost shyly.

"He's being modest," Elizabeth said. "He's really good."

He shrugged. "It's been a while."

The way he said it carried something heavier. Maybe nostalgia. Maybe grief.

Before I could ask, Willie hollered from across the crowd, "Let's see if he still remembers how! Still got it, Charlie?"

Laughter rippled through the marina. Charlie's jaw flexed, but his eyes softened. "Guess I'm out of excuses."

He nodded toward the stage. "Wish me luck."

"Don't need to," I said. "You've got this."

The crowd gathered as he sat on the stool, adjusting the strap over his shoulder. The first few notes floated out—clear, intricate, familiar. "Blackbird."

The conversations quieted one by one until the only sounds were the fire and the guitar. His fingers moved like memory, like every note carried its own story. It wasn't loud or showy. Just honest. Beautiful in a way that hurt.

When his voice came, low and unforced, something in my chest tightened.

I'd never heard the song like that.

He wasn't performing. He was remembering. And maybe healing.

The lake mirrored the firelight in broken ribbons. The air was cold enough to make breath visible, and still, no one moved.

I felt tears prick my eyes and blinked them back before anyone could see.

He played a few more songs. One I'd never heard before, something old and aching. Then came "Tennessee Whiskey," his voice low and rough at the edges, the kind that pulls you in without asking. He eased into "Forever and Ever, Amen," and even Willie went quiet. He followed it with "Take Me Home, Country Roads," and the crowd joined in, off-key and happy. When he began "Simple Man," the crowd stilled, and every word felt lived-in—like he'd carried that song through a thousand airports just to bring it home here.

When he finished, the crowd erupted—cheers, clapping, even a few whistles. Willie yelled, "He's still got it!" again, and someone handed him a sparkler like it was an award.

Charlie smiled, shook his head, and stood. His gaze found mine through the crowd, and the noise dimmed again, at least for me.

He handed his guitar to someone who picked up the tune as he crossed the dock, the music trailing him like an echo that didn't want to let go.

"That was amazing," I said when he reached me. My voice came out quieter than I intended.

He didn't meet my eyes right away. He looked down instead, thumb brushing the edge of his flight jacket like it was a habit he didn't notice. A small, almost shy shake of his head. Then he lifted his gaze to mine.

He nodded once. "Thanks. It felt good to play again."

"It sounded like it," I said. "Like you meant it."

"I did," he said simply.

For a moment, neither of us spoke. The crowd thinned as people drifted toward the tables. The fire threw gold across his face, catching in his hair. He looked both younger and older in that light—someone who'd seen too much but still carried wonder somewhere inside him.

"Stay right there," he said suddenly.

Before I could answer, he walked toward Ute's table. A minute later, he came back with a paper plate dusted in powdered sugar.

"Funnel cake?" I asked.

He grinned. "You looked like you needed it."

I laughed. "That's a lot of sugar for one person."

"Let's share it," he said, tearing off a piece.

We sat on the edge of the dock, legs dangling above the water. The cake was warm, sweet, and messy. The sort of thing that never stopped tasting like childhood.

"It's just like the ones they used to make when I was little," I said.

He smiled. "They're still the same because Willie still runs the fryer. He hasn't changed a thing in thirty years."

I laughed. "That checks out."

He brushed at his chin, leaving a smear of sugar. I pointed. "You've got—"

He beat me to it, touching his lip and missing.

I reached out without thinking, swiping it away with my thumb. The moment stretched. His eyes caught mine, dark and steady.

"Thanks," he said quietly.

"Anytime," I said, just as softly.

A sharp spark snapped in the fire, making us both flinch. The spell broke for half a breath. The air smelled like pine, burning wood, and something warm I couldn't name.

"I should probably thank you," he said after a moment. "For what you said last time. About the freedom thing."

"What about it?"

"You were right," he said. "It's not all it's cracked up to be."

I studied him. "Do you miss home?"

He looked out over the lake. "Sometimes. But when I'm here too long, I start thinking about leaving again. Like I'm wired for motion."

"Maybe you're just not used to stillness," I said.

He glanced at me. "And you are?"

"Trying to be," I said. "It's not easy."

"No," he said. "But you make it look that way."

I smiled faintly. "That's the trick. Act as if."

We watched the last of the kids roast marshmallows in the fire. The laughter had thinned into murmurs and music. The lights from The Oasis glowed on the cliff above, mirrored in the black glass of the lake.

"You'll be gone again soon," I said before I could stop myself.

He didn't answer right away. "Yeah. Maybe a week. New York, then Paris."

I nodded, trying to sound casual. "That's... impressive."

"It's a lot of airports," he sighed. "A trip like this used to thrill me."

I wanted to say I'd trade anything to see what he's seen. But the way he said it made me realize it wasn't the same kind of seeing.

He shifted, resting his elbows on his knees. "You ever wish you could just start over somewhere completely new?"

"I did," I said. "Then I realized new isn't better. Just different. You still wake up with yourself."

He looked at me like he understood every word. "That's the hardest part."

Someone called his name from the other end of the dock—Elizabeth, waving him over to help load her van.

He stood slowly, dusted sugar from his hands. "You need a ride?"

"No, I drove. But thank you," I said.

He nodded, hesitated, then said, "I'll see you soon, Rose."

"Soon," I said.

He walked away, his stride easy, unhurried. I watched him lift a crate into the van with the same calm focus he had when he played.

Mom called something about leftovers. Granny yelled at Willie to quit sneaking jars of moonshine into purses. Laughter rolled through the crowd again.

Normal life resumed. But for me, everything felt quietly altered.

I wrapped my arms around myself and looked out at the lake one last time. The reflection of the fire rippled across the dark surface, fading and reforming with each breath of wind.

A guitar string twanged faintly as someone packed up equipment.

The night settled, soft and sure, over Tunbridge. Laughter rose and fell like waves, and for a moment it felt like I belonged to it all.

Then the wind off the lake shifted—cooler, sharper—and I wondered how long belonging lasted before life asked you to prove it.

CHAPTER 16
Choosing It Again

Winter arrived the way it always did in Tunbridge—quiet, beautiful, unbothered by hurry. The lake held a muted, pewter glow, as though someone had washed the world in soft watercolor grays. Frost silvered the dock boards and the air smelled like chimney smoke and pine. Bare branches etched the sky, delicate and stubborn, remembering the weight of leaves but not mourning them.

I stood at the kitchen counter, phone face up beside my mug, watching the weather app draw a blue smear across north Georgia. Wind advisory. Possible outages. The kind of forecast you shrug at until the power clicks off mid-sentence and you're left staring at your own reflection in a black screen.

Mom's watercolor hung above my desk, soft as breath. It steadied me. I set the mug beneath it and opened my laptop.

New e-mail stacked like a dare.

One subject line lifted its chin above the rest: *Opportunity—Let's talk next steps.*

Richard.

I didn't have to open it to hear his voice, all slick confidence and borrowed credit. I clicked anyway.

Rose, hope you're well. We're at a pivotal point with Helios. I need your leadership to push the campaign across the finish line. Contract. Executive title. Compensation to match. You'll have autonomy and my full support.

My stomach cramped.

My work. My career. All the nights, weekends, and the pieces of myself I'd handed over like dues. Autonomy now, because the house he stole is on fire.

I scrolled, then sucked in a breath. There it was: a number that would have made me dizzy a year ago. More than I made in two. The kind of number that buys a roof and fixes the things under it. I read it twice. Then I read mom's painting instead—the way the light reached between trunks like careful fingers.

I drafted a reply.

Richard,
I'm not available. Wish you the best with Helios.
-Rose

I left it unsent. Not because I didn't mean it. Because hitting send would make it real, and I wanted the moment of choosing to stretch a little longer. To feel it.

The number pulsed in my mind like a warning light. I thought about the rent, my retirement account, the way my savings app had stopped congratulating me months ago. Stability was a soft word for a hard thing to turn down.

My phone buzzed.

> Charlie: Are you home?

I smiled without meaning to.

> Me: Yes. Why?

> Charlie: Wind's picking up. Sam needs a space heater ferried to Sundancer. You want out of the house for 20 minutes? I'm passing by your place.

I looked at the sky. It was the kind of gray that makes you pull on sweaters just to see if it helps. My inbox loomed.

> Me: 20 minutes. No detours.

> Charlie: Pulling up now.

I reached for lip balm, considered mascara, even tugged at the hem of my sweater like that might turn me into someone more put together. I grabbed my coat and a knit hat from the basket by the door. The hat smelled like fabric softener. I pulled the door shut behind me and locked it.

He idled at the curb in an old truck that sounded like it had a story. Black, reliable, paint dull from honest weather with rust around the fenders. The passenger handle stuck for a second before it gave. Heat rolled out, grateful and immediate.

"Hey," he said.

"Hey," I said back, and the word felt warm between us.

He wore a baby blue sweater and a jacket that had seen airports on three continents. There was stubble on his jaw and the pale, stubborn line of a healed cut near his temple I hadn't noticed before. His hands looked like they'd fixed things that weren't supposed to be fixed.

He handed me a spare knit cap from the bench seat. "Yours is thin," he said. "Wind's mean."

"You carry extra hats around like a Boy Scout?"

"Like a man who hates cold ears," he said, and the corner of his mouth moved.

He drove with easy attention, one hand on the wheel, eyes on the road and also everywhere else—the wind, the trees, the way the light shifted on the lake as if testing boundaries. Down by the shore, the water wore a skin of chop.

"Busy day?" he asked.

"Emails," I said. "A logo tweak. And a generous blast from the past."

"Corporate?"

"Yeah."

He waited. Not a push. An open door.

"They want me back as a contractor," I said. "Big title. Bigger check. My campaign's off the rails and they're looking for someone who knows where the tracks are."

"How's it feel?" he asked.

"Equal parts infuriating and... flattering," I said. "Which is a gross combination."

"True things usually are."

We reached the marina and parked. High above the lake, The Oasis shimmered on the cliff's edge like a crown set upon the mountain—glass and stone catching the last gold light until it glowed from within. It looked almost alive up there, suspended between heaven and water, holding its own reflection like a secret. Down at Sundancer, staff moved portable heaters like chess pieces, readying for the cold.

Wind tugged at the truck when we opened our doors. Cold slid under my coat sleeves like a clever thief.

"Come on," he said. "We'll make it quick."

Inside, the heater waited like a small metal dog with a bad attitude. He lifted it without ceremony. I caught the cord so it didn't drag. We moved like we'd practiced—down the service hall, through the side door, onto the deck where wind threaded itself through everything that wasn't nailed down.

The lake was darker here. The water wore the weather's face.

Sam met us halfway, hair flattened by the wind, cheeks bright with work.

"You're a saint," he told Charlie, then tilted his chin at me. "And you're a better one."

"I'm transactional," I said. "I was promised hot chocolate."

"Hot chocolate's for tourists," Sam said. "You're getting the real contraband."

Ten minutes later, we stood under the covered end of the deck with two mugs of decadent liqueur-enhanced cocoa. I warmed my fingers and pretended I didn't see the huge basket of fries just go past us on a tray.

A gust rattled the string lights hard enough to make them clack. The air smelled like something deep-fried and impending rain.

"You said twenty minutes," he murmured, eyes on the water.

"I did."

"Good," he said. "We've got fifteen to kill."

I followed his gaze across the lake. Whitecaps shouldered toward the far shore. The wind bit his cheekbones pink and flattened my hair back from my face. I should've been cold. I wasn't.

"Tell me you're not considering it," he said after a minute.

"The job?" I shrugged. "I considered it for the length of one deep breath. Then I thought about fluorescent lights, calendar alerts, people clapping for theft, and the breath turned into a choke."

"And now?"

"I'm going to say no," I declared. Saying it made my ribs loosen. "I'm building something here. It's small, but it's mine."

Saying it out loud felt like handing the truth to someone who might actually take care of it.

"Good," he said simply. The word landed like a hand at my back, steadying me forward.

A kid tore past us in a puffy red coat, his laughter pinwheeling in the wind. His mother called after him and the sound got snatched sideways. Sam yelled something to a bartender, who then laughed like help was on its way before he even moved.

"I forgot how much I missed this," I said.

"What?" Charlie asked.

"People going about their day without consuming themselves to do it."

He huffed a laugh. "You make a mean case against airports."

"Airports serve their purpose," I said. "Get you home. Take you away."

"Usually both," he said quietly.

I glanced at him. "Are you flying soon?"

"Two days," he said. "Rome and back. Then Rio."

"Sounds glamorous."

"It was," he said. "Now it's just far."

We let that sit. The wind sent a scatter of dry oak leaves skating along the deck. One landed against the toe of his boot and spun until the air gave up.

"I love this." He smiled.

"Me too."

We didn't look at each other. It felt like we were both renting the same view for a minute, and that was enough.

Sam reappeared with a plate of fries big enough to qualify as a sin. He thrust it toward us. "A little tip. Thanks again," He rushed off, already three crises ahead.

Charlie set the plate on a barrel table and grabbed a handful. Steam curled up from the fries, sharp with salt and oil. He dunked one in ranch and handed it to me, grease warm against my fingertips, and I didn't bother pretending to be polite. We ate with our fingers, trading dips and quiet laughter, the wind teasing ripples across the lake.

"Childhood in one bite," I said.

A gust swept across the deck, sharper than the last. My hair whipped straight across my eyes. Before I could reach for it, Charlie's hand was already there, fingers brushing it back, tucking it behind my ear with surprising care.

The world narrowed to that one touch.

For a second, neither of us moved. The wind kept pushing. The lake kept shifting. His hand hovered by my cheek like he wasn't sure whether to let go.

Just then, someone yelled his name from the dock. He looked over the rail, cupped his hand to his mouth, shouting back. He belonged to motion in a way that didn't make me tired watching it.

"Time's up," he said, checking the sky. "Let's get you home before you miss any important emails."

The heater glowed like a loyal dog now, doing exactly what it promised. He walked a half step ahead of me, not blocking the wind so much as absorbing it. A sharp gust hit, cold enough to steal breath. The lake below us churned, restless under the weight of wind—like it couldn't decide whether to fight or surrender.

I braced, but before I could reach for him, his hand found mine.

"Got you," he said quietly.

His thumb traced the inside of my wrist once—barely pressure, just warmth. A question, an answer, and something neither of us was ready to name.

The drive back was a slow crawl past trees bowing to whatever wanted them. He turned the heat up without asking. I watched his hands on the wheel and realized I'd learned the way he moved without meaning to—the economy of it, the steadiness.

He idled at the curb in front of my building and put the truck in park.

"Thanks," I said. I didn't reach for the door handle.

"You still owe me for the hat," he said.

"I'll knit you a scarf with all my extra time."

"I would wear it every day."

I laughed. The wind shoved at the truck like a big kid trying to pick a fight.

"Hey," he said, and my laugh softened without instruction. "You did the hard part, you know."

"What part's that?"

"Leaving what was killing you," he said. "The rest is just figuring out what you really want now."

I thought of my unsent email. The number. The painting above my desk. The breath that had turned into a choke.

"I'm figuring it out," I said.

He nodded once. "Good."

A silence that wasn't empty filled the cab. Every cell in me leaned toward him and I told all of them to relax. Not here. Not yet. Not because wind made the world feel smaller and trucks feel safe.

"I'll see you," he said.

"When?" It slipped out before I could decide if wanting to know was smart.

"Tomorrow, maybe," he said. "I told Sam I'd help tie down the upper docks. If not, the next day. If not—" He shrugged. "I'm two days out."

"Rome," I said.

"Yeah."

"Bring me back a sky," I said. "I'll trade you a lake."

He smiled. "Deal."

I climbed down with the hat still on my head. He waited until I was at the door. I looked back over my shoulder just as a gust came. He lifted a hand in a small salute and pulled away.

Inside, the loft sighed the way old buildings do—complaining and also comforting. I set the borrowed hat on the counter, wiped salt from my sleeve, and opened my laptop.

The unsent email waited, polite and persistent.

I read it again. Then I hit send.

Outside, the wind climbed the building and poked at the windows with curious fingers. I made hot cocoa and snuggled into the couch with a book.

"Choosing it again," I told the painting.

The first low rumble lifted from somewhere over the ridge, rolled across the lake, and set the glassware to humming. The lights flickered, caught themselves, and steadied.

I breathed in. I breathed out. And I let the thunder answer for me.

CHAPTER 17
The Calm Before

Tunbridge felt suspended.

The air carried a quiet tension, like the town was holding its breath after the first shiver of winter. Even the lake looked different—still and metallic, rippling in slow motion beneath a gray sky that couldn't decide between rain or snow.

From my window, I could see the lights strung along Main Street swaying in the wind, pale against the coming dusk. Someone down the block was splitting wood, the rhythmic crack of the axe echoing faintly through the cold. Every sound carried a kind of intimacy this time of year. Closer, sharper, as though the world were smaller and listening harder.

Inside, my space smelled like coffee and cedar. I'd been working since morning—website mockups open on one screen, photos on the other, a dozen browser tabs scattered like thoughts. My Tunbridge clients were sending me consistent business. Small work. Honest work. Each project carried the same kind of quiet satisfaction that came from fixing something you could hold in your hands.

My phone buzzed near the window, the screen lighting with a name I hadn't expected to see until next week.

> Lydia: Hey Rose! Totally random favor. Any chance you could swing by Grace Hill later? We're setting up for the Winter Market this weekend, and the social media page needs a few good photos. The light's perfect tonight.

I smiled. Lydia Harper was a few years older than me, part of the Grace Hill Church volunteer crew, and one of those people who turned even the smallest event into something warm and festive. Her voice always sounded like sunshine.

On my way after dinner, I responded.

> Me: You're just using me for my camera skills, aren't you?

> Lydia: 100%. Also... I have Lindor truffles, I know you love them.

> Me: On my way!

I laughed and tossed my phone onto the couch. Outside, the first slant of dusk had turned the lake pewter. The air through the cracked window smelled like pine and something electric—the sort of weather that whispered about what was coming.

It was always like this before a storm, the stillness that wasn't still at all.

Grace Hill sat on a rise overlooking the edge of town—white brick, unassuming and simple. By the time I parked along the gravel lot, the place was alive. Pickup trucks lined the drive. The sound of boxes being shifted and laughter echoing through the open doors carried all the warmth of a small town getting ready for something.

Inside, the fellowship hall looked like controlled chaos. Lydia stood at the center of it all, clipboard in hand, scarf unraveling as she gave orders to anyone within earshot.

"Rose!" she said, spotting me. "You're my hero. These decorations aren't going to photograph themselves."

I grinned. "You said truffles."

"Over there," she said, pointing toward a table draped in plaid. A red bag sat front and center beside a paper cup of cocoa.

"You really know how to motivate a girl," I said.

"I know your currency."

A deep voice answered from somewhere behind her. "Chocolate is universal currency."

I turned.

Charlie was at the far end of the hall with Sam, both carrying a table that looked like it had no business being lifted by two people.

My pulse found a new rhythm.

It wasn't attraction so much as recognition—the kind that reminds you what your heart sounds like when it remembers itself.

Emerson trailed behind them, arms full of folded blankets, her light hair twisted up messily like she hadn't planned to stay but somehow had.

"Oh, look who decided to show up," Lydia said, waving toward the guys. "Our very own heavy-lifting crew."

Sam grinned. "We were bribed with chili."

"Hot chocolate," Emerson corrected. "And community service brownie points."

Charlie lowered the table with the ease of someone who'd done a hundred quiet favors in his life. When he straightened, his eyes found mine across the room. Not fast, not surprised—just focused. Like he'd been expecting to find me there eventually.

I lifted my camera as a shield. "Don't move," I said, aiming toward him.

He smiled a little. "Am I decoration or documentation?"

"Both," I said. "Hold still."

The shutter clicked. He didn't look away.

"Mom, that's our cue to look busy," Elizabeth said from the next table, arms full of mason jars and pine garland. Beside her, Helen Warren—though I could only ever call her Mrs. Warren thanks to school—sorted donation bins with the same calm steadiness that had once quieted a roomful of nine year-olds.

Mom walked in a few minutes later. "Granny insisted on sending her pecan bars," she said by way of greeting. "If she asks, everyone loves them."

"I know I do," I said, smiling.

She set the dish near Lydia and joined the others arranging centerpieces. The room buzzed with motion—voices overlapping, laughter spilling between them. It smelled like cinnamon, pine, and fresh paint from the crafts table in the corner.

I snapped photos as I moved: children tangled in string lights, Lydia gesturing dramatically with her clipboard, Sam carrying another box like it weighed nothing, Emerson sneaking marshmallows from the cocoa station. The kind of small-town chaos that photographs itself.

When I turned, Charlie was beside me, close enough that I caught the scent of his cologne and cold air clinging to his jacket.

"Need help?" he asked.

"I'm good," I said, though my hands were trembling slightly, the way they did when I was too aware of someone standing near.

He nodded toward the wreath she'd hung crookedly above the stage. "That one's threatening to fall."

I followed his gaze, laughing softly. "It's fine."

"Mm," he said, already reaching up to fix it. "You say that like you're not about to take fifty photos of it."

I tried not to smile. "Perfectionist tendencies die hard."

He adjusted the wreath until it sat straight, stepped back, and met my eyes again. "Better?"

"Better," I said quietly.

Someone called his name and he turned, one hand brushing my shoulder as he passed. The touch was nothing. Barely there.

But my pulse reacted like it had been waiting for that exact nothing all along.

Outside, the sky had darkened. The light through the windows turned soft and gold, warming the wood floors. A gust rattled the glass, and for a second, the whole world felt caught between breaths.

"Hey," Lydia said, appearing at my elbow with a cookie tin. "Don't forget these."

Inside, perfect circles of chocolate and sugar waited, dusted like snow.

"Bribery part two," she said, smiling.

I took one. "You're a saint."

"I prefer genius," she said. "You'll post these photos tonight? The Winter Market announcement needs a little sparkle."

"Already on it," I said, though I wasn't sure she heard.

My phone buzzed on the table—Richard's name lit the screen. I silenced it without looking. Not tonight. Not here.

Charlie had reappeared—carrying a crate toward the doors with Sam. His sleeves were rolled now, a faint smudge of dirt along his forearm. He caught me watching and didn't look away.

Lydia followed my gaze and smirked. "You know, for someone who claims to hate being photographed, he's surprisingly photogenic."

"Don't start," I warned.

"I didn't say a word."

"Your face did."

"Fine," she whispered, grinning. "But if he ends up in your next post, tag me. I want credit."

We laughed.

Lydia lowered her voice. "But seriously, did you see the way he looked at you?"

"No, I didn't. Let's move on." I shook my head.

By the time the last box was loaded, the wind outside had started to howl. Lydia called everyone in to pray for a safe weekend and a cooperative sky. People gathered in loose circles, mugs in hand, voices low and hopeful.

Charlie stood near the door, his jacket zipped, talking with Sam and Emerson. The lamplight hit him from behind, outlining his shape in gold. He turned when I moved toward the exit.

"Did you get a good one of me?" he chimed.

He lifted his chin a little, like he was offering up his most heroic angle. Then he planted his hands on his hips in a mock Clark Kent pose. It would've been ridiculous if it hadn't also been unfairly charming.

I snorted. "Absolutely not. Try again."

His mouth curved, slow and knowing, before he dropped the pose and stepped aside so I could pass.

"Just kidding, I got a lot of good ones," I smiled.

"I'm assuming that doesn't include the one where Sam sneezed on the wreath."

I laughed. "That one's staying in the archives."

He smiled, the kind that reaches the eyes before the mouth catches up. "Good. Wouldn't want the internet to think Tunbridge's hero is allergic to Christmas spirit."

"I think it's the pine," I said.

Sam chimed in, "I have allergies!"

Everyone smiled.

Charlie tilted his head slightly. "You heading home before the storm?"

"Yeah. Lydia promised I'd make it back before the sky decides to do anything dramatic."

"Text me when you get there," he said.

It wasn't a question.

"Okay," I said softly.

He nodded once, the kind of gesture that carried more weight than words, and held the door open. Cold air rushed in.

As I stepped outside, I caught his reflection in the window—a blur of light and stillness. He looked like someone who'd seen every horizon and still hadn't found the one that fit.

The wind tugged at my scarf, playful and insistent. The smell of cocoa and pine lingered on my hands.

By the time I reached my car, the first drops of rain had started to fall—light, deliberate, like the sky was warning us to pay attention.

I looked back once. The church windows glowed gold through the dark, and for a second, I almost wished I'd stayed.

CHAPTER 18
What Broke Open

The rain had started by the time I left Grace Hill, soft at first, more suggestion than downpour. But the wind was shifting—urgent now, whipping through the trees as if the sky couldn't make up its mind whether to break wide open or hold the weight a little longer.

Lydia yelled after me as I ran to my car. "Drive safe!"

I waved with my fingers still curled around my camera strap. "I will!"

She disappeared into the chaos behind her—clipboards, cocoa, voices tangled in preparation and warmth.

The cold hit fast. My coat caught the gust and flared behind me like a warning. I pulled the hood up, shoved my gear into the car, and climbed in. The wind slammed the door shut for me.

For a moment, I sat there in the silence, fingers hovering over the ignition. The streetlights swayed above the gravel back lot, making long, distorted shadows across the windshield. My reflection was a flicker in the glass. Pale. Unsettled. The kind of face that could still be undone by a look, a word, a memory.

I turned the key.

The drive home wasn't far, but the weather didn't care about mileage. Rain came hard and fast—sheets of it, drumming the roof, turning the world into motion and blur. The wipers worked furiously and still couldn't keep up. Every curve of the road vanished before I reached it. I leaned forward, white-knuckled, the headlights cutting through walls of water.

By the time I reached the bottom of the hill, the sky had opened wide. Main Street was a river, shop lights flickering against the storm. The lake to the east heaved and frothed, a restless black mirror that caught every flash of lightning and threw it back at the sky.

I eased into the narrow lot behind the lofts, heart pounding. The wipers squealed once and froze mid-swipe when I cut the engine. The world outside was chaos—rain slanting sideways, the wind howling through the alley.

I waited, hoping it would lighten. It didn't. It got worse.

The parking lot reflected the streetlight, a pool of moving silver. When I finally opened the door, the storm swallowed me whole. I ran for it, one hand clutching my bag to my chest, the other holding my hood down. My shoes splashed through puddles so deep they felt bottomless.

By the time I reached the steps, I was soaked through—hair dripping, coat heavy, water running down my spine. I reached for the door, fumbling for my keys—

And headlights swept across the lot.

Charlie's truck.

He parked fast, the door flying open before the engine even stopped. He didn't bother with an umbrella. Rain hit him in full force, but he didn't slow down.

"Rose!" he shouted, his voice barely cutting through the wind.

"Charlie—what are you doing here?"

He covered the distance in a blur, rain streaming from his hair, his jacket dark and slick. "I wanted to make sure you made it home safe."

Lightning flashed behind him, thunder breaking close enough to rattle the glass. The storm raged around us.

His hand found my arm, steadying me against the wind. His palm was cold, but the second he touched me, I stopped feeling it.

We just stood there—two soaked silhouettes under the streetlight, faces inches apart, the storm pulsing around us like a heartbeat.

Without warning, his hand went to my cheek, his thumb trailing down to my jaw.

Something in me gave up pretending I didn't already belong to this moment.

He kissed me.

The world tilted. The rain hit harder, fierce and cold, but I didn't feel any of it. I felt him—his hands, his mouth, the warmth breaking through the chill. His jacket brushed my fingers, drenched and rough, his heartbeat pounding against mine.

It wasn't soft. It wasn't careful. It was the kind of kiss that feels like truth finally breaking its silence.

My hand slid up and grilled the collar of his jacket. His mouth deepened against mine, rain running between us, lightning throwing flashes of silver across his face.

When we finally broke apart, breathless, he pressed his forehead to mine.

"Come inside," I said. "It's freezing."

The power was out. I pushed the door open and grabbed the flashlight out of the drawer. I lit the candle on the island.

The storm thundered beyond the windows, rain still streaming down his hair and jacket as he stepped in behind me.

We peeled off wet layers, left puddles on the floor, laughed under our breath because it felt unreal—like the whole world had narrowed down to this one moment that neither of us saw coming.

I lit another candle. Shadows danced along the walls. The air smelled like rain, wax and him.

He rubbed his hands together and met my eyes. "You're shaking."

"I'm fine."

He didn't believe me. He crossed the room, tugged the blanket from the back of the couch, and draped it around my shoulders. Then he hesitated—only a second—before pulling me closer.

He kissed me again.

It was warmth and breath and pulse, the kind of kiss that tells you the space between two people has been lying about how small it really is.

His hands slid into my hair, holding me just enough to make me feel safe in it. The kiss deepened. My fingers found the front of his shirt and curled there, anchoring myself to the only steady thing in the room.

His mouth moved to the corner of mine, to my cheek, to the place below my ear where no one had touched me in years. His breath was warm. His control was sharp.

When his lips touched my neck, just once—soft, reverent—I felt my whole body pull toward him like gravity was something personal.

I said his name, and it came out like a plead.

My chest rose and fell like I'd run a mile.

We stood there in the flickering candlelight, neither of us moving. The storm hissed at the windows. Somewhere, a shutter banged. His thumb brushed the edge of my cheek.

He pulled back, breath uneven, his hand still tangled in my hair. I could feel him fighting it—the pull, the permission. Wanting to say something that would make it less real. He didn't. He just looked at me, every muscle wired between stay and go.

If he'd touched me again, I wasn't sure I'd have let him stop.

"I should go," he murmured.

The wind rattled the window hard enough to make the candle flame bow.

"Not in that," I said quietly. "Stay. Just for tonight."

Something in him gave way then—resistance, maybe, or reason.

He exhaled and nodded. "Okay."

We ended up on the couch, the storm pressing close on the glass. A blanket between us at first, then not. I laid my head on his shoulder. His arm came around me slowly, deliberate, as though he was memorizing the shape of where I fit.

The world outside went dark and wild. Inside, it felt impossibly still.

His thumb traced idle circles against my hand, comforting and unguarded. I felt the tension leave him with every breath.

When he leaned in and pressed a kiss to my forehead, it wasn't a promise—it was something quieter, deeper. The kind of touch that says, *you're safe.*

I closed my eyes and let the storm speak for us.

The candles flickered. The wind softened. And somewhere between thunder and quiet, my hand found his chest. His heartbeat was slow and steady.

We sat like that, wrapped in candlelight, each other, and the hum of the storm for a while. It felt grounding and electric all at once.

"You should get some sleep," he murmured. "I'll take the couch. I'm right here."

I nodded, too full to speak.

Then lit a candle in a jar, its flame bowing as I carried it toward the stairs. I brought him some towels, blankets, and an extra toothbrush.

At the top of the stairs, I turned back once. He was watching me from the couch, hair still damp, light flickering over his face.

"Thank you," he said quietly. "For letting me stay."

His fingers brushed mine—barely there, but enough to make my pulse forget itself.

He smiled faintly. "Goodnight, Rose."

"Goodnight, Charlie," I said quietly.

I went to bed with the sound of rain against the glass and the warmth of his kiss still breathing on my skin.

CHAPTER 19
The Morning After

The world was quiet when I woke.

Not silent, exactly—just hushed, like the house itself was still deciding whether it wanted to wake up. Light seeped through the blinds in pale gold stripes, touching the edges of the blankets I hadn't really slept under. I could hear the faint hum of the heater again, a reminder that the power had returned sometime before dawn.

Downstairs, something shifted. The creak of a floorboard. The soft clink of a mug.

Charlie hadn't left.

I sat up too fast, pressing a hand to my heart, as if I could calm the way it reacted to that simple fact. He was still here. I brushed my teeth, my hair, and threw on a hoodie. I could smell coffee.

He was standing in the kitchen when I came down, barefoot, in a T-shirt, hair tousled. The storm had left his curls wild, a few darker than the rest. He looked... comfortable. Like he belonged here.

He looked up when he heard me. "Morning."

His voice had the rough edge of sleep, and that one word did something to me.

"Morning," I said. My throat felt dry.

He nodded toward the counter. "Power's back. I made coffee."

"You found the good beans," I said, noticing the bag.

"I guessed," he said, smiling a little. "You don't seem like the instant kind."

He handed me a mug. The brush of his fingers was casual, but I still felt it.

"Did you sleep?" I asked.

He gave a half-laugh. "Yeah. The couch was comfortable, but the best part was that quilt. It made me feel like I was sleeping under a field of roses."

"It's hydrangeas," I said. "My granny embroidered them herself."

He smiled. "Explains why I woke up feeling judged."

"She's a perfectionist."

"Then I was definitely sleeping under her watchful eye."

He sipped his coffee, leaning against the counter. The air between us felt different now—still soft, still quiet, but charged in a way that didn't feel temporary.

"Do you need anything?"

He held up the toothbrush. "Nope. You've already changed my life."

I lifted a brow. "That's all it took?"

"Well, it's been a while since a woman gifted me dental hygiene."

"High standards, I see."

"Ruthless."

When I turned back, he was watching me—not in a way that made me self-conscious, but in a way that made me feel seen. Really seen.

He cleared his throat softly. "You hungry?"

I nodded.

"The Rusty Skillet's probably up and running. I'll buy you breakfast to make up for the imposition."

"You think breakfast will cover that quilt comment?"

"Depends on how good the pancakes are."

"Good thing I keep a change of clothes in the truck," he said, glancing down at his now-dry flannel.

"Prepared for every emergency?"

"Pretty much. Jumper cables, clothes, and apparently now—romantic thunderstorms."

He said it lightly, but something in my chest tightened anyway. Like the storm hadn't actually passed—it had just changed form.

The air outside smelled like rain and pine. The sidewalks were littered with leaves and small branches, the aftermath of the night before. My breath fogged as we walked.

Charlie shoved his hands in his pockets. "So, do you always invite guys in to make out during storms, or am I just special?"

"Statistically speaking, you're my first."

He glanced down at me. "Good. I like those odds."

At The Rusty Skillet, the bell above the door barely jingled. The place was packed—half the town seemed to be there, swapping storm stories and warming up over coffee. Ute gave me a look the second she spotted us. One eyebrow arched. A smile she didn't bother hiding.

Charlie noticed and leaned in. "Do I want to know what that look means?"

"It means she's about to tell everyone we came in together," I whispered.

"Good," he said.

My stomach did a small, traitorous flip.

We slid into a booth near the window. The table felt too small for how much air seemed to move between us.

He picked up his menu. "All right, serious question. Pancakes or waffles?"

"Pancakes. But only if they're slightly undercooked in the middle."

He pretended to think. "You like a little chaos in your breakfast. Noted."

"And you?"

"Waffles. Crispy. Predictable. Stable."

I laughed. "You? Stable?"

He smiled. "Touché."

We ordered pancakes, eggs, and two refills of coffee before the food even came. Somewhere between bites of toast and the scrape of forks, the conversation shifted.

"What do you do for fun?" I asked.

He leaned back, thinking. "Flying used to be the answer. But now it's... habit. The kind that's hard to shake. I like music. Languages. I read when I can. Mostly travel books. I've seen half the places they describe, but I still want to know how other people see them."

"That's very *pilot* of you."

He laughed. "Your turn," he said, smiling. "What do you do when you're not out here rescuing Tunbridge one small business at a time?"

"I love photography," I said first, then hesitated. "And design. I used to read a lot—really read. The kind of books that take over your whole weekend and leave you different afterward." I gave a small shrug. "Then work took over instead. I keep telling myself I'll find my way back to it." I smiled faintly. "Maybe I just need the right book."

He studied me. "I've been meaning to ask... what were you doing on the road that night? One in the morning."

I froze for half a beat, then exhaled. "I was coming home. To Tunbridge. For my mom's birthday."

He nodded once, quiet encouragement.

"I should've left earlier, but there was this dinner meeting. One that starts with fake smiles and ends with everyone pretending they're not exhausted." I gave a small laugh that didn't stick. "By the time I got on the road, I'd been up since before dawn. Twelve hours at work, maybe more. I don't even remember leaving the parking lot. Just... brake lights. Gravel. And then... you know."

He didn't say anything at first. Just looked at me—like he was cataloging every word, trying to imagine the parts I hadn't said.

"I thought it was a deer at first," he said finally. "I was a few car lengths behind you. I saw you swerve. It looked like you hit black ice."

I could've blamed the road, the rain, the exhaustion. But the truth was simpler. Harder.

"It wasn't the road," I said softly. "It was me. I fell asleep."

His gaze found mine. "I still can't believe you walked away from it."

"I know."

The words hung there. My throat tightened. "I remember waking up in the hospital, staring at the ceiling, and thinking, if I'd died, that's what my life would've been. Dead tired. Always chasing something that didn't want me back."

He didn't say anything right away. He just reached across the table and brushed his thumb over the edge of my hand, grounding me without a single word.

"I'm glad you're here," he said quietly.

I nodded, swallowing hard. "Me too."

He gave a small smile. "For what it's worth, I've been the guy burning out at thirty thousand feet. It's not as glamorous as it sounds. Flying gets lonely. You start to feel like a ghost that just visits places other people live in."

"That's poetic for someone who likes waffles."

He laughed. "I contain multitudes."

"Do you have a favorite place?" I asked.

"Lisbon," he said without hesitation. "The air smells like salt and oranges, and the people stay out late, but not to rush anywhere. They linger. The whole city feels like it remembers what it means to rest."

"That sounds amazing."

"It is. You'd love it."

"Maybe someday," I said. "I've never left the country."

His eyes softened. "Then I hope the first time you see it, I'm the one showing you."

When the plates were cleared and the check came, I reached for it, but he was faster.

"Don't even try," he said.

I raised a brow. "You think buying me pancakes means you're off the hook for floral quilt jokes?"

"I think it buys me a second date."

My heart stuttered. "That assumes there'll be one."

He leaned forward, smiling. "There will be."

The walk home was slow. The air had that just-after-storm smell. He stopped at my door, his hands tucked into his jacket pockets, looking like he wanted to say something and couldn't quite find the words.

I saved him the trouble. "Thank you. For checking on me last night. For breakfast. For... everything."

He nodded, stepping closer. "You don't have to thank me."

"I do."

He reached up, cupping my face the same way he had the night before. "Then you're welcome."

I smiled, and before I could say anything else, he leaned in. The kiss was soft, warm, slow enough that I felt it before I processed it. His hand brushed my jaw, gentle but sure.

When we pulled back, I whispered, "Safe flight."

He smiled against my mouth. "Always."

I watched him walk away, hands in his pockets, and wondered if it was possible to miss someone who hadn't even left yet.

. . .

A few days passed. The rhythm of life filled back in—work, meetings—but everything felt different. My phone lit up with his name mid-afternoon.

> Charlie: Back Saturday. Dinner?

> Me: Yes.

> Charlie: The Oasis?

> Me: Perfect.

I stared at the screen like a teenager, biting my lip. Then I called Abby.

She answered on the first ring. "Tell me everything."

"It's just dinner," I said, already smiling.

"Dinner with the man who looks like he walked straight off the cover of a romance novel?" she said. "Rose, he's hot. And tall. And broody in a way that could fix the global economy."

I laughed. "You're ridiculous."

"I'm right," she said. "Now, what are you wearing? You can't show up in a sweater. This is your first real date in how long?"

"I'm not answering that."

"Exactly. It's been *that* long."

My phone buzzed again. Grant.

"Hey," I said, dropping onto the edge of the bed.

"Just checking on you," he said. "You crossed my mind."

That was Grant in a nutshell. A man who lived buried under deadlines, yet always made time to call.

"I'm okay," I said. "Really."

"You sound... lighter," he said. "Haven't heard you like that in a while."

My throat tightened. "It's been a good week."

"Good," he said quickly, as if collecting proof. "You deserve those."

There was a pause—comfortable, familiar. The kind we grew up speaking fluently.

"Hey," he added, voice softening. "I'm proud of you."

"For what?"

"For choosing a life that feels like yours again."

The words landed somewhere deep. Somewhere rarely touched.

"I needed that," I whispered.

"I know," he said. "That's why I called."

Another beat of silence. Then, his usual dry humor. "Don't get sappy on me, Sis."

"Too late."

He chuckled, warm and tired and home. "Alright, go do your thing. And call me this weekend, okay?"

"I will," I said. "Love you."

"Love you more."

When the line clicked off, the air in the room felt steadier. Like someone had reached in and tightened the bolts that held me together.

When Saturday came, Abby insisted I FaceTime her. Within five minutes she had vetoed half my closet.

"No wild patterns. Try the black wrap dress. It's sexy without screaming, 'Please propose immediately.'"

"Got it."

"And hair down. Always hair down. The man needs to suffer."

I snorted, but my cheeks hurt from smiling.

By the time we hung up, my room looked like a boutique exploded across it—shoes, jewelry, the curling iron already heating on the dresser. I caught my reflection in the mirror: flushed, nervous, alive.

I hadn't felt like this in years.

Somewhere inside, a voice whispered that I was getting in too deep. That men like Charlie didn't stay. But another voice—the louder one—told me that for once, I didn't need to protect myself from what felt good.

I looked at the dress laid across the bed, then at my phone glowing on the nightstand. His last text was still open.

> Charlie: The Oasis. 7:00.

I smiled, heart thudding, and reached for my lipstick.

CHAPTER 20
Learning How to Stay

The mirror kept arguing with me—lipstick softened, a curl coaxed behind my ear, then freed again. I hadn't cared this much about a first date since I was twenty. Maybe not even then. That felt like someone else's life. But I was ready fifteen minutes early.

The sun had already dropped low, casting a cold, golden light over Tunbridge.

When Charlie's truck pulled in, I was staring out the window like a child watching for fireworks. I opened the door before he even reached the steps.

Black sweater. Dark jeans. That easy, unguarded smile that started in his eyes before it reached his mouth. The porch lights were already on with a low hum, washing everything in amber. For a heartbeat, I just stood there, memorizing him against the soft halo of light.

"You look beautiful," he said, his voice quiet but sure—like he didn't need to rehearse it.

"You look... dangerous," I meant to say, but what came out was, "You look great." Heat rose to my throat anyway. Because what I really meant was *you just took the air out of the night.*

Then he handed me a book. Not just any book.

A vintage copy of *Gone With the Wind*. Maroon leather, gold-engraved spine, edges kissed in gilt. Heavy in my hands—because all old stories are. I ran my fingers over the cover, the texture soft and worn in places where other hands had loved it first. The pages were creamy linen, faintly perfumed with time.

"Wow," I breathed. "This is... gorgeous."

He watched me, that steady warmth in his eyes. "You said you just needed the right book."

For a second, I couldn't speak. The words caught somewhere behind my throat. He remembered. Of all the things I'd said, he'd held onto that.

"I did," I whispered finally. "And this is it."

He smiled faintly. "I found this in a little antique shop in Savannah a few years ago. It felt like it was waiting for someone who'd understand it."

I laughed softly, but my heart felt too full. "You have no idea how perfect this is. I'll never forget the first time I read it—I lost sleep for days because I couldn't stop turning pages." I looked up at him. "It's still the longest book I've ever read."

He smiled, the kind that reached past his mouth and settled somewhere deep.

"Thank you," I said, stepping closer. "For remembering."

Then I kissed his cheek—light, brief, but charged enough to make both of us still for a second too long.

We walked to his truck, and he opened the door for me. The air had that clean, cold bite—the kind that wakes every sense. Our fingers brushed when I climbed in, a small, deliberate touch that neither of us pretended was accidental.

The drive wound upward through the hills, the world wrapped in silver and shadow. Night had settled early, the kind of December dark that shimmered faintly with mist instead of stars. Patches of fog clung low to the trees, curling through the headlights like smoke. Each turn revealed a new sliver of the lake below—black glass catching bits of reflected light, trembling like it was still remembering the storm.

Charlie drove with one hand on the wheel, the other resting near mine on the console. The space between our fingers buzzed, full of quiet possibility. He was humming—something low and familiar, a slow country song that matched the rhythm of the rain that had started.

"Is that George Strait?" I asked, smiling.

He gave a small nod. "Guilty. Old habits. My mom used to play him when she cleaned the house. I think it's permanently wired into my brain."

"It suits you," I said.

He glanced over. "You mean I have cowboy energy?"

"More like... steady energy," I said. "Like the song knows where it's going before it gets there."

He smiled at that—just barely—and then reached over, his thumb brushing the back of my hand before lacing our fingers together. I forgot to breathe.

Neither of us spoke for a while after that. The hum of the engine and the soft patter of rain against the windshield filled the silence, steady and intimate. It felt like a heartbeat.

As the road curved higher, the woods thinned, and a soft amber glow began to appear through the trees—warm, flickering, alive. Then the sign came into view, lit from beneath so the gold letters gleamed like fire against the dark.

THE OASIS ON EMERALD RIDGE LAKE
450 FEET ABOVE THE LAKE
THE SUNSET CAPITAL OF GEORGIA

I smiled, the sight washing over me like déjà vu. The entrance was transformed for winter—stone walls dressed in frost-laced ivy, lanterns swaying from iron hooks, each one glowing with soft, golden light. Evergreens framed the path, strung with tiny white bulbs that sparkled like stars caught in their branches. Where summer had bloomed in pinks and peonies, December had traded color for candlelight and quiet grace. Ornamental grasses bent beneath blooming camellias, their petals soft as silk against the cold air, and somewhere above, music drifted faintly through the night.

Charlie slowed the truck as the road leveled out. The Oasis came into view—terraces tiered along the cliff, their windows spilling gold onto the night. Strings of lights traced the railings like constellations, their reflections rippling across the black mirror of the lake below. It looked like a dream perched between sky and earth, glowing against the winter dark.

He cut the engine and turned to me. "You ready?"

I nodded, though my heart had already said yes.

He smiled, climbed out, and came around to open my door. The air was sharp with pine and woodsmoke, the kind of cold that made everything feel clearer. But when his hand found mine, warm and steady, I didn't feel it.

The Oasis waited above us—glowing, golden, and impossibly beautiful. Like the kind of place where stories don't just begin. They're remembered forever.

He opened the door and let me step in first.

The Oasis was warm and golden, its beauty the kind that didn't need to announce itself. Candlelight glowed against polished wood and stone, catching on the gold fixtures and glassware. The scent of rosemary and something sweet drifted through the air, carried on a low hum of conversation and laughter.

A live trio played near the bar—just a guitar, a brushed snare, and a woman with a clear, caramel voice that wrapped itself around the room like silk. The sound blended with the clink of glasses and the soft scrape of silverware, the kind of effortless harmony that made the place feel timeless.

People from town turned their heads when we passed. Not everyone. Just enough to make me aware of us. Enough to remind me that Tunbridge remembered things for a long time.

Sam lifted a hand from behind the bar and tipped his chin at

Charlie. There was a grin tucked under it that I chose not to think about.

The hostess led us to a table near the windows, where the lake revealed itself in fragments of silver and shadow. Candles already lit. Linen napkins soft beneath my fingertips. The whole place seemed to hum with light and memory—like it had been waiting for this moment as much as I had.

"Still pancakes?" he asked when we sat. It broke the ice and made me smile.

"Tonight I can be talked into real food."

He looked almost relieved to have permission to slow down. Or maybe I was projecting. He ordered a bottle of wine like he knew what he was doing. He probably did. He glanced at the label and passed it to me. I pretended to read it instead of watching his mouth while he talked to the server.

We ordered simple things. Grilled salmon for me. He chose the lemon chicken that everyone loved. While we waited, the nerves ebbed and something steadier took their place.

"So," I said, resting my chin on my hand. "Tell me something people never ask you on a date."

He looked surprised and thought about it. "Great questions." His eyes moved, counting memories, choosing one. "No one asks me what I miss," he said finally.

"What do you miss?"

"Not the obvious things. When I'm away too long, I miss little markers." He looked at the window. "The way this lake looks right before winter. The smell when it's about to snow, even when it never does. How my mom leaves the porch light on for everyone like it can find them all the way from the highway." He smiled. "I miss being the person a place recognizes when I walk in."

"That's not little," I said.

"It feels little compared to flying into somewhere new and pretending it matters that I'm there."

"Does it not?"

"Sometimes it does. Sometimes I'm only moving through. Lately the movement feels louder."

I let the shape of that sit between us. "Then what would quiet it?"

He looked at me and didn't look away. "Learning how to stay," he said. "Or, if I can't yet, learning how to come back to the same someone on purpose."

My breath found a careful rhythm. I didn't say anything because the wrong words could break it. The server poured wine and slid away again. The trio shifted songs. The room dimmed almost imperceptibly as the evening settled around us.

He watched me for a moment, eyes soft, curious. "Your turn," he said. "What do you think is harder—trusting someone, or letting them trust you?"

I looked out the window, the lake below us reflecting moonlight. "Letting someone trust me," I said after a moment. "Because it means they've given you something fragile. Something they can't take back if you drop it. And I've spent most of my life proving I can be trusted. It's different when someone just... does."

He nodded, gaze steady. "That's a beautiful answer."

"What about you?" I asked.

He thought for a second, then exhaled. "Trusting someone," he said. "Because I've seen how quickly it can vanish. You can give everything to a person, and in one second, they remind you that love isn't a contract. It's a risk you take every day."

The air between us thickened—quiet, charged, real.

I smiled faintly. "We're getting dangerously close to the kind of conversation that ruins small talk forever."

"I'm okay with that." His voice was low, unguarded. "Tell me something else, then. What was your longest relationship?"

"Four years," I said. "If you count the parts that were good."

"What happened?"

"I kept showing up. He stopped." I swirled the last of my wine, then met his eyes. "What about you?"

He hesitated, then gave a soft, almost rueful smile. "Two

years. We were better apart than together. I think she fell in love with the idea of the man who was never home."

Something in my chest twisted. "That must've been hard."

"It was," he said quietly. "But it was also fair. I never made an effort to stay long."

I leaned forward, chin resting on my hand. "Do you always want to live like that? Always somewhere new?"

He studied me for a long moment before answering. "I hadn't thought about it much before."

I nodded, half smiling. "I'm sure it's exciting. You see the world. It's romantic." I hesitated. "But... will you ever want more than that?"

"Every day lately," he said softly. "But it's complicated. Flying isn't just what I do—it's where I disappear when everything else feels too close."

Something in me twisted—wanting to believe him, already believing him, and knowing belief was exactly how people got broken.

Neither of us spoke for a while. The music floated around us —slow, tender, threaded with the hum of conversation. The candles flickered between us like they'd been listening, too.

He smiled after a moment, that low, crooked smile that felt like an answer. "You ask questions like someone who's not afraid of the truth."

The candle between us flickered, catching on the curve of his wrist, the faint callus at his thumb. He didn't look away. "That's what makes you different."

The words hit deeper than they should have. I felt my pulse trip, the air between us thick with something unspoken. He reached across the table, his fingers brushing mine, slow and deliberate. When I didn't move, he laced them together—palm to palm, warm, sure. The noise around us faded until there was only the steady rhythm of the music and the weight of his hand around mine.

Our food arrived and gave us a way to look down. We ate in

intervals, talking between bites, laughing when we reached for the salt at the same time.

"Favorite food?" I asked when the plates had shifted from full to warm remnants. "If you say airplane peanuts I'll walk out."

He chuckled and reached across as if I might actually do it.

"Fresh croissants in Paris that come alive the second you touch them. Where the outside is whisper-thin and shatters into golden flakes that cling to your fingers. Peaches in August from the farmer's market here in town, when the air around it smells like sunshine and sugar before you even bite into them. Your turn."

"My granny's home-made tomato soup. With elbow noodles," I said. "And sourdough bread. I could *live* on bread."

He smiled. "Favorite subject in school?"

"Math," he said, smiling a little. "Anything that made sense once you stopped fighting it."

He glanced over at me. "I had this teacher who used to say numbers don't lie, people just get emotional about the answers. She made us recite the multiplication tables like it was gospel."

I laughed. "You probably loved that."

"I did—until I corrected her on the board once." He paused, smirking. "Turns out, teachers *do* lie. About detentions."

I covered my mouth, laughing. "You were that kid."

"The annoying one who actually liked proofs," he said. "I guess I just liked finding patterns where everyone else saw chaos."

His eyes softened a little. "Still do."

I pressed my napkin to my mouth to smother a laugh. The laugh turned into something softer.

"Do you want children?" he asked gently, and it startled me because it felt like a question someone asks when they want a life with you someday, not a first date topic.

"I do," I said. "I want a house that smells like Sunday pancakes and fresh laundry. I want laughter coming from every corner. I want little hands leaving fingerprints on windows, and a porch light that's always on for whoever needs to come home."

He drew a slow breath, like I'd opened a window in his chest. "Absolutely. I always have. It was never about not wanting a family. Just... waiting for the person who made the waiting make sense."

"Isn't it hard to find her if you're never around long?" I asked, my voice careful—not accusing, just honest.

He didn't flinch. Didn't deflect. He leaned forward, elbows on the table, studying me like he wanted to answer right. "It is. I've dated. I've cared. But I kept my distance because it felt safer that way. I told myself if I never stayed, I couldn't disappoint anyone."

I let it sit. The kind of silence that hums with things neither of you are ready to say.

When the waitress passed, Charlie caught her eye. "Two crème brûlées," he said, then glanced at me. "With extra berries."

It felt deliberate—soft, grounding. Like he was giving the moment somewhere to land.

"So," I said finally, tracing a circle on my napkin, "what are the next few weeks like for you?" Because the thing about truth is once you start inviting it, it expects a chair at the table.

"Busy," he said, and he didn't pretend otherwise. "Lisbon again next week. A charter to Tokyo the week after. I might pick up two hops while I'm there. Someone's talking about a Madrid job that runs close to Christmas. It's not decided, but it's out there." He looked sorry even as he said it. "I want to see you. I can build around it. I won't make promises I can't keep, but I'll try."

There it was. The schedule itself felt like a third person at the table, uninvited and unavoidable. I tasted something metallic behind my teeth that I recognized as fear.

"I don't want to be a layover," I said, quietly.

"You're not," he said at once. "Don't ever think you are."

"I'm trying not to," I said, and I meant it. "I like you, Charlie. I like you more than I meant to when this started. I'm not asking for a map. I just need to know that when it gets hard, we don't disappear into our old habits. Mine is to bury myself in work. Yours is to fly farther."

He exhaled. "Then do me a favor," he said, and the corner of his mouth lifted. "If I start to run, tell me to turn around."

"And if I start to hide, tell me to step out."

"Deal."

The trio slid into a standard I recognized from Granny's kitchen radio. Couples stood and swayed near the bar. It made the room feel like someone had opened a door to a softer hour.

"Dance with me," he said.

"I don't dance well," I said, out of habit.

"I don't care."

He stood and held out his hand. I let him lead me to the pocket of open floor. His palm was warm. His other hand settled at the small of my back. He didn't pull. He didn't steer. He let the music find our feet and we moved without deciding to.

I rested my cheek against his shoulder for one measure and then lifted my head because being that close made my bones hum. He smiled down like it wasn't a problem worth fixing.

"Is this where you tell me I'm stepping on your toes," I teased.

"You can step anywhere," he said. "I'm not going anywhere."

"Don't promise that," I whispered before I could stop myself. His hand tightened at my back, like he wanted to.

I knew he was. That was the cruel part. He'd go, because his job was a runway and a sky. I knew I'd stay, because my life here was finally more than a pause. But there, in that circle of light, with my heart beating where he could feel it, I believed for a breath that we could make a third thing between those truths.

When we stepped outside, the night was colder and brighter. The stars were clear—scattered like someone had placed each one by hand. The air held that crisp, pine-scented stillness that only comes after a storm.

The drive home was quiet but alive. The kind of quiet that feels full, not empty. Headlights stretched ahead in ribbons of white, glinting off wet pavement. He drove with one hand on the wheel, the other resting over mine. His thumb traced my skin, and every touch felt deliberate. He hummed now and then—some old song that made the truck feel smaller, warmer, like we were sealed off from the rest of the world.

When he parked in front of my place, neither of us moved right away. The dashboard light softened his face, made his eyes darker, more thoughtful.

He turned toward me. "You make quiet feel easy," he said.

Something in my throat tightened.

"Text you when I land," he added.

"Good."

"And I'll find a way to see you before I go again."

"I'd like that a lot."

He walked me to the door and when we reached it, he leaned down and kissed me. It was different this time—slower, certain, like both of us had come to it carrying everything we'd said and were still choosing yes. His hand framed my jaw; my fingers curled in his sweater because I needed somewhere to put the ache of wanting him to stay.

When we parted, our breath fogged the air between us—soft, visible, fleeting.

"Thank you for dinner." I smiled.

"Goodnight, Rose," he said.

"Goodnight," I whispered, watching as he walked down the sidewalk, the porch light holding steady until he turned the corner and disappeared into the dark.

Inside, the loft held the echo of him. The couch. The kitchen. His toothbrush was still on the bathroom counter. I put my shawl on the chair and stood in the quiet with my hands on the back of it, trying to let my heartbeat slow.

I was happy. Not loud-sparkler happy. This was the quiet kind that sits low in your ribs and changes the way you stand. And braided into it already was the ache I'd expected. The stop-and-go of a life tied to a sky. I wanted him to want this town, this table, this porch light. I knew that wasn't a thing I could force.

I chose to want it anyway.

I washed my face and set my phone on the bathroom counter while I reached for a towel. The mirror was still fogged when the screen lit up. I looked down and froze with the towel in my hands.

A name I hadn't seen since Buckhead filled the display. *Dieter Fluke*

The phone buzzed again. The sound felt like a hand closing around my wrist.

Why would Dieter be calling me at eleven on a Saturday night? I didn't answer.

The buzz faded. A moment later a message appeared, short and surgical, the way only my old life knew how to be.

Dieter Fluke: PLEASE CALL ME TONIGHT. URGENT.

Water ticked in the pipes. The house held its breath.

I stood there with the towel pressed to my collarbone and felt the new life pressing forward while the old one reached back. The porch light glowed on the other side of the wall. My phone lit again on the counter, waiting for me to decide what type of woman I was going to be.

I didn't call him back.

Not that night. Not with Charlie's kiss still warm on my lips and the scent of pine still clinging to my hair. I put the phone face down on the counter and told myself it could wait—that whatever he wanted belonged to a life I'd already buried.

But I didn't sleep. I lay there listening to the house breathe, watching the shadows move across the ceiling, waiting for the past to get tired of knocking.

It didn't.

CHAPTER 21
The Call That Tried to Claim Me

The email came first. *Subject: URGENT—CALL ME*

Dieter never used lowercase letters. It was one of the many things that used to make me tense before I even opened a message. He wrote like every word was an emergency and every delay was an insult.

I didn't open it.

The first day, I told myself I'd reply later. The second, I decided ignoring it was its own kind of answer. By the third morning, when his name started flashing on my phone instead of my inbox, the weight in my stomach felt like lead.

I let it ring out. Then again. And again.

When he called the fourth time—ten seconds apart, like persistence was loyalty—I answered.

"Rose. Finally."

His voice hadn't changed. Smooth, rehearsed, like a man who'd spent too long talking over people who couldn't afford to interrupt him.

"Dieter," I said flatly. "You're persistent."

"I've been trying to reach you for days. We're in a situation. The launch collapsed. Richard's out. Engineering's in chaos. They've lost confidence. No one knows the campaign like you do."

I said nothing. Just stared out the window at the street below, the empty stretch of Maple where the leaves skated by like they had somewhere to be.

"You built that campaign," he continued. "Richard was never right for it. But you weren't exactly easy to manage, Rose. The board wanted stability. You made things... complicated." He paused. "You're the only one who can fix it."

"Fix it?" I repeated. "You mean *save* it."

"Call it what you want. The point is, we need you."

"You needed me five months ago," I said. "You let someone else take over."

"That was a different situation."

"No, Dieter. It wasn't."

"You were emotional," he said, cutting me off. "And I couldn't have you unravel in front of clients." A pause. The sound of him exhaling, impatient. "Look. I know there were issues, but we're talking about a new deal. Permanent return. Full senior management privileges. We'll restructure the department around you. Name your salary."

He said it like it was generous. Like money could buy back the part of me that almost died trying to please him.

"I already had that job," I said. "Minus the respect."

"You're angry. I get that."

"No," I said quietly. "I'm actually not angry at all." But my voice betrayed me. A tremor, small but real. He'd always known how to find it.

"Good. So, what do you say?" He asked.

"No, thank you."

"Don't do this," he said, his tone dropping into the voice that used to get under my skin. "Rose, I *made* you. I mentored you. You wouldn't have your résumé if it weren't for this company."

Something in me snapped.

"You're right," I said. "You *made* me. You *made* me the woman who worked sixteen-hour days for a title that meant nothing. The woman who thought exhaustion was proof of worth. The woman who kept defending people who didn't deserve her loyalty. Congratulations."

"Be reasonable."

"Reasonable?" I laughed. "Dieter, you stabbed me in the back. Your plan fell through and you're begging me for help." I took a deep breath. "You didn't just give Richard the greatest project of my career, that would have been bad enough. But you gave him my *promotion*. No one would have given more to you or that company than me. Bad decisions have consequences."

He went quiet for a moment. "You left us stranded, Rose. One day you're leading a multi-million dollar launch, the next you vanish without warning. No handover, no update. Do you know what that did to morale? To our reputation?"

My blood went cold.

"You're blaming *me* for that?"

"I'm saying you disappeared without ensuring continuity."

"Continuity?" My voice shook, but not from fear. "Dieter, I documented every step of that campaign. Every strategy, every file, every vendor contact. You had everything. Engineering, the marketing team, and the agency all knew the plan forward and backward. The reason it failed is because Richard didn't execute. You gave my job to a liar, and you got the result you earned."

"That's not fair—"

"Do you want to know why I got in that accident, Dieter?" I cut him off. "Because you called a six a.m. meeting that day. I'd already worked twelve hours. Then I agreed to a last minute dinner with leadership that ran until midnight. You knew I was driving to Tunbridge that night. You knew I was trying to get to my mom's birthday in the morning. I fell asleep at the wheel, Dieter. I didn't crash because I was careless. I crashed because I was killing myself for your approval. You didn't just drive me into that wall, Dieter. You built it."

Silence.

"I didn't even care that Elaren never sent flowers or made a statement," I said. "But pretending I was replaceable the same week I almost died? That was its own kind of obituary."

When he finally spoke, his voice had that low, measured tone that meant he was recalibrating. "No one forced you to do all that, Rose. You could have said no."

"You're right," I said. "I could have refused to attend the early meeting, and the leadership dinner. That's on me. But you don't get to weaponize my loyalty now."

"You're being emotional."

"Emotional?" I laughed again, harder this time. "You're the one calling four times in a row." I took a deep breath to lower my blood pressure. "You trained me to kill every feeling I had so I could fit into your version of strong. Maybe that's why this one scares you."

"You're making a mistake," he snapped. "This is your chance to step back into real power. I'm offering more than you ever asked for. The salary alone—"

"I don't care."

"You will."

"I won't," I said again, louder. "Character matters more to me than money now. You'll do the same thing again. You'll find another Richard when it's convenient. And I'm not going to let you."

He sighed, that heavy, patronizing sound that used to make me shrink. It didn't anymore.

"You've changed," he said.

"Thank God."

"Keep the door open, Rose," he said, softer. "When you come to your senses, you'll see what you're walking away from."

"I know exactly what I'm walking away from," I said. "And I hope you remember this conversation the next time your company burns down around you."

He didn't answer. Just breathed once, slow and careful, like he was deciding whether to apologize or detonate something else.

"Goodbye, Dieter," I said. "I hope you find someone else to save you."

Then I hung up.

The sound of the disconnect clicked sharp in my ear. For a second, I just stared at the screen, waiting for it to light again. It didn't. The silence came rushing in—thick, total, alive.

I didn't realize I was shaking until the phone slid out of my hand and hit the rug. The silence that followed wasn't peace. It was heavy. My heart was pounding hard enough that I could hear it in my ears.

I sat on the couch, staring at the dark screen, every muscle locked tight.

For years, that man's voice had been the sound of authority in my head. It was the voice I heard when I second-guessed myself, when I wanted permission to rest, when I wondered if I was enough.

Now it was just noise.

Still, the anger didn't fade. It twisted and climbed until it had nowhere to go. I stood, pacing the length of the room, then stopped by the window. Outside, the streetlight flickered like it was remembering the storm.

My chest tightened. The silence in the house felt sharp at the edges. I promised myself I wouldn't reach for him. That I could hold this alone.

Five seconds later, that lie cracked.

I picked up my phone, thumb hovering over Charlie's name. I wasn't someone who asked for help. Not from men. Not from anyone. But the ache under my ribs pulsed like a question.

> Me: Are you anywhere near town?

The dots didn't appear right away. I almost put the phone down. Then:

> Charlie: Fifteen minutes. Is everything okay?

I hesitated. Then told the truth.

> Me: Can you come over?

> Charlie: On my way.

I set the phone down and pressed my palms to the counter, breathing slow. I wasn't falling apart. I was reaching out. There was a difference.

My heartbeat kicked hard, a mix of relief and embarrassment. I wasn't used to being someone's soft place to land—or letting someone be mine.

When he knocked, he didn't look worried or intrusive. He looked like someone who understood being summoned after a hard day. His jacket was damp from the mist. He held a grocery-store bag with two cans of ginger ale and a small box of shortbread cookies like he'd grabbed the first things that looked comforting.

"I didn't know what you needed," he said. "So I brought options."

That tugged at something tender.

I stepped aside and he came in, moving quiet, not scanning the room for clues, not demanding explanations. He nodded toward the couch. "Sit with me?"

I did. Not close, not far. The space between us felt like an invitation instead of a test.

He opened a ginger ale and handed it to me. "You don't have to talk. Just... let me be here."

The kindness of that settled me more than anything else had all day.

After a minute he said, "If you want to talk about it, I'm all ears." His voice soft, giving me room.

I nodded. "It was my old boss," I said. "Someone who took advantage of me for years and never admitted it. He called trying to pull me back in."

He didn't ask what happened. "And?"

"I said no," I whispered.

"Good." He touched my knee, gentle and brief. "You deserved better than whatever he tried to drag you back into."

That reassurance felt good.

The room stayed silent. He didn't fill it. He didn't fix anything. He just stayed.

And it made it easier to breathe.

After a while he said, "Want to walk for a bit? Sometimes that helps."

I nodded again.

We walked the loop around Maple Street, our steps hitting the wet pavement in a slow rhythm. He didn't take my hand right away. He waited until we reached the corner, like he was letting me decide if I wanted the closeness. When I reached for him, he laced our fingers together like it was instinct.

By the time we circled back to my porch, something inside me had settled. Not healed. Just steadied.

He paused at the steps. "I'm sorry to cut this short, I'm leaving for Lisbon," he said. "I wish I didn't have to go."

I nodded. "It's okay. Thank you for coming."

"Always," he said quietly, like he wanted that word to land somewhere inside me and stay.

He cupped my jaw with one hand, his thumb warm against my cheek.

"Text me later?" he asked.

Before I could answer, he leaned in and pressed a slow kiss to my mouth—nothing urgent, just certain.

The kind of kiss that said I'm here, even when I'm not standing in front of you.

When he pulled back, he rested his forehead against mine for a second. "Let me know you're okay."

Then he left me with a quiet house that didn't feel quite so sharp anymore.

CHAPTER 22
The Silence That Tested Me

I wandered through town by late afternoon, just to hear something other than my own heartbeat. The air smelled like rain again. The streets were slick, the kind of cold that bit your skin before you realized you were shivering. People nodded as I passed—small-town reflex. I nodded back, polite, distant.

By the time I reached the lake, the wind had picked up. The water looked mean—choppy, gray, alive. I sat on a bench near the pier, the same spot I used to come when I first moved back. Back then, I was numb. Tonight, I was burning.

The wind stung, but not as much as the thought that Dieter knew exactly which bruise to press and I still felt it echoing in my bones.

I replayed the call, every word, every tone. His manipulation, his condescension, his complete inability to see me as human. I thought of the years I'd traded for that company, the holidays I'd missed, the way my stomach used to knot before Monday mornings.

And still, part of me ached for the stability. The paycheck. The illusion of being indispensable. That was the most dangerous part of all.

I pulled my knees closer to my chest and whispered it out

loud, like saying it might make it stick. "I'm not that woman anymore."

But even as I said it, my throat tightened.

That night, I couldn't sleep. Every time I closed my eyes, I saw Dieter's name on the caller ID. I kept checking my phone—half-expecting another email, half-hoping for a text from Charlie.

For a heartbeat, I wished he were here. Or wished he were someone whose life stayed in one place. I hated that the thought felt disloyal and true in equal measure. Needing him felt dangerous, because he could be in a different country by morning. I didn't want my heart learning how to brace for departure.

I grabbed my phone again without thinking and hit my dad's name.

I didn't expect him to answer. He almost never did on the first try—not with the hours he kept or the places he worked, half the time on bases he wasn't allowed to mention.

It rang once.

Twice.

Then his face filled the screen, grainy from some overseas satellite connection, a dim light behind him and the hum of generators in the background.

"Hey, Peach," he said, voice low, calm, threaded with that steady intelligence that had carried him through twenty years of military service and another ten working defense contracts in places I tried not to picture. "Is this a good surprise or a bad one?"

My throat went tight. "Bad day."

He leaned closer to the camera. I could see the fatigue under his eyes, the kind that came from weeks of twelve-hour shifts on foreign soil. Still, he was fully present, scanning my face the way he used to after I scraped my knee as a kid. Assessing. Reading. Understanding.

"Work?" he asked.

"Old work," I said. "Someone who shouldn't have access to me anymore."

He nodded slowly, like he already knew the shape of the wound without needing the details. "People like that don't want you back," he said. "They want the version of you they could control. You walked away from that girl. Let her stay gone."

I swallowed. "It's harder than it should be."

"Of course it is," he said. "You gave them years. Routine has gravity. Even the wrong kind."

A faint shift of noise behind him—metal, boots, some distant machinery—reminded me he wasn't calling from a porch or a living room. He was somewhere he wouldn't name, under a sky I couldn't see, probably running on four hours of sleep and strong coffee. Yet still, he answered.

"You listen to me, Peach." His voice softened but didn't lose its weight. "You didn't leave a job. You left a life that was shrinking you. That takes brains and backbone. I'm proud of you."

Something steadied inside me. Not fixed—just less breakable.

"I wish you were here," I said quietly.

"I wish I was too," he answered. "But you're stronger than you think. Text me tomorrow. Even if it's just to tell me you're breathing easier."

"I will."

"That's my girl," he murmured. "Now get good sleep. It makes everything better. Love you."

The call ended.

The ache didn't vanish, but the sharp edges dulled. Someone in the world was on my side, even from thousands of miles away.

The next morning, I made coffee I didn't drink. Answered three inquiries I barely read. I spent half an hour entering figures into my budget spreadsheet, watching my hands work like they belonged to someone else.

At noon, I sent Charlie a message.
Me: Just thinking of you. Hope Lisbon's good to you.
The dots didn't appear.

I tried to focus on invoices, but my phone stayed silent. The longer it stayed that way, the louder the other voice got—the one that sounded too much like Dieter's. *You'll come to your senses. You'll see what you walked away from.*

A few hours later, I went to The Rusty Skillet just to be around noise. The diner was full—families, laughter, clinking dishes—but I couldn't tune any of it out enough to feel better.

Dixie waved from behind the counter. "You look like you need pie."

"I need a new brain," I said.

The truth was simpler. I needed air. A heartbeat that wasn't my own. A reminder that people like Dieter weren't the whole world.

"Apple or pecan?"

I almost smiled. "Surprise me."

She set down a slice the size of my hand and poured coffee without asking. I stared at the steam, wishing it could quiet the buzzing in my chest.

When my phone lit up, my pulse jumped.

> Charlie: Long day. You okay?

I swallowed hard. The words blurred.

> Me: Yeah. I'm fine.

He didn't reply again. But seeing his name on my screen softened something sharp inside me.

For the first time all day, I exhaled without shaking.

. . .

When I got home, I opened my laptop. Dieter's email was still sitting there at the top of my inbox like a warning label.

Subject: URGENT—CALL ME

Below it, a line of text I hadn't noticed before: *This could change your life, Rose.*

I stared at it until my eyes burned, then deleted it. Permanently. No archive. No safety net.

The quiet in the loft felt too loud, like the walls were holding their breath.

A sharp knock broke through the quiet.

Three quick taps. Then one more. Elizabeth's pattern. She always knocked like she was entering a secret treehouse.

I opened the door to find her standing there with her hair in a loose braid and her coat half-zipped.

"Get your shoes on," she said. "Now. No questions."

"I look that bad?"

"You sound that bad. Move."

Before I could argue, she was already halfway down the sidewalk. I grabbed my jacket and followed, confused.

The sound hit first—trumpets, drums, a wavering tuba. Elizabeth shot me a grin over her shoulder.

"Tunbridge High's marching band is rehearsing in the square," she said. "And half the town showed up with baked goods, because of course they did."

She wasn't wrong.

Three blocks away, under a pale winter sky, the band huddled in coats and scarves. Folding tables overflowed with brownies, pumpkin bread, cinnamon rolls the size of my face. Parents handed out samples with the solemn urgency of surgeons.

It felt like the whole town had wandered outside at once—not for anything official, just because someone started playing music and everyone remembered they were neighbors.

We walked toward the square. A sax squeaked. A flute player burst into giggles and dropped her sheet music. Ute waved at us over a tray of lemon bars.

Something in my chest loosened—small, but real.

Then a golden retriever wrenched free from its leash.

He barreled straight toward the brass section, tail whipping like a helicopter blade. Half the trumpet line jumped back. A kid shouted "Pepper!" in pure, helpless panic.

Elizabeth sprinted.

I sprinted after her.

Pepper dodged left, then right, gleefully, like chaos on four legs. Elizabeth lunged. I reached. We both missed by a breath.

A trumpet blasted.

A cymbal crashed.

Someone yelled, "He's going for the cookies!"

Finally, Elizabeth snagged the leash and I blocked his escape with my entire body. Pepper skidded to a halt, panting like he'd won something.

The kid rushed over, breathless. "Thank you! He thinks rehearsal is snack time."

"He's not wrong," I said, rubbing Pepper's ears.

Elizabeth returned the leash, then nudged my shoulder. "That was kinda fun."

We stayed as the band fought through a wobbly but enthusiastic version of "Georgia On My Mind." Parents clapped. Kids laughed. Someone handed me a brownie I didn't ask for.

Life, unpolished and ordinary, moving whether I was ready or not.

When the wind picked up, Elizabeth hooked her arm through mine.

"Come on. Let's walk."

We wandered a few blocks, letting the night settle around us. Then she slowed. "Look."

The town shifted as we moved away from the square. The music faded, replaced by the soft hum of Main Street settling into evening. Storefronts glowed in warm pockets of light. It all felt small and steady and impossibly safe.

Tolliver's Bookshop glowed like a lantern against the early

dark. String lights traced the windows in amber loops, and through the glass I could see the fireplace flickering beneath the mantel Lila decorated for every season. Tonight it held pine boughs, little wooden stars, and a chalkboard that read *cozy up with something new.*

Elizabeth nudged me with her shoulder. "Still open. Come on."

Inside, warmth wrapped around us instantly. The air smelled like old pages, pine, and whatever candle was burning. A few locals browsed the front tables, murmuring about holiday picks, their coats steaming lightly from the drizzle outside. The crackle of the fire softened everything, turning the shop into its own little world.

"Rose?"

Lila appeared from behind the counter, cheeks flushed and her hair was pinned up with an antique brass clip. She took one look at me and hurried around to pull me into a hug.

"Good grief, you scared ten years off me," she said into my shoulder. "How long are you in town?"

"Long enough," I said. "And your window is gorgeous."

She beamed. "I redid it this morning. The weather won't commit, so I figured the bookstore should." Her eyes softened. "Really... how long are you back?"

"For awhile," I smiled. "I moved back."

She pulled me into a hug. "That's the best news," she chimed, slipping an arm through mine. "Come here, I have something you are going to love."

She brought me to the display table by the fire and lifted a cloth-wrapped book from beneath a stack. 'Found this at an estate sale in Athens,' she said. 'A red leather edition. I knew you'd appreciate her.'

Soft, worn leather. Gold lettering faded in all the right places. The kind of book someone once loved enough to keep close.

"Oh, Lila," I breathed. "It's beautiful."

She grinned, proud and a little emotional. "You should've

seen me bargaining for it. Nearly scared the poor old lady at The Queen."

"The Queen? As in The Queen of Hearts? You're on a first name basis with the antique store?" I asked.

Lila smiled and nodded, "Absolutely."

Elizabeth laughed. "By the way, she's not exaggerating. She negotiates like she's fighting a dragon."

"We all have our gifts," Lila said, waving her off.

"Speaking of... Lila, your cake will be ready first thing in the morning. I'm pretending not to know it's for James's birthday tomorrow." Elizabeth added.

"Thank you," Lila whispered. "And please don't tell him. It's a surprise. I also got him a clock that has algebraic expressions for each hour. Is it too geeky?"

Elizabeth snorted. "No. James will love anything from you. He's a goner."

We ended up by the hearth, sitting on the old sofa while Lila made us hot cider in mismatched mugs. The warmth, the soft lamplight, the murmur of a customer flipping through a book across the room—it all wrapped around me like a cozy blanket.

Tunbridge at its best.

When we finally stepped back outside, the night air chilled my hands, but something inside me stayed warm. Like the light from Tolliver's followed me all the way home.

"Tonight was so good. I didn't know I needed it."

She looked at me, eyes warm. "You don't have to do this town alone, you know. You've got me now."

I swallowed hard. "I'm really glad we're friends."

"Me too," she said. "You fit here more than you think."

As I let myself inside, the quiet didn't feel empty anymore. It felt like a place I could return to. A place that might hold me while I learned how to hold myself.

CHAPTER 23
What I Didn't Say (Charlie)

I touched down in Lisbon just after sunset, the sky fading from gold to that deep blue that made the river look like glass. I'd flown here fifty times, maybe more, but the place still hit me the same way. A spark in my chest. A lift under my ribs. Like the minute the wheels kissed the runway, something unclenched.

Flying gave me that feeling the whole way down. Cities blooming under the nose of the plane, runways lighting up like they were waiting just for me. Most people got used to routine. I never did. Every landing still felt like the world was bigger than I would ever figure out. I liked that. I needed it.

By the time I'd signed off the logbook and stepped out of the jet bridge, warm Portuguese air wrapped around me. Jet fuel. Stone. Salt off the river. The kind of smell that woke something in my blood.

I should have been buzzing. Usually I was. But the first thing I did was pull out my phone like an idiot and check for messages.

I locked the screen before I could think too much about it.

The crew bus dropped us near the hotel. The guys chattered about dinner plans and the bar. I nodded along, but my head was somewhere else. Atlanta. Tunbridge. A lake at the edge of a small town where I once belonged.

My room was identical to every other Lisbon layover. White sheets. Hard mattress. A balcony that stuck when I slid the door open. I forced it anyway and stepped outside.

The city stretched out under me. Terracotta roofs stacked like uneven steps. A tram clanged its way uphill. Some couple was arguing three balconies over in rapid Portuguese, then laughing a second later. I used to love standing on balconies like this. A place where no one knew me. Nothing expected. I could be anyone. Drift in and out without consequence.

Now all I could think about was her.

The way she looked at me like she saw too much. The way she tried not to. The wreck. The way her nose wrinkled when she smiled. How quiet she got when she was deep in thought. How that quiet crawled under my skin and stayed there.

I pulled up our message thread. My thumb hovered.

Landed.

Too simple.

Wish you were here.

Too much.

You'd love the light tonight.

What did that even mean?

I deleted every version and shoved the phone in my pocket.

I wasn't good at this. I could land a jet in a storm with one engine out, but send a text to the woman who'd been in my head for months? Apparently impossible.

We walked over to A Tasca do Chico, a cramped little tavern that had become our unofficial layover headquarters. Just a table full of pilots and flight crew with lived-in laughter.

"Look who finally made it," Marco called, raising his glass. Captain Marco Silva had been flying for twenty-two years and acted like he'd invented the sky. "The American who thinks he's Portuguese."

"Please," I said, dropping into the chair. "Sou mais português do que vocês todos."

"Only in appetite," Rui shot back. First Officer Rui Andrade—loud, loyal, built like he still played football on weekends. He slapped a hand on my shoulder hard. "Sit. Eat. Tell us how many passengers tried to stand during landing this time."

"Four," I said. "A record. One tried to take a selfie."

The table groaned in unison.

Paulo snorted as he passed me a plate. He flew cargo for a different airline and swore he preferred boxes to people. "This is why I don't fly commercial. Cargo never argues. Cargo never unbuckles."

"Cargo also can't compliment your smooth landings," Marco said.

"Exactly," Paulo replied. "Peace."

We'd all met years ago. Different airlines, different routes, same exhaustion and same addiction to altitude. Most friendships took time. Ours had taken one bad overnight delay in São Paulo and a shared bottle of cheap whiskey.

We passed plates down the line—grilled sardines, caldo verde, bread so fresh the steam still rose off it. This was the part I always forgot I needed until I was sitting in the middle of it. Voices overlapping. Men who understood the strange hours, the jetlag, the anonymity, the freedom. The way time blurred when you lived half your life above the clouds.

"Charlie," Marco said with his mouth full. "Tell Rui about the Tokyo approach last month."

"It wasn't a big deal," I said automatically.

"That crosswind could've taken your wings off," Rui said. "The man is a machine. A legend."

"Please don't inflate his ego," Paulo said. "Last thing we need is another American thinking he was born with God's thumbs."

The table erupted. I even laughed.

This world—the jokes, the language only pilots understood, the way these men lived on instinct and adrenaline and solitude—had built me. I belonged here. I'd earned that belonging.

And it felt good.

Too good.

At one point, I felt my phone buzz. For a split second my pulse shot up. Ridiculous. I didn't take it out. I didn't want to be the guy who checked his phone in the middle of this. I didn't want them to see how easily one message—one person—could pull my attention off the runway.

Marco leaned back in his chair and eyed me. "You're quiet tonight."

"Jet lag," I lied.

"Uh huh," Rui said. "He's thinking about someone."

I didn't rise to it. These men were wolves—they smelled blood and emotion from a mile away.

Paulo lifted his beer. "Don't bother denying it. We've all been ruined by someone at some point."

"That's the problem," I said quietly. "This job doesn't leave room for being ruined."

Marco's expression softened. "Then you better decide whether she's an anchor or a compass."

The conversation shifted after that—someone telling a story about a Barcelona layover that started with missing luggage and ended with a tattoo—but the words stuck under my ribs.

Later, when we broke off into smaller groups, Rui slung an arm around my shoulder.

"You know why we all love this life, Charlie?" he said. "It's simple. No responsibility stays with us for long. Not flights. Not people. Not places. We move. That's freedom."

He meant it as a good thing. And it *was* good. Most days.

But I heard the other half of the truth.

The part he didn't say: you can't build anything real if you're always airborne.

I stepped outside for air. Cool wind off the river. Music from a nearby bar drifting up the street. My phone sat heavy in my pocket. I reached for it and pulled up our text thread, but stopped.

I told myself I was protecting her from the chaos of my life. But part of me knew I was also protecting myself. If she wrote back, I'd want more. If she didn't, I'd feel it in my chest for days.

Inside, the guys were shouting for me to come back in. Someone had ordered another round. Someone else was singing badly.

This was my life.

The noise. Freedom. The sky. The camaraderie.

A world where nothing holds you down.

So why did it suddenly feel like something was missing?

After a while I slipped away from the table, telling the guys I needed air. Lisbon at night had its own pulse. Narrow alleys glowing under hanging lanterns. The river catching the last light like spilled metal. Normally it grounded me.

Tonight it just made the quiet louder.

I walked until the noise thinned out and found a low stone wall overlooking the city. I pulled out my phone before I could stop myself.

Typed: *I miss you.*

Deleted it.

Typed: *Thought about you when we flew over the river.*

Deleted that too.

I hated how hard it was. I hated how much I wanted to get it right. I hated knowing that if she texted back, the wanting would spike so sharp in my chest I wouldn't sleep. And if she didn't? I knew exactly what that silence would do to me.

I set the phone beside me and ran both hands through my hair.

For years, the sky had been the safest place I knew. Constant motion. Constant reinvention. No one is close enough to disappoint. No one was close enough to lose.

But now all I could think about was a woman on the other

side of the ocean who made solid ground feel like something worth learning.

I picked up the phone again.

Typed, almost without thinking: *Someday, I'll bring you here.*

I stared at it for a full ten seconds.

Then deleted every word.

The city spread out below me, warm and bright and familiar. A place that usually filled me. Tonight it felt like a backdrop.

Even in Lisbon, she was everywhere.

And it scared me how much I didn't want to outrun that anymore.

CHAPTER 24
When the Waiting Hurt

Three days passed before I realized I hadn't heard his voice.

It started small. The first morning after Charlie left for Lisbon, I woke up expecting a text. Nothing elaborate—just something simple, something him. *Good morning.* Or *drink your coffee before it gets cold.*

Instead, there was nothing.

I checked his Instagram, which I hated myself for. No new posts. His last story was about an airplane wing and a caption in some language I couldn't translate. I stared at it too long anyway, hoping it meant he was thinking of me.

A memory flickered—his hand on the back of the couch the night of the storm, the way he had leaned close without crowding me. His eyes steady. Quiet. Present.

I had never met someone who listened like he did.

Maybe that was why the silence now felt louder than it should.

By the second day, I told myself he was busy. He'd said his week in Lisbon would be packed. Pilots, ex-military friends, people from all over the world—the kind of men who thrived on chaos and camaraderie. I pictured him in a crowded bar somewhere, laughing with people who understood him in ways I never could.

By the third day, it wasn't curiosity anymore. It was ache.

A faint, nagging pressure pulsed behind my left eye, not painful, just persistent.

The house felt different when I walked into my kitchen that morning. Quieter. The hum of the refrigerator filled the space like static. I opened my laptop, rewrote a project outline three times, then reorganized my desktop folders just to have something to control.

When my email pinged, my pulse jumped—but it was spam. I deleted it, emptied the trash, and kept staring at the blank screen.

The coffee on my desk went cold before I remembered to sip it. Every few minutes I checked my phone, pretending I was only keeping an eye on the time.

By noon, I gave up pretending. I scrolled through old messages, rereading the easy rhythm of our conversations—the teasing, the warmth, the way he always made me laugh when I was too serious. I stopped at one from a week ago.

> Charlie: Wish you were here.

"Me too," I whispered.
Then I typed it. *Me too.*
And stared at it for a long time.
Then I deleted it.

Abby had called earlier in the day, right after I told her about the Dieter situation. She said I needed to get out of my head for a while—and that the Winter Market setup at Grace Hill was the perfect distraction. She was driving whether I liked it or not. "You need sugar, noise, and twinkle lights," she'd said. "And I need funnel cake."

By the time I pulled into the parking lot, the sky was soft gray and the air smelled like cinnamon and pine. Rows of stalls stood half-built under the big oak trees, strings of white lights draped from branch to branch, the bulbs glowing soft against the frost. Someone was selling cocoa from a metal thermos, steam curling like breath into the gray air. Volunteers carried boxes of garland and mason jars filled with candles, their laughter spilling through the chill.

Abby's voice carried before I even spotted her. "Rose!"

She waved from across the lot and hurried over, her scarf bright red against the early winter gloom.

I smiled, really smiled, for the first time all day.

"You look like you've been through it," she said, looping an arm through mine.

"Talk."

I rubbed my temple without thinking. The headache pulsed again.

I hesitated. "It's nothing dramatic."

"You say that every time something is very dramatic."

I laughed softly. "I haven't heard from Charlie."

"Ah." She drew the word out. "The handsome, mysterious pilot vanishes into the clouds again."

"Don't make it sound romantic."

"It's romantic," she said. "Unless he's a jerk, and then it's tragic. Which is it?"

I shook my head. "Neither. He's just... busy."

"Busy men still text," she said. "Unless they're not the texting kind. Or unless they're thinking too much about what to say."

"Or unless they're not thinking about you at all," I said quietly.

Abby frowned. "Rose. You're spiraling."

"I know."

Abby squeezed my arm. "Then ask yourself something real.

What kind of relationship do you want, Rose? Not what he wants. Not what you're afraid he'll avoid. What do you want?"

We helped string garland for a while, our fingers going numb from the cold. When someone turned on a speaker and "Landslide" started playing, my throat closed. Abby noticed but didn't say anything.

As we headed toward our cars, Mrs. Hayworth from Grace Hill called out that they still needed volunteers for the candlelight walk next weekend. Abby nudged me until I signed my name. I didn't know why I did it—maybe I needed something to look forward to, something rooted, something that didn't depend on anyone else's schedule.

By the time I left, the wind had turned sharp enough to sting. She hugged me tight before she left, her scarf smelling like cinnamon and perfume. It lingered even after I got in my car. I drove home slowly, my breath clouding in front of me.

Back home, I lit a candle just to have company. The scent was something warm—balsam and cedar wood—and it filled the silence enough to make me believe I was okay.

I sat at the table with my laptop open, but I was too distracted to work.

Outside, the power flickered—just once, but enough to make me hold my breath. The hum of the refrigerator went silent, then kicked back on. For a second, it was like the storm had returned, reminding me what it sounded like when someone was there.

I walked into the living room and sat on the couch. The same couch where we'd fallen asleep during the storm. The blanket was still folded where he'd left it.

I picked it up, pulled it over my knees. It smelled faintly like him—soap and rain and something that made my heart hurt.

Hours passed.

The candle burned low. My phone stayed dark.

At one point I thought about calling Abby again, but I couldn't stomach hearing my own voice say the same things.

What if he met someone?

What if I scared him off?

What if I built the whole thing up in my head?

A sharper thought slipped in, the one I'd been avoiding.

What if distance didn't scare him because he lived there?

What if the sky felt safer to him than anything on the ground—including me?

I hated myself for needing answers. I hated how easily silence turned into self-doubt.

But maybe that was the cost of caring about someone who could leave at any moment. You never stopped checking the sky.

When the phone finally buzzed, the sound made me jump.

My pulse kicked like I'd touched a live wire. Every thought I'd been holding back surged at once.

I grabbed it so fast I almost dropped it.

> Charlie: Long week. Still standing. Thinking of you.

A second bubble appeared, then vanished. Appeared again. Vanished.

He was trying to explain something and couldn't figure out how.

That alone told me more than silence ever could.

I stared at the message, at the little time stamp beneath it. Three days. Three days of nothing, and now this.

I typed *Miss you too,* hovered, deleted. Then *I'm glad you're safe,* then erased it. My screen kept returning to blank like it knew better.

I set the phone down and made myself a promise.

I would not chase someone who hadn't chosen me yet—not the way I chased jobs, approval, and purpose.

If he wanted to be here, he would find his way back.

And if he didn't...

I would still be standing.

I looked out the window. The lake was silver in the moonlight, rippling with wind.

Somewhere, a plane blinked across the dark sky—a speck of light moving away from me.

I set the phone down, leaned my head against the glass, and whispered what I couldn't send.

"I miss you too."

I woke before dawn.

I made coffee and stood barefoot in the kitchen watching the sky shift from black to gray. My body felt heavy in a way that had nothing to do with sleep.

I replayed every word of Dieter's call and every text Charlie hadn't sent. My past and present felt like two ropes pulling in opposite directions, and I was the knot between them.

At seven twelve, another text came in.

> Charlie: Sorry I've been off the grid. I owe you breakfast when I get back. Deal?

I smiled before I could stop it. Then I hated myself for smiling.

Deal, I typed back. Then I put the phone down before I could reread it a hundred times.

The ache didn't vanish, but it softened—like a bruise fading.

I looked out at the lake again. The sun had started to rise, turning the surface to gold. Somewhere, wind brushed through the sycamores, and for the first time in days, I felt a tiny flicker of peace. Not the kind that erased the loneliness, but the kind that reminded me I was still here.

Still choosing.

Still waiting, even if I didn't want to be.

Outside, a plane blinked across the sky—slow, steady, patient.

For the first time all week, I didn't tense when I saw it.

I just watched it cross the sky, steady and sure, and let the ache settle without owning me.

I didn't know what Charlie and I were becoming yet. But I knew one thing as the morning warmed the lake.

I wanted to find out.

CHAPTER 25
The Space Between

On mornings when Charlie was home, time felt slower. Maybe it wasn't, but we acted like it was—moving through each hour as if we could stretch it out by noticing it.

The Rusty Skillet opened at seven. We were there by seven-fifteen, the bell over the door giving us away. The air inside always carried the same warmth—coffee, butter, maple syrup, and the low rumble of people who knew each other's names. It steadied something in me I hadn't known needed steadying.

He liked the corner booth where light slid across the table and turned everything golden. He ordered black coffee and Belgian waffles he swore would ruin him for all others. I ordered oatmeal with brown sugar and pecans and stole half his bacon without asking.

We talked about beginnings. Not the glossy kind—the ones that leave a soft bruise you press just to see if it still hurts.

"Third grade," I said, stirring my coffee. "Your mom kept a jar of river stones on her desk. Good choices lived there. I spent a whole year trying to earn one. When I finally did, I slept with it in my pillowcase."

His mouth curved, like the memory found him too. "She'd love that you remember."

"She taught me to slow down when I read. That not every word needed to be outrun."

He looked at me like he knew that was about more than reading.

"What about you?" I asked. "Where do your beginnings live?"

"In a hangar that smelled like oil and old stories," he said. "I was eight the first time I touched a plane. Elizabeth swears I've been chasing that feeling ever since."

He told me about the paper route that led to a summer job, then a scholarship. The first solo flight. The sound of silence at altitude that scared him in a holy way. He talked about the places he'd slept—hotels, crew houses, borrowed apartments—never quite belonging to any of them.

"Home is a language," he said. "I keep learning pieces of it. Still speak it like a tourist."

"What does it sound like here?" I asked.

He looked at my hands instead of the room. "Slower. And less lonely."

His thumb traced one slow line over my knuckles, like he was learning a map.

We split the fruit salad. He taught me a Portuguese phrase that melted off his tongue like honey. I tried to repeat it and made it too sharp. He grinned and said there were worse things than being sharp. Then he said it again, slower, until I almost had it.

Love is a romantic language. Care is a patient one. He was careful with me. I wanted to be careful with him back.

After breakfast, we walked past the square where garlands still clung to the railings and wreaths on shop doors had already begun to brown. The quiet of January made everything feel softer somehow. The air smelled of sugar, reminding me to stop by the bakery for some sweets later. He took my gloved hand, folding our fingers together like it had always been that way.

"What did you want to be when you were little?" he asked.

"In the Army, like my dad used to be," I said. "Or anything that meant I wouldn't have to sit still long enough to build a life I didn't want."

"And did you?"

"I did the opposite," I said. "I sat still. I called it ambition. Really it was fear wearing a suit."

He didn't correct me. Just walked beside me until the words lost their sting.

"What about you?" I asked.

"Architect," he said. "I liked the idea of building something people could live inside. Then I realized I loved the lift of a plane and the places it could take me, and I never looked back."

He kissed me on my front steps that morning—soft, deliberate. Not the storm's heat, but something steadier. Then he told me he had a late check-in and a dawn departure. Denver. Then Vancouver. Then back through Atlanta before Frankfurt. A week, maybe ten days. He said it the way pilots said weather: expected and out of his hands.

"Walk with me for a minute?" he asked.

I almost said no. He had a flight to catch. I didn't want to make goodbye harder. But then he slid his hands into his coat pockets and waited like it mattered, like the minutes between now and leaving were negotiable.

"Yeah. Okay."

We cut through the square, the air sweet with the last of the bakery's morning batches. He bought one cinnamon roll "for the road," then tore off a piece and held it out to me first, like it was a rule he'd made quietly for us.

"That's unfair," I said, taking it. "You pick the warm center."

He smirked. "Seniority."

We walked without rushing, sharing the roll like two people who weren't supposed to be on opposite sides of the sky. A few townspeople waved. He waved back like he belonged here and wasn't flying thousands of miles away in a few hours.

"You good?" he asked after a minute.

"Yeah. Just... wishing time was slower."

"It is," he said. "Right here."

I didn't know what to do with that. So I slipped my hand into the pocket of his coat, curling my fingers around his instead of holding his hand outright. His thumb brushed the back of my knuckles—one soft, sure pass that felt like a promise he hadn't said yet.

We stopped at the edge of the lake. The water was pale and still, winter light glinting across the surface. He let out a low breath.

"Every time I leave," he said quietly, "I wish I had ten more minutes like this."

"Then stay ten more."

He closed his eyes for the length of a heartbeat. "If I stay ten more, I'll want twenty."

I didn't know whether to be comforted or crushed by that.

He kissed my forehead, warm and steady.

I nodded. "Go. Before you make it harder."

He hesitated—just a flick, barely a breath—then walked backward a few steps before turning toward his truck.

"Text me when you land," I said.

"I will. And text me even when I don't. I like knowing how your day is."

I watched him until he disappeared around the curve of Maple Street, my hand still warm from his coat pocket.

The days we had were bright. The ones we didn't were full of trying.

I kept replaying the little things. That night we slow danced in my kitchen to a song that wasn't playing. In the afternoon he fixed the crooked curtain rod without being asked. The way he always checked the lock on my door on his way out. Quiet acts. No speeches. A man showing up in the simplest ways before life pulled him away again.

He sent photos from windows I couldn't see through—wings over clouds, sunrise over the Pacific, a bookstore in an airport that looked like art. A pastry with a name I kept mispronouncing. He corrected me in voice notes, his laugh soft in my ear. Each message hummed across time zones, a fragile string of proof. *Good morning, wherever you are. I'm here. I'm thinking of you.*

I had work. Real work. Meetings at the orchard that smelled of cinnamon and apples. Calls with Lydia about the Winter Market. Emerson invited me to The Oasis for tea that made you feel cared for before you even took a sip. I kept moving, telling myself I wasn't waiting by the phone. But my phone still felt like company in the room.

I put it in a drawer to prove a point, lasted nine minutes, then took it back out.

One night he sent a video from a crew van—darkness outside, laughter behind him. "Red-eye," he said. "Tell me something good so I don't dream about pretzels."

I sent him a photo of the twins at the fair, powdered sugar all over their faces, Sam grinning like he'd finally figured out how to be at peace. I told Charlie about the neighbor's cat who had claimed my porch. About the viral wedding at The Oasis. Ordinary things. He thanked me like I'd handed him warmth.

We set a date for the night he'd be back. Thursday. He'd land mid-afternoon, shower at his place, pick me up at six. I cleaned the kitchen like company was coming. It felt silly and right all at once. I tried on the black dress that made me stand taller and the sweater with the sequin bows.

At three-twenty, my phone buzzed.

> Charlie: Grounded in Newark. They're trying to reassign us, but it's not looking good. I'm so sorry, Rose. Best case, I land late tonight. Worst case, tomorrow.

I stared at the message until the words blurred.

> Me: It's okay. Just get home safe.

Another ping.

> Charlie: I'm mad about it. I wanted tonight. I wanted you.

The warmth of that lingered, followed by the cold behind it.

> Me: It's okay.

> Charlie: It's not. But thank you for pretending.

> Me: Tell me when you know.

I set the table like he was still coming, Hope can be stubborn when it wants to be. I kept rearranging the silverware like it mattered, like precision could keep disappointment away. I blew out the candle last. Then I sat on the couch in a dress that had run out of purpose.

For a long moment, I just sat there, hands useless in my lap. Then I reached for my phone. Habit. Weakness. Something in between.

The photos from the Harvest Fair opened before I even realized what I was doing.

There he was.

Caught mid laugh, a paper cup in his hand, sunlight warming every line of him. Leaning in on the dock, the wind carrying his hair and half his restraint. Focused, steady, lifting that saucepan as if strength came naturally to him. And in the last photo, looking at me like he understood something I hadn't said out loud.

That version of him felt so close I could almost touch the moment. The present Charlie. The grounded one. The man who pulled up to my house because the wind picked up. The one who showed up with a space heater and hot chocolate like it was a love language he didn't know how to name. The one who kissed me like he'd been waiting for permission he didn't think he'd ever get.

I stared at the photos until my vision blurred. Missing someone who wasn't even gone felt like the cruelest kind of trick.

I put the phone down.

But the ache didn't move with it.

At seven-thirty, another message.

Charlie: Wheels up in ten. If I make the connection, I'll land. If not, I'll be in Charlotte. I'm trying.

I pictured him in the gray airport night that looked the same everywhere. I pictured myself in a living room that never changed and didn't need to. Somewhere between those two pictures was the line we kept walking.

At nine-fifteen:

Charlie: Charlotte. I'm sorry.
Me: For what?

I regretted it as soon as I hit send.

Charlie: For wanting what I can't give you easily.

I sat with that. It was honest. It didn't fix anything.

He called from an airport hotel where the TV in the next room bled through the wall. His voice did something to my shoulders—they dropped, and I could breathe again.

"Next Saturday," he said. "I can be human next Saturday. I'll make you dinner that will be questionable at best."

"You have too much faith in my standards."

"I have faith in you," he said. "Probably not helpful right now."

"It's something," I said.

He told me about a kid who clapped when the plane landed. "Like I'd invented gravity," he said.

"Tell me something true," he added.

"I'm mad," I said. My jaw ached from holding the good-sport smile in place all afternoon. "Not at you. At the way this makes me feel like I'm standing in a doorway waiting for someone to come home. I worked hard not to be that woman."

"I don't want you to be that woman either," he said. "But I don't know how to do this without asking you to be her sometimes."

"I know." I heard the soft thud of his head against the headboard. Then silence.

A beat passed.

Warm. Awkward. Honest.

"Tell me something good," he said finally, gentler now.

"The cat brought me a leaf," I said. "It felt like an offering."

"Accept it," he said. "We should all bring you offerings."

"Bring me next Saturday," I whispered.

"Done," he said. "Save me a morning."

"Always."

We hung up. I didn't cry. It wasn't a crying night. It was a night for putting leftovers in glass containers, stacking them like order still mattered. For washing my face until the lipstick disappeared. For lying awake, not from fear but from keeping him close by thinking him here.

CHAPTER 26

The Saturday He Comes Home

He came back Saturday, scraped and smiling, like the world had finally given him a day off. He knocked once before I even reached the door, his hair wind-ruffled and his cuff unbuttoned like he'd run straight from the airport.

"Hi," he said.

Everything in me settled. "Hi."

"Come on," he added. "I'm stealing you for the day."

We ended up at Sundancer because Tunbridge had decided it was a good night for line dancing. Lanterns hung low from the rafters. The band warmed up with a fiddle tune that sounded like August trying to remember itself.

Johnny spotted us first. "Well look who crawled out of the clouds," he called.

Alice sat next to him and called, "Hey, you guys!"

Hutch lifted two beers in greeting.

Charlie leaned close, his voice low against my ear. "They're going to make fun of me, aren't they?"

"Yes." I giggled. "They absolutely are."

They did. In the gentlest way possible.

Charlie gave the first line dance a shot. He could glide through a slow song, but this was chaos. He failed spectacularly.

Nearly took out a chair and apologized to it. Johnny laughed so hard he had to bend over the table. Hutch taught him the steps, slow and patient, like they'd known each other forever.

He wasn't self-conscious.

He wasn't cool.

He was *present*.

When the music changed, he reached for my hand.

"Help me?" he asked.

So I did.

We moved clumsily at first, then closer. His palm found the small of my back, warm and steady. The whole room blurred into lantern-light and laughter. Someone whooped when he spun me. He flushed. I kissed his cheek without thinking.

Tunbridge noticed. Tunbridge always notices.

During the break, we sat with the guys. They talked shop—engines, call schedules, a prank involving a rubber snake and Merriweather's locker. Charlie fit there like he'd been folding into this town for years, not just in between trips.

Emerson passed by with Sam, both carrying paper baskets of fried pickles. "Come by The Oasis later," she said. "We're going to have a special dessert."

I nodded. Charlie stole a pickle from Sam. Sam pretended to be offended.

It felt easy.

It felt like belonging.

Later, we walked out into the cool night, the music still thumping behind us. My breath curled in front of me. His hand stayed in mine like it was instinct.

"Want to see something?" he asked.

I nodded.

We drove to the lake. Not the public dock—the quiet cove nobody used. He spread a blanket across the grass. The sky stretched wide and dark, scattered with stars that looked close enough to touch.

"This is why I fly," he said quietly. "It looks like this up there."

He lay back. I followed.

The hush between us felt full, not empty.

"What do you need from the person you end up with?" He asked.

It wasn't a small question.

It was the kind you only ask if part of you is already hoping it might be you.

"Honesty," I said. "Even when it's hard. And presence. Not constant, but real. Someone who shows up on purpose."

His jaw flexed like the answer hit him somewhere true.

"I can do purpose," he said quietly. "I'm learning the rest."

I breathed out. "What do you need?"

He didn't look away.

"To stop feeling like I have one foot on the ground and one in the sky. To feel like someone knows me, even when I'm gone."

The wind lifted the edge of the blanket.

My hand settled against his chest, just over his heartbeat.

He turned to face me. The starlight caught his eyes, soft and unguarded. He didn't rush. He never rushed. But when he kissed me, it was slow and certain and full.

A kiss that said: *I see you. I'm here. I'm trying.*

We didn't move for a long time, not until the grass chilled and the night closed in around us like something alive.

Later, he walked me to my door. He kissed me again, gentler, like he was memorizing something.

"I'll text when I land Wednesday," he said.

"Okay."

"And text before that too," he added, smiling.

I smiled back. "Good."

. . .

The week began kindly and then unraveled the way weeks do. Tuesday, I designed three logos and ate cupcakes from Elizabeth's bakery. Wednesday, I fell asleep with the lamp on. Thursday, we planned a long-distance movie night—phones propped, pretending it was the same couch.

He texted at nine: *Delay*. Then again at ten-thirty: *Pushed*. At midnight, he sent a picture of an airport floor and wrote: *Wish you were here*.

I wanted to be, and hated how quickly the wanting rose.

Thirty minutes later he sent a second photo, then nothing. The quiet after felt earned and also like a bill I would have to pay.

Sometimes it felt like loving him came in weather patterns. When he was here, the world sharpened in color. Everything tasted sweeter, moved slower, opened wider. I remembered who I was when someone looked at me like I wasn't an afterthought.

Then he left, and the sky thinned. Hours filled with quiet I pretended didn't bother me.

A day would pass. Then another. Sometimes he texted, sometimes he didn't, and I found myself inventing reasons that felt generous so I wouldn't feel foolish.

This was the rhythm we were building without meaning to—bright flame, long shadow.

I wasn't sure yet which one I was supposed to learn to live inside.

Friday before dawn, I walked down to the lake. The world was undecided about the day. The water was the color of pewter; the dock boards bit through my shoes.

When I turned to walk home, the neighbor's cat appeared, trotting down the path with the confidence of ownership. She rubbed against my leg, claiming me for the morning. Her tag caught the light—*Isa*.

We walked home together, a woman, a cat, and the braver

thought that I could learn this. Not the waiting, but the part where I didn't disappear inside it.

By the next morning, the pattern sat heavier than I wanted to admit. The sweetness of Saturday felt far away, like something I'd watched instead of lived. I tried to brush it off, to focus on work, but the silence kept tugging at the edge of everything. This was the part I hadn't accounted for—the whiplash between closeness and distance. Between being seen and being... paused. I kept telling myself it wasn't intentional, that this was just his life and I'd stepped into it mid-stride. But part of me wanted him to notice the shift too, to feel the gap before I said a word.

That afternoon, Charlie FaceTimed from a bright hotel room that looked like it wasn't meant for rest.

"I'm not asking you to wait for me," he said, quiet, like it was both apology and truth.

"I'm not waiting," I said. "I'm living. You're just in it."

He smiled. "I want to be in it."

"You are. You just have to be in the sky, too. I'm learning how to love both."

"I'll try to meet you on the ground more," he said. "Next Saturday. The one after. As many as I can string together."

"Okay," I said. It wasn't a promise. It was a step.

That night, I lit a candle and made a list I didn't intend to show him—what I needed, what I could give, what I wouldn't trade again. I wrote that I needed honesty before romance. That I could give grace, but not at the cost of myself. That I wouldn't hold my breath for anyone, not even for love. Then I tucked the list under the book he'd given me, a prayer that had already done its work by being said.

We never said we were together. We were. It lived in the toothbrush in my cabinet, in the way my kitchen looked like a place meant for two for a few hours at a time. It lived in the quiet that softened when his name appeared on my screen.

The space between us wasn't empty. It was full—of trying, learning, and all the things we hadn't yet said.

He sent me a photo of the Mediterranean at sunrise. I sent him a new logo I was working on. We kept showing up however the week allowed.

On Sunday, the church bell carried across the lake like a hand on my shoulder. I sat on the porch with a blanket and a mug, Isa curled at my feet. The air was cold enough to sting, but it felt clean.

I didn't have answers. I had a heart stretched and alive and a little sore. A man who wanted to be two things at once and was trying to be good at both. A town that held the tranquility without asking it to explain itself.

I wrote his flight number on a sticky note and pressed it under a magnet on the fridge, because I'm that kind of woman. Then I made pancakes that weren't as good as The Rusty Skillet's and ate them anyway—one forkful at a time, until the sweet was more than the wanting.

Wanting stayed, but it learned to sit.

CHAPTER 27
The Sky Went Quiet

I sent Charlie a picture of myself in the black dress—half-joking, half-serious.

He texted back a plane emoji and *see you soon, gorgeous.*

Two hours later, the same phone vibrated with a news alert that tore that promise in half.

A Fox News alert popped up on my phone. I nearly swiped it away. The headline fixed me in the doorway between normal and not.

Lisbon-bound flight makes emergency landing in Reykjavík after mid-air mechanical alert.

There are many flights to Lisbon, I told myself. There are many mornings. I clicked on it anyway. The writing was careful, the way it gets when no one is ready to say more. *The crew reported an engine anomaly and diverted as a precaution. No injuries reported at this time.* A flight number lived halfway down the page, small as an afterthought.

It matched the one Charlie had texted me before dawn.

Something bright and cold opened in my ribs, the exact second before a glass hits tile. My hands felt too far away. The room narrowed until it was just me and the screen and a heartbeat that didn't know how to count.

I called him. Rings went unanswered. Voicemail, polite and wrong.

I set the article in the center of the screen and made the font bigger and read the same lines again. Diversions are precautionary. Reykjavík is a standard North Atlantic stop. My brain repeated what he had taught me, like prayers with hand motions. I didn't believe any of them long enough to feel relief.

I texted him.

> Me: Are you okay?

Nothing.

Rain started in a thin whisper against the windows. A steady yes to my fear.

I stood so fast the chair scraped. The sink ran. I watched water run because I needed something that obeyed. Off. On. Off. I wasn't crying. I was very calm while my heart measured out a different story.

The phone didn't light up. I turned every sound up. I turned them all off. I turned them up again. My sweater felt too heavy and not enough.

I didn't call Abby or Emerson. I didn't call Elizabeth. Putting panic in their hands without facts felt like knocking on a stranger's door and asking them to hold an animal you had already let loose. I stayed in the house and tried to make the space smaller. I folded the throw on the couch. I lined a spoon exactly with the edge of the counter. I closed the laptop and opened it again. Still nothing.

I stared at the phone again and then I called Grant.

He picked up on the second ring. "Hey. What's up?"

My breath shuddered. He always heard it first. "Did you see the news?"

"No. Talk to me."

"A flight to Lisbon was diverted. Mid-air mechanical issue." My voice cracked. "It's his flight, Grant. I know it is. He's not answering."

There was a quiet beat, the sound of him shifting into big-brother mode, the version of him that had talked me down from a hundred cliffs.

"Rose. Listen to me." His voice was calm, steady. "Panicking won't help him. It won't help you. These crews are trained to handle everything. Charlie's been doing this for years. He knows what he's doing."

"I just—" My throat tightened. "I don't want the worst thing to be the last thing."

"I know." His voice softened. "I know. But you need to breathe. It's probably a precautionary thing."

I closed my eyes. "I'm scared."

"I'm here," he said simply. "Have some faith in the guy. And in the people flying with him."

A shaky exhale left me. "Okay."

"Go stand by a window. Get some air. I'll stay on the line if you need."

"I'm okay," I whispered, though it wasn't fully true yet.

"You will be. Text me if you hear from him."

"I will."

We hung up, and the house felt a little less hollow, as if someone had opened a window and let the air move again.

The article refreshed itself, then pretended it hadn't. A sentence changed by half a word. No one said anything new. The battery icon slipped down a fraction that felt like a dare.

I remembered the second before my accident. The soft break of it, the meniscus of wakefulness giving way. Terror had been a clean, cold noise then. This was different. This was a silence that pressed its hands over my ears.

I carried the phone to the window. Pines stood dark and still along the hill. The lake held its breath. Somewhere a siren far off started and ended without meaning. I pressed my forehead lightly to the cold glass and counted to ten, to twenty, to sixty. Numbers calmed him. They didn't know what to do with me.

I called again. Rings. Voicemail.

I wanted to drive to the airport, any airport, just to be near a runway. I wanted to stand under a sky with a name and order it to give him back. I wanted to do something that would change something. There was nothing to change.

Breathe, I told myself, like Abby would have said if she were here. Don't borrow pain from a future that has not arrived. Stay in this minute. Then the next one.

So I breathed, and I waited, and the minutes grew long legs and walked away without me.

The heater clicked off. The house admitted it was cold. I put on shoes without looking. One had a darker lace. It didn't matter. I walked to the door and back. I lifted the phone and put it down. I poured coffee and forgot to drink it. I stood in the doorway of every room like a security guard who could not guard anything.

A plane flew overhead, miles too high to hold meaning. Its sound crested and faded. I told myself he was under a ceiling of professionals and checklists and calm. I told myself a hundred crews had done this exact dance and called it a day. I told myself all of it until the telling turned thin.

The phone rang.

I answered on the first slice of sound. "Hello."

"I'm okay," he said.

Everything in me dropped and rose in the same second. The chair found me. The room steadied.

"Oh, thank God," I said, and heard the small in my voice.

"Are you sitting?" He asked, soft enough to make it almost a smile.

"Yes."

"Everything is fine, we landed safe," he said. "But it was a scary situation, I won't lie."

"What happened?"

"Engine two took a bird," he said. "Compressor stall. Loud

enough that the passengers heard it. We went through the shutdown checklist. The engine windmilled but wouldn't relight." He paused.

"We were too far out to turn back. Reykjavík was the only smart option. Solid runway. Good weather. We landed heavy, but clean. Could have been a lot worse."

I pictured his hands where they live when the world tightens, steady on a checklist, steady on a throttle, steady on a human shoulder when steadiness is the only currency. The image fit. My body loosened by inches.

"I've had engine failures before," he said quietly, "but never out over that much water. We train for it, but training doesn't give you the weight of three hundred people behind you."

"When did you land?"

"A little while ago. Debrief. Paperwork. Maintenance. Making sure the machine is the thing we say it is." A slow breath through the line. "Also wanting to call you and not being allowed to be a person yet."

"You can be a person now."

"I can," he said, and went quiet for a beat like he was listening to his own heart and deciding what language to answer in. "I kept thinking about you," he said. "Not in a last words way. In a practical way that somehow hurt more. When the engine wouldn't relight, all I could think was: I never told her the truth. Not once. And I hated the idea of leaving this world with that silence between us."

I closed my eyes. Relief turned into something that lifted heat to my face. For a moment I hated the ocean itself for being between us.

"What am I to you?" I asked, because there was no point walking around the thing we both stood inside.

"A place I want to be," he said. "It's simple. It's all I have that is true."

"It's enough," I said, and meant it.

"I hate that I scared you."

"Were you scared?" Trying to hide the nerves in my voice.

"Yes," he said. "Not of the work. Of leaving with stupid sentences still in my mouth."

"What sentences?"

"That your porch light looks like a decision. That my toothbrush in your cabinet is the best view I've had in months. That when I say goodnight to you, I say it to the part of myself that has finally chosen to land."

I sat with my hand pressed flat to the table because if I didn't I might float up like steam. I let the words settle in the room where fear had been.

"Tell me something not poetic," I said, because the air in me needed a place to go.

"The coffee in this break room tastes like it lost a fight," he said. I laughed, shaky and real. "And my hands are clean," he added. "We did our job. Everyone is safe. But now that I'm sitting still, my body is catching up. The adrenaline... it's loud when the danger is gone."

"You did an incredible thing." I said, and took the slow breath I had been trying to talk my body into since the headline.

"I don't scare easily," he said. "Today rattled me."

"I can only imagine. Are you headed home?"

"Not today. They will room us. Maintenance will sing to the bird and decide if it flies. I may be here tonight. I'll call when I know."

"Call anyway," I said.

"I will."

We stayed on the line. He said the sky changed in bands as they descended—slate giving way to milk, then ocean—each layer so exact it looked brushed on by hand. I told him the cat on my porch chose violence with my fern. He said his co-pilot had three grandchildren and two of them were aboard that flight. I told him The Rusty Skillet added pecan waffles to the menu. The quiet between our sentences changed temperature. It stopped being a cliff. It started being a couch.

"Sleep when you can," I said when voices rose behind him in the way rooms do when paperwork is done.

"I will. Text me your coffee later. Pretend I am there telling you not to burn your mouth."

"I don't do that."

"You do," he said, and I could hear the shape of his smile. Then softer. "Goodnight, for now."

"Goodnight."

The line clicked clean. The house breathed again. The rain let up to a mist fine as flour. I set the phone on the counter and leaned my hips against the wood and let the shaking I had been borrowing from the future pass through. Not violent. Not small. Just the body letting go of what it had been holding.

I made hot chocolate and sent him a photo. Steam rose in a pale ribbon. He replied with a single word that wasn't English and didn't need to be. *Here.*

I walked to the window. Pines dancing in the wind. The movement of a cloud that had work to do elsewhere. The sky was silent again. Not an empty silence. A held one. The kind that happens after a storm chooses not to break.

I thought of the headline and the flight number and the minute that split the day in two. I thought of the sentences he hadn't wanted to leave unsaid and how they had found their way to me anyway. I thought of how love sometimes announces itself like a brass band and sometimes slips into the room and sits down, sure as gravity.

My phone buzzed a last time.

> Charlie: Still here.

> Me: Me too.

I flipped the porch light on long before dark. Not because he needed it to find me, but because I needed something in this house to stay lit.

CHAPTER 28
Still Here

The air felt changed, lighter somehow. I didn't. Relief had weight. It sat on my shoulders like a coat that fit and also made me tired.

The tears didn't come right away. They came later, in small honest drops, not a storm, just the overflow that happens when your body realizes it's allowed to feel again. I wiped my face on the sleeve of the sweater I should've changed hours ago and let myself sit on the floor for a minute with my back against the cabinet. The tile was cold and clean.

I toasted bread because it felt like an instruction I could follow and not a metaphor. The butter pooled in the middle. I watched it disappear. I ate it standing up.

I thought about texting Charlie again. I wanted to say all the things the news story had shaken loose. I wanted to say I can't lose you—not now, not when I've only just found the part of myself brave enough to let this be real.

I didn't.

I'm not good at waiting. I'm learning. I don't want to live in a doorway, even when the person I'm waiting for feels like gravity. If this is the life we're building, it needs a floor that doesn't shake every time the sky does.

I went out to the porch because the air had a softness I needed. The lake held a thin skin of light. Someone somewhere mowed a lawn too late in the season and the smell of it stirred something in me that wasn't grief. I wrapped the blanket around my shoulders and listened to birds who didn't know about headlines. I pictured Charlie lying on a bed in a city that would never belong to him, staring at a ceiling he couldn't claim, and I wanted to fold time. I wanted to drive him a bowl of the soup I still hadn't had the appetite to eat. I wanted to put my hand on his chest and feel the steady proof of him.

I stayed there until my toes got numb and then made myself move. My body still hummed with leftover panic, like it hadn't gotten the message that we were safe.

Warm socks. A shower hot enough to redraw my lines. I changed the sheets because the morning had turned the old ones into a place I didn't want to sleep. The fresh cotton smelled like a house that keeps its promises.

When I lay down, I didn't turn on a show. I turned off the lamp and let the dark be soft. The quiet was different now. It had edges I recognized. He was safe. He was far. I could hold those two truths at the same time and not break. That felt like growth and also like new pain.

I didn't want this to be my life forever. I wanted Saturdays that weren't negotiated with time zones. Dinners that didn't depend on a maintenance sign-off.

The thought didn't make me run. It made me honest.

I rolled onto my side and put my hand on the other pillow like a child. I didn't apologize to the dark for it. I fell asleep with my phone face up on the nightstand, not because I was waiting, but because I wanted to see the light when his name found me.

When the phone buzzed some time later, a message slid into the thin place between sleeping and awake. A picture of an ugly break room mug with coffee the color of stubborn. His hand around it.

I stared at it until my eyes stung and then smiled like a person who'd been given a life-sized thing in a small package. The sky outside the window held. Morning would come with or without either of us asking. For the first time since the headline, I believed it might come to find me still whole.

I'd felt fear like this before, but never tied to someone else's heartbeat. That was the part that undid me. Not that he could've been hurt. That I would've had to live without him. I lay there in the dark, fully awake for a moment that felt like confession, and admitted to the ceiling what I hadn't said to him yet.

I tried to swallow the thought, the way you do when something too bright hits too soon. It didn't go.

I *loved* him.

The word wasn't soft. It was heavy, true and scary. It didn't make the distance easier. It didn't make the sky kinder. It made both feel like places we'd have to cross with more care. I closed my eyes and let the slow rhythm of my breath count out the promise I could make tonight. I wouldn't disappear inside the waiting. I would love him in the spaces we were given and keep a life going in the ones we were not. But part of me still waited for the sky to break again.

Sometime before dawn, I woke to the quiet fact of myself and didn't feel like an empty room. The sky outside the window wasn't light yet, but it wasn't endless either. It held a shape. I pulled the blanket higher and told the dark what I'd tell him when the time was right.

CHAPTER 29
When the Sky Held Still

The air outside Queen of Hearts carried that February hush. Cold, metallic, the kind that makes even laughter sound distant. Behind me, the antique shop glowed soft amber through the windows, a square of warmth against the brick. Across the street, the mill lights blinked like tired eyes.

A truck idled at the curb. Headlights off. Engine low.

I knew before I saw him.

Charlie stepped out and closed the door with that quiet precision of his, like noise cost something. He looked a little worn, travel still clinging to him, but his smile was steady.

"I wanted to practice patience," he said. "I made it four minutes."

I laughed, relief catching in the sound. "You're home."

"For tonight," he said, and it landed like both a gift and a warning.

My smile dropped. For a second, the word tonight felt like the sky narrowing again. The same kind of borrowed time I'd already lived through once.

A small, nagging headache pulsed at my temples, the kind that had been coming and going all week. I pressed a hand there without thinking.

He took my hand—warm even in the cold—and we walked to the truck. The cab smelled like cedar and leather and something that felt safe. A guitar pick glinted in the cup holder.

"You're quiet," he said.

"I'm listening," I said.

He smiled like he liked that answer. "Good. Because I have a plan."

"Should I be nervous?"

"Yes."

Golden Lotus was already expecting him. The bag waited on the counter, steam curling from the paper. The girl behind the register told him to tell Elizabeth she loved the pastries she sent. He promised he would. It sounded easy, that exchange. Domestic. Dangerous.

He didn't drive me home. He turned instead toward the far edge of Tunbridge, where the houses still wore the bones of another century. White siding. Blue shutters. Wind chimes that sounded like old secrets.

"This is me," he said when he parked behind the farmhouse.

The porch swing still held frost. The light over the door burned steady.

"You live in a postcard," I said.

He shrugged. "I like quiet when I'm home."

Inside, everything felt intentional. Books and flight manuals. Black-and-white photos of clouds that looked like continents. A map over his desk threaded in red routes—some looping, some crossing, like paths that couldn't stay apart. Two plates waited on the table beside a jar of unlit candles.

When he lit the candles, the air turned honey-soft.

Music drifted from a speaker—Spanish guitar, low and intimate. It felt like Córdoba at midnight.

"This is beautiful," I said. "I didn't picture it like this."

"How did you picture it?"

"A sleek, modern bachelor pad. With coffee cups in the sink. Suitcase on the floor."

He smiled. "You caught me on a good day."

He unpacked dinner like it mattered how it looked—bowls lined in a neat row, chopsticks crossed like ceremony. No hurry. No performance. Just quiet, careful motion.

My shoulders dropped without asking permission. My pulse stopped measuring distance.

"Sit," he said.

I did. We passed dishes, chopsticks, and laughter.

He broke the rhythm first. "When the plane dropped," he said, voice even, eyes steady, "I thought about the sound of you saying goodnight."

The air left my lungs. The candle flame flickered hard.

"You don't have to say anything," he added. "I just needed it said out loud."

I managed a breath. "I'm glad you did."

We ate without words for a while. It wasn't silence; it was breathing.

When I spoke again, my voice was smaller. "I told you how I've never left the country."

He looked up, curious.

"I used to think I didn't need to," I said. "I told myself I could build the best version of my life from the inside. Promotions. Paychecks. Proof I mattered. I think I was afraid the world would make me small."

He set his chopsticks down. "You're not small."

The words landed somewhere I didn't know how to name.

"Your turn," I said.

He thought for a second. "My favorite word in Portuguese is *saudade*. It means missing something you still love. Longing with memory in it."

"That's us," I said quietly.

He nodded once.

He reached for my hand and drew me close. Between the table and the counter, there was barely room to breathe, but somehow it was enough. I felt the warmth of him through it, the quiet steadiness of a man who didn't rush what mattered—and the pulse of a woman who wasn't sure she could keep from falling.

We moved without rhythm, the kind of dance you do when standing still feels impossible. His cheek brushed mine. My pulse answered. The room felt suspended—heat and breath and the sound of fabric meeting fabric.

Then my phone buzzed.

He closed his eyes. "Ignore it."

It buzzed again. Harder this time.

I reached for it, and the world tilted. *Mom.*

"Hey," I said, as I put it on speaker.

Her voice came tight, too controlled. "Grant had a scare."

Cold prickled up my spine. "What happened?"

"He was at work and his heart started racing. Couldn't catch his breath. They took him to urgent care to be safe."

I felt a jolt run through me.

And before I could stop it, the memory of my last exchange with my brother flickered through my mind. How he'd stayed on the line with me without hesitation. How he'd felt like a lifeline when I hadn't even realized I needed one. I hadn't asked him how he was. Not really. I'd been so wrapped up in my own storm that it never occurred to me he might have one too. A small sting of guilt pierced through the panic rising in my chest.

"Is he okay?" My voice felt too thin.

"They ran an EKG. Everything looks normal. They think it was a stress response, like an anxiety or panic attack."

A shaky exhale. "He's exhausted, Rose. He lives on caffeine and pressure. It finally caught up to him."

I braced a hand on the counter, needing something solid. "Thank goodness it wasn't a heart attack."

"Yes, thank God. They're sending him home with instructions to rest." A pause, softer. "Maybe this will be the wake-up call he needs."

I stared at the candle flame until it blurred. My chest tightened with that old, familiar fear—the kind that came from watching someone push themselves past their limits.

"He just needs to slow down. Really slow down," she added.

Slow down.

The words echoed somewhere deep.

"You okay?" she asked.

"Yeah," I managed. "Just keep me posted. Please."

When the call ended, I stayed still. The window held my reflection—pale, blurred, like someone trying to become solid again.

Charlie moved closer but didn't touch me yet. "Come here," he said quietly.

For a heartbeat, I was back in the wreck—hands gripping air that wouldn't hold. Fear doesn't vanish; it just changes faces.

His arms wrapped around me, steady and warm. My body trembled once, then eased. He didn't tell me it was fine or offer clichés. He just held me until the shaking passed.

"He's going to be okay," Charlie murmured.

"I know." My voice was thin but steady.

He studied me for a moment. "Do you want to call him?"

I shook my head. "Not yet. He'll just brush it off. He always does."

Charlie nodded, something quiet and understanding passing between us. "Then stay right here. Breathe. I've got you."

He nodded.

"I'll make you tea," he said.

"You're bossy."

He winked. And then he moved with that same quiet focus—kettle, honey, lemon, mug. When he handed it to me, his fingers brushed mine, warm and grounding.

I drank. The heat went down slowly, settling the wild in my chest.

He leaned against the counter so I could lean back against him.

The world wasn't steady; it never would be. But for the first time, I didn't need it to be.

Everything in me stood down.

The candle burned low. Outside, a wind started through the trees. It was the night exhaling.

CHAPTER 30
The Days I Disappeared (Charlie)

I flew out of Atlanta on a gray morning that looked like it had been washed out. Low ceilings. Wet tarmac. The kind of sky that held you down before it let you go. Rose had hugged me before she left yesterday, and for a second I came close to saying something I didn't trust myself to say yet.

Then the airport swallowed me. It always did.

By the time I cleared the jet bridge and stepped into the cockpit, the shift had already happened. Work-brain. Flight plans. ATIS reports. Fuel numbers. Crew dynamics. The noise level inside me changed. It always had. It was the only way I knew how to function.

Halfway to Denver, I realized I hadn't texted her all day. I told myself I would as soon as we parked.

I didn't.

A passenger issue took twenty minutes. The next crew had a delay. Someone needed help coordinating a medical bag that ended up being nothing. My phone stayed in my pocket through all of it, and I never noticed the vibration.

By the time I got to the hotel, exhaustion hit hard. I showered. Dropped onto the bed. Meant to check my phone.

I woke three hours later with the sun already sinking.

One text from her.

> Rose: Miss you. Let me know when you're settled.

There was a second one. And a missed call I hadn't heard.

My gut tightened, but I brushed it away. She knew this job. She knew my schedule. She knew this rhythm.

I texted back.

> Me: Long day. Talk later.

I waited for the three dots.
They never showed.

The next morning we had a repositioning flight and a short hop into Chicago. The weather had us holding thirty minutes. I spent most of it watching the wings shake slightly under us, thinking about the way Rose had looked in my kitchen, her hair slipping loose near her cheek. The way she had breathed against me when the news about her brother came in.

I should have texted right then. I should have checked on her.
I didn't.

Not because I didn't care. But because the Chicago approach was talking fast, a new pilot was shadowing the jumpseat, and by the time we broke through the clouds and got clearance to land, my entire brain had locked into the procedure.

We parked. Deboarded. My phone buzzed twice, but I was helping a passenger find her connecting gate. When I finally checked it, there was a message.

> Rose: Everything okay?

Two hours later she had written again.

> Rose: Ignore me. Long day.

Guilt. I typed out three messages and deleted every one. Anything I said sounded like an excuse.

I told myself I'd call her once I got to the hotel.

Instead I ended up at dinner with the crew, because the new FO looked like he needed someone to talk to, and then someone suggested one more drink, and by the time I got back to my room, it was past midnight and my phone was dead.

I plugged it in. Turned it on. Stared at the blank screen like it owed me something.

No messages from her.

For a moment, the room felt strangely quiet. Not peaceful. Just empty.

I told myself she was sleeping. That she was tired. That she didn't want to bother me.

The truth punched through before I could block it.

She was hurt. Because anyone would be. Because I forgot her. Because I let the job swallow everything like it always did.

Because when I wasn't in Tunbridge, when I wasn't physically near her, the world around me charged forward and she faded back. Not in my heart. Not in what I felt. But in the part of my brain that never learned how to stay connected to anything I couldn't touch.

I sat on the edge of the bed and pressed the heel of my hand to my eyes.

I loved her. I knew it. God knows I knew it.

But I didn't know how to be the man who remembered to text from airport gates. I didn't know how to be the man who made someone feel chosen when I was three states away and living inside a cockpit schedule that changed by the hour.

I didn't know how to be hers the right way yet.

My phone buzzed suddenly. I snapped it up.

Just a weather alert.

Not her.

I set the phone down and leaned back against the headboard, staring at the cracks in the ceiling paint, wondering how a man could care this much and still fail in all the small ways that mattered.

I told myself I'd call tomorrow.

I meant to.

I really did.

But morning came early. Dispatch rerouted us. Crew scheduling called twice. The day slid out of my hands before I even realized it had started.

And every time I checked my phone, the screen was empty.

Every time I meant to send something, a new task pulled me away.

By the time I landed back in Georgia, two full days had passed.

Two days.

And all I had to show for it was a long list of reasons she probably felt alone.

I stepped off the jet bridge, pulling my bag behind me, scrolling back through her last messages with a pressure in my chest I hadn't felt in years.

She deserved more than what I had given her.

She deserved more than absence dressed as love.

She deserved someone who remembered her even when the world grew deafening.

I walked toward the parking deck telling myself I'd fix it. I'd explain. I'd apologize. I'd give her every honest part of me.

I'd start tonight.

Except I had no idea she'd already reached her breaking point.

CHAPTER 31
The Night We Stopped Pretending

The air was damp and sharp, touched with woodsmoke and the faint green smell of something waking underground. March hadn't decided what season to be—half thaw, half freeze. Half holding on, half letting go.

Emerson and I had lingered over dinner at The Oasis for hours, the way you do when you don't want to go home to your own thoughts. We'd shared a bottle of wine, talked about festival plans and small-town gossip, and laughed until it felt easy. When we hugged goodbye under the string lights, she said, "You're good?"

"Yeah," I lied.

Then I saw him.

Charlie.

Stepping out the side door with Sam, both of them laughing. He looked good in the kind of way that still hurt—sleeves rolled, hair pushed back, eyes that lived in time zones instead of rooms. When he saw me, the laugh fell off him. Not dropped—just gone.

Sam read the air instantly, gave a two-finger wave, and slipped back inside. The door shut behind him, leaving only the hum of the cooler and the night between us.

"Hey," he said.

"Hey."

We stood there like the world had already decided one of us would leave first.

He started to speak, but I beat him to it. "Don't," I said quietly. "Please don't start with small talk."

He stopped. Waited.

"I can't keep doing this," I said. "Not the way we are. I'm not built for almost."

The words felt like pulling glass from my own skin.

Something in his expression flickered—pain or understanding, maybe both.

"I'm not asking you to change," I said. "I know who you are. I fell for the man who can't sit still, who carries the sky like a second skin. But I can't be the woman who waits for the world to give you back to me. I deserve more than what's left over after your departures."

He exhaled, slow. "Rose—"

"No." I shook my head. "I've been here, Charlie. I've been *all the way here.* You live with one foot in and one foot out. Maybe that feels like freedom to you. I want someone who's *in the room.* Every day. Not someone who texts from airports and calls from time zones I'll never touch."

He rubbed the back of his neck, that tell he had when he wanted to fix something he couldn't. "You think I don't want that?"

"I think you want the *idea* of it," I said. "The warmth, the gravity. But not the stillness it takes to hold it."

He stepped closer. "You think I don't love you?"

"I think you do," I said, my voice shaking and sure at once. "I just think you love the sky more."

Silence. Only the faint click of the sign light above us cooling in the dark.

He looked at me like a man trying to memorize the moment before impact. "Say you don't love me," he said quietly. "Say it, and I'll go."

I laughed once, soft and breaking. "You don't get to make me the villain because I finally learned to walk away."

He looked down, jaw set. "I don't know how to stay," he said, voice low. "Every time it gets quiet, I hear it—this voice in me that says move. It's been there since I was a kid. I can't shut it off."

"You don't shut it off," I said. "You talk over it. You choose louder."

His eyes found mine, sharp with regret. "You make it sound simple."

"It's not," I said. "But it's *clear*. At least it is for me."

Wind slid through the patio, lifting a napkin across the stones. I watched it spin into a corner and wished I could go with it.

"I can't keep living like this," I said. "Loving you and calling it patience. You're gone more than you're here, and I keep pretending it's enough, like I can fill the empty space with stories about what it means to be strong. But I'm tired of being strong. I'm tired of fighting for half a life."

He stepped forward, eyes wet but steady. "You're asking me to stay."

"No," I said. "I'm telling you I'm done waiting for you to."

That broke him a little. His hands twitched at his sides. He almost reached for me—almost—but stopped himself like he always did.

"I don't want to lose you."

"Charlie, I've been here. If you think this is the way I wanted things to be, you haven't been paying attention."

He closed his eyes. Then looked into mine.

"Do you think it's fair?" I said. "Is this what you think I deserve?"

The words tasted sharp, but the ache underneath was worse. Because the irony sat there between us like a bruise. The one person who understood me without trying. The one who pulled me safety when I was in danger. The one who comforted me in ways he'll never fully grasp... was also the one tearing holes in my life without even meaning to. Loving him had steadied me. Wanting him was slowly undoing me.

I didn't know how to reconcile both truths in the same breath.

He flinched like the words were truth hitting bone.

"We talked about both wanting to share our lives with someone. Have a family one day. All the beautiful things that come along with setting down roots." I took a deep breath. "I love you. But love should never leave this much doubt."

I wanted to reach for him so badly it felt like fire under my skin. But I didn't. Because this was the moment I'd been avoiding—where love wasn't enough to save what fear had already ruined.

He hesitated, shoulders tightening like he was holding back something that might break loose if he said it wrong.

"I thought we were getting there," he said finally. "I thought... this was us, working toward something real."

"Charlie—" My voice cracked once, but I didn't look away. "How far in the future do you think 'working toward something' is supposed to be?"

He blinked, stunned. "I didn't realize you felt like this."

"I know." The quiet hurt. "That's part of the problem."

He ran a hand over his jaw, exhaling hard. "I don't know why I'm like this. I've spent half my life leaving before anyone can ask me to stay. It's not about you."

"It always ends up being about me," I said. "Because I'm the one standing still when you go."

He nodded once, slow, like the truth had landed but hadn't fully found its home yet. "I don't want to lose you."

"I've always been here, Charlie," I said. "I'm still here."

The wind moved between us, cool and sharp. His eyes searched mine, as if he could still fix this by looking long enough.

"Rose..." His voice was raw now, low. "I love you. You know that."

The air between us went still. He looked at me with a kind of reverence that hurt worse than anger.

"It's not love we're missing. It's the part where it turns into a life."

For a long moment, neither of us spoke. Somewhere down the street, a car door slammed, a dog barked twice, the kind of ordinary noise that felt cruel against what was happening here.

He reached for me then—hesitant, halfway. "Tell me what to do."

I shook my head. "I want you to do whatever makes you happy."

Something broke across his face then—not anger, not despair. Just the quiet realization of someone who'd been given one last chance to change and didn't know how.

"I will call you tomorrow," he said, almost to himself.

"Don't," I said softly. "I'll be okay."

The words hung there like breath in cold air.

He didn't argue. He just stood there, motionless, as I turned and walked toward my car. I felt his eyes on me all the way across the lot, like gravity refusing to let go.

When I opened the door, I looked back once—just once—and saw him still standing where I'd left him, his hands in his pockets, the light from The Oasis spilling over his shoulders like something he didn't know how to step out of.

It hit me then, sharp as breath on cold glass. All those weeks ago, he'd told me a view had never looked the same until I was in it. And now here I was, memorizing one of him without even trying. The way the lamplight curved around him. The way the night folded quiet at his feet. The way his presence could anchor a moment so completely it felt stitched into me.

This was a view I would carry—whether I wanted to or not.

I started the engine, and the headlights cut through the dark. He didn't move.

Neither did I, for a beat too long.

Then I shifted into drive.

The night stayed behind with him.

CHAPTER 32
The Quiet Between Flights

Spring came dressed in contradictions—dogwoods in bloom, frost still ghosting the edges of the grass. Tunbridge looked alive again, but I didn't.

My heart still carried that hollow burn—the kind you get when something's been pulled out and the space hasn't closed yet.

At Queen of Hearts Antiques, the air smelled like furniture polish and old cedar. I sat at the counter, hunched over my laptop, trying to finish a layout for the shop's spring campaign. Pastel banners. A tagline about *timeless pieces for a new season*. It all felt fake. Nothing about this season felt new.

The owner, Marlene, leaned over my shoulder.

"That's lovely, sweetheart. You've got such an eye for warmth."

"Thanks." My smile didn't reach anywhere real.

She patted my arm and went to rearrange a table of teacups. The heavy door opened, letting in a sweep of cool air and laughter from the street. I didn't look up. Laughter had a way of cutting when you hadn't heard your own in a while.

By noon, I'd re-written the copy four times and erased every trace of him in my mind at least twenty. But he still found ways in —the coffee shop song that played when we first sat together, the word *flight* showing up in an email subject line, a plane carving across the sky outside the window. Each one small, ordinary, brutal.

When the door chimed again, I expected another customer. Instead, it was Elizabeth, cheeks flushed from the wind, her hair braided and messy. She waved and walked straight to me.

"I was hoping you'd be here," she said. "My mom needed a lamp, but I think I just needed a break."

"You picked the right store for both." I forced a smile. "How is she?"

"She's good. Baking too much. The freezer's full of lemon bars again."

"Dangerous."

We laughed softly, then the silence stretched.

Elizabeth traced the rim of a glass bowl on the counter. "He's been flying too much," she said. "Morocco, Iceland, back again. He talks less now. Like he's trying to outfly his own head."

I looked down at my hands. "He'll run out of sky eventually."

She sighed.

"He's not himself, Rose. I mean, he's never exactly been predictable, but lately it's worse. He barely talks. When he does, it's like his mind's somewhere else."

"Maybe it's just work."

"Maybe," she said, but she didn't sound convinced.

The door opened behind her and a couple walked in—hands intertwined, sunlight catching the gold band on the woman's finger. I watched them drift through the aisles, heads bent together over some trinket, laughter soft as breathing.

Elizabeth followed my gaze. "He misses you," she said quietly.

I looked away. "I wouldn't know."

She reached across the counter, squeezed my hand. "He's scared."

"Of what?"

"Of needing something he can't control."

Her words hit too close. I laughed under my breath, shaky. "Yeah. I know the feeling."

After she left, the store felt smaller. The ticking clocks seemed louder. I closed the laptop, packed my things, and told Marlene I'd finish the ad tomorrow. She didn't ask why. I think she saw it on my face.

Outside, the sky had dimmed to pewter. The air smelled like wet clay and new grass. Rain was coming. I walked the long way home through the square, past The Oasis with its patio lights already glowing, past Tolliver's where I'd once seen Charlie flipping through travel guides. Everything looked the same, and none of it felt the same.

A man bought flowers from a street cart and handed them to his wife, who looked at him like it was the first bouquet she'd ever been given. My throat tightened. I wasn't jealous, exactly. Just aware of the space inside me where something used to live. I was just beginning to understand the difference between being alone and being left.

At home, I tossed my keys on the counter and let the silence fill in. The heater clicked on. I turned on the kettle for tea and forgot to pour it. My phone buzzed.

> Abby: Checking in. Haven't heard from you. Are you okay?

I typed *Fine* and erased it.

> Me: Just busy with work.

> Abby: Call me when you can.

I didn't. I couldn't talk about nothing, and I wasn't ready to talk about him.

Another buzz.

> Mrs. Warren: Thinking of you, honey. Hope you're well.

My fingers hovered. I wanted to write, *I miss him*, but instead I typed, *You too* and hit send before I could regret it.

I carried my mug to the couch and stared out the window. The street lamps had come on, halos of gold in the mist. A car splashed through a puddle. Across the street, someone's curtains glowed with the flicker of a TV. Domestic noise. Ordinary life. The kind that used to bore me and now felt like salvation.

I thought about calling him. Just hearing his voice. But I knew how it would go—small talk, polite, his tone clipped around the edges like he didn't want to say too much. Then the ache would double, and I'd be back here again, staring at my reflection in the window.

So I whispered instead. "Please."

It wasn't for him to come back. It was just... please. Let this hurt mean something. Let it lead somewhere good.

The kettle clicked off behind me. I ignored it and went to the window, cracked it open an inch. The night air smelled like rain and honeysuckle. Somewhere a dog barked twice.

A low hum rolled overhead—a plane, faint but steady, a sound I'd know anywhere. My breath caught. I could picture the cabin lights, the hum of engines, his face half-lit by some glow thousands of feet above me.

I didn't look up. I didn't need to.

"Fly safe," I whispered.

The wind slipped through the opening, cool against my skin. For a moment, it felt like an answer.

The next morning dawned gold and gentle. I stood in my kitchen with the window open, coffee cooling in my hand, and realized I'd slept through the night for the first time in weeks. Not peace exactly—just exhaustion that finally gave in.

I worked from home that day, designing a flyer for The Maple Street Mercantile's Spring Soirée. Soft greens, watercolor florals, the words *New beginnings start here.* The irony made me laugh. Then I left it that way.

A dull headache pressed behind my eyes, the kind that came from too much pretending I was fine. I took a Tylenol and forgot about it.

By noon, the square outside had come alive. Music floated up —something bright and fast. I watched people come and go, weaving between tables and tents. For a second, I imagined walking down there, slipping into the crowd, pretending I belonged to that kind of easy joy.

Instead, I grabbed my jacket and headed for the lake. The walk took me past the bakery, the feed store, and the flower shop. Every face I passed seemed lighter than mine.

Emerald Ridge Lake shimmered under a pale sun. The water was still, the air heavy with the scent of pine and dirt. I sat on a bench and let the quiet stretch. The breeze lifted strands of my hair, brushing them across my cheek like a touch I almost recognized.

I thought about what Elizabeth said—*He's scared of needing something he can't control.*

Maybe I was too. Maybe that was why we found each other in the first place. Two people fluent in running, trying to learn the language of staying.

When I stood to leave, the first drops of rain began to fall— soft, steady, cleansing. I tilted my face up and let it hit, cool against warm skin. It didn't fix anything. But it reminded me I was still here.

That night, I wrote a note on a scrap of paper and tucked it in my journal: *Some love stories aren't lost. They're just waiting for better timing.*

I didn't know if I believed it yet. But it felt like something to hold.

CHAPTER 33
The Light at Grace Hill

The air over Grace Hill carried that early-April weight—half chill, half bloom. Lilies perfumed the courtyard, their scent drifting through Grace Hill's open doors. Inside, laughter ricocheted between the folding tables where Lydia, Elizabeth, and I worked beneath a row of paper crosses strung with twine. The fellowship hall smelled like coffee, wax, and spring trying its best.

I told them I was fine. Just a headache. Too much screen time, probably.

It wasn't a lie at first.

We'd been there since morning, setting up banners for the Easter market—Grace Hill's yearly attempt at both revival and bake sale. Lydia fussed with a microphone cord while Elizabeth knelt by the donation table, tying pastel ribbons around jars of jam.

At the other end of the hall, Mom directed volunteers with her usual mix of poise and thinly veiled panic. "No, Grant, that tablecloth is ivory, not white," she said, exasperated. "We don't mix tones."

Grant rolled his eyes, setting down a box of plastic cutlery. "Remind me again why I let you talk me into this?"

Mom swatted his arm, but he was already grinning.

It felt strange seeing him here in the flesh. I hadn't in almost a year. His sales job kept him pin-balling between cities, airports, and conference rooms—always another client dinner, another quarter to hit.

"Be grateful," Mom said, smoothing the corner of the tablecloth. "Your family finally gets you in the same zip code."

Grant shook his head with a soft laugh. "Honestly? I forgot what it felt like to slow down. To, I don't know—stack plastic forks in a church basement instead of fighting traffic on I-285 or giving a pitch at midnight." He glanced around at the bustle of volunteers, the cinnamon rolls cooling on wire racks, the spring sunlight spilling across the tile. "These little happy things... I didn't realize how much I missed them."

Something warm flickered in my chest. He looked tired, but lighter somehow—like being home let him breathe in a way nothing else did.

Granny swatted him with a dishtowel. "And because you love your old Granny. And because your father bribed you with barbecue. Don't pretend he didn't."

Dad stood by the window with a hammer, fixing a loose nail on the display board. He hadn't said much—he never did—but when he looked up, his eyes found mine with a quiet kind of pride. The same look he'd given me when I left for Buckhead and bought the condo.

It should've felt good, having them all here. But the sound of their voices seemed too far away.

Light from the stained-glass window fractured across the floor, turning everything into pieces of color. I watched it too long and the room wavered.

"Rose?" Elizabeth straightened. "You need water?"

"I'm good." I smiled, because that's what you do when your head feels full of thunder.

The laughter started again, and it echoed wrong—too bright. Mom called my name from across the room, but her voice bent, slurring at the edges.

When I bent to plug in the lights, the light from the windows doubled, then blurred. Sound thinned to a hum, like the drone inside a shell. I pressed a hand to the floor to steady myself, but the boards seemed to breathe. My pulse pounded in the base of my skull.

Just stand up, I told myself. Just breathe.

I made it halfway down the steps before the air left me. The sky blurred to white.

Elizabeth's voice chased me—"Rose?"—but it came from miles away. My knees went first, then my hands. The cup of lemonade slipped from my fingers and shattered the afternoon.

When I opened my eyes, the ceiling was a blank field of light.

Hospital light. Too bright, too still.

A low hum filled the room, steady and mechanical—the same sound that had swallowed the world when I fell. For a second, I couldn't tell if I'd woken up or drifted somewhere in between.

Machines ticked and hissed in steady conversation. Lydia sat curled in a chair by the window, her chin on her chest. Elizabeth paced with her phone to her ear, whispering fast. Mom was on the other side of the bed, perfectly still, hands folded like prayer. Dad stood behind her, one hand on her shoulder. Grant leaned against the wall, arms crossed, trying to look unaffected but failing completely.

I tried to speak, but the air caught in my throat.

A nurse appeared, soft-voiced, practiced. "You're in Tunbridge Regional, honey. You collapsed at the church. We've been watching you."

"What... happened?"

The doctor came in then, the kind of calm that only comes from bad news delivered too often.

"You have acute subdural hematoma," he said. "A slow bleed near the surface of your brain. Likely from your previous accident. Sometimes these stay quiet for months before pressure builds."

He paused, reading my face. "It's treatable. You'll need a minor procedure to drain the blood. The prognosis is good."

A slow bleed. Quiet for months. My body had been holding danger like a secret.

I nodded, because that's what you do when your world tilts but the walls don't move.

"It's the kind of thing that hides until it doesn't," he added.

That line found a place inside me and stayed.

Grant exhaled hard.

Mom gasped.

Dad stepped closer, resting a hand on my blanket. "You'll be okay," he said softly, certainty wrapped in gravel. "They know what they're doing."

Granny sniffled and patted my arm. "You gave us all a scare, sweetheart. Don't do that again."

Mom's voice was sharp again, the way it gets when she's scared. "You shouldn't have been lifting things. You should've told someone about those headaches."

"It wasn't that bad," I said.

She blinked hard, her voice catching. "It was."

They wheeled me through sterile corridors smelling of antiseptic and old air. I drifted in and out, the gurney wheels a lullaby of metal. Lydia's voice floated somewhere behind me, brave and breaking at once.

When the world came back, it came in fragments: the pulse monitor, the ache behind my eyes, the scent of disinfectant and lilies someone had smuggled in from the church.

Then—footsteps. Familiar.

Charlie.

He stood in the doorway like someone who hadn't yet decided if he was allowed inside. Wrinkled T-shirt, jeans, travel fatigue still on his skin. His eyes were rimmed red, like he hadn't blinked since hearing my name.

Lydia looked up, relief washing through her face. "She's awake," she whispered. Then, to me, "He came straight from Atlanta. I called him."

He stepped forward slowly, a man crossing a thin bridge. "You scared the hell out of me."

"You're not supposed to be here," I managed.

"Exactly why I am."

He sat, close enough that I could feel the heat of him, but not touching. My hand lay on the blanket between us, IV taped to the back. He stared at it like it was fragile glass.

"They said it was small," he said. "That you'll be fine."

"I will be." My voice rasped. "It just... hid too long."

His jaw tightened. "I know the feeling."

We stayed like that, silence layered with machines and breath. Finally he spoke again, voice lower.

"I was boarding for Lisbon when Elizabeth called. I didn't think. I just... turned around. Thirty years of reacting to alarms, and this was the first one that felt personal."

"You don't have to—"

"I do." His hands flexed, empty. "I kept moving my whole life because standing still felt like dying. But seeing you here—" He broke off, swallowed hard. "I realized leaving was the thing killing me."

The words hit something soft and bruised inside me. I wanted to believe him. I did.

But believing meant opening the door again, and I wasn't sure my body could take another fall.

"Charlie," I whispered, "you can't fix everything by showing up after."

"I know." His eyes flicked toward the monitor, then back to me. "I'm not here to fix it. I'm here because I finally understood what leaving costs. And I'm never doing it again."

Tears slid, silent. Not from pain. From the impossible weight of hearing what I'd needed all along. Something in my chest loosened, the way ice cracks when the sun finally finds it.

He reached out then, hesitating just long enough for me to nod. His fingers brushed mine—warm, careful, real.

"I don't know what happens next," he said. "But I'm done flying from the things that scare me."

I smiled, small and shaky. "You wouldn't lie to a woman with stitches in her skull, right?"

"Not one I hope keeps me around," he said.

He leaned closer, forehead resting gently against my hand. The monitor kept time for both of us.

Morning crept in through the blinds, thin and gold. Lydia and Elizabeth slept in the corner chairs, their heads tilted toward each other. Mom sat by the window now, staring out at the parking lot, phone in her lap, unread messages open. Dad stood beside her with coffee, quiet sentinel. Grant snored softly in a chair against the wall, his arm slung over his eyes. Granny's knitting lay folded neatly on her lap, one half-finished square of soft blue.

Two arrangements waited on the counter.

The first was a small bundle of deep red and blush peonies from Beloved Blossoms. Emerson had dropped them off that morning, saying they were her favorite. They were lush and layered. Beside them sat a mason jar of sunflowers Alice had left on the porch. Bright, open-faced, hopeful in that stubborn way sunflowers always are. Seeing them felt like a bridge between the woman I'd been before and the one still here.

Charlie sat exactly where he'd been all night, elbows on his knees, head bowed. His shadow stretched long across the tile. I reached out, slowly, and touched his shoulder.

He startled, then smiled. "Hey."

"Did you sleep?"

"Didn't need to."

"You should go home," I whispered. "Get some rest."

"I will," he said. "But I'm not leaving."

Something shifted in me at those words, quiet but unmistakable. A break in the fear. A break in the dark.

Maybe this was what the light at Grace Hill really was... not a beam through a window, but the moment something finally steadies after a long season of shaking.

The words were simple, unpolished, and absolutely true. The man who'd spent his life moving had finally stopped.

I looked past him to the window. Sunlight spilled across the wall, catching the silver hook of the IV pole until it glowed like a tiny cross. Outside, the church steeple gleamed wet against a sky the color of forgiveness.

For the first time in months, I let myself close my eyes—not out of surrender, but trust.

The light held.

And so did he.

CHAPTER 34
After the Falling

They wheeled me to the curb just after noon. Sunlight sat mild on the brick. My head felt cotton-soft around the edges. The discharge folder lay across my lap, fat with instructions that all said the same thing in different words. Go slow. Listen to your body. Call if the world tilts.

Charlie stood beside the chair, not behind it. Present without hovering. He thanked the nurse, took the folder, and crouched to my eye level.

"Ready?"

"As I'll be."

He helped me stand with one hand and buckled the belt with a care that made me smile inside.

The drive home was soft. Pine shadow. Two stoplights. Radio low. His hand found my knee at the first turn and rested there, warm and quiet. I watched sunlight flicker through the windshield and counted mailboxes to keep the small wave of nausea from winning. At the lake road he slowed without asking, as if the curve might be too much today.

"You good?" he asked.

"I'm good."

He didn't tell me I looked pale. He didn't tell me to sleep. He just kept the car moving like a promise.

At the loft, he killed the engine and studied the stairs. "We take them like a song. One line at a time."

I laughed once. "Are you listening to yourself now?"

"Apparently."

We climbed. One hand on the rail, one hand in his. He let me set the pace. At the landing I stopped and breathed. The air had that rain-after smell, wet stone and green. Somewhere a neighbor's wind chime offered three notes and quit.

Inside, the rooms felt like they had been waiting with their hands folded. He opened the curtains, then left them half-closed so the light stayed kind. He set a glass within reach. He didn't touch anything else. The respect in that did more for me than any speech.

"Couch or bed?" he asked.

"Couch," I said. "I don't want the bed yet."

He found the soft throw I liked and shook it loose. He tucked it over my knees with a touch that remembered the shape of my bones. His phone buzzed once. He didn't look.

"Work?" I asked.

He nodded. "I told them I needed personal days."

"How many?"

"As many as it takes."

The room went still around that. Not grand.

It shouldn't have felt like love, that sentence. But it did—the kind that doesn't arrive with fireworks, just a quiet weight that fills the room until you finally notice you can breathe again.

He moved to the kitchen and read the list on the discharge summary like it was a new language he planned to learn. No heavy lifting. No screens for long. Call if the headache spikes. Call if the world brightens wrong. He set his palm over the paper, then over the side of my head for a second as if to say I am learning both.

"Tea?" he asked.

"Half a cup."

He brought it in my favorite mug. With honey and a wedge of lemon. The first sip settled the nervous flutter in my chest. He sat in the chair opposite instead of the far end of the couch, his knees close enough that if I reached out I could hook my fingers into the denim and not let go.

"Mom and Granny are coming by later," I said. "With soup. And correction."

His mouth tilted. "I can handle correction."

"They were born for it."

"I know." He rubbed the seam of his jeans with his thumb. "Your mom texted me. She said not to let you out of my sight."

I smiled. "Wow, you exchanged numbers with my mom? That's serious."

A quiet hour followed. No TV. No phone. Just the clock and the low hum of Sunday traffic and the small sound I made when the headache tugged and then let go. He dozed once, head tipped back against the chair, jaw unguarded. He woke when I shifted and offered water without opening his eyes, like he had trained his hands to listen.

The knock came midafternoon.

Granny entered first like a weather system. Apron still on. Hair pinned like a crown. "You look like you did a hard day's work," she said, which was her version of sympathy. She put a cool hand to my cheek and then to my wrist, counting a beat as if she might disagree with the monitor I no longer wore. She approved of my pulse, my blanket, and the way the light hit the rug. She disapproved of my lack of socks and fixed it in ten seconds.

Mom followed with a Dutch oven that made the house smell like rosemary, chicken, and the promise of minutes that would pass. Her eyes were already wet before she spoke.

"You should have called me sooner," she said, then kissed my forehead the way she had when I was eight and had a fever. She turned to Charlie and surprised us both by hugging him. "Thank you for bringing her home."

He hugged back, gentle. "There was nowhere else to be."

Granny eyed him, assessing in the way of queens. "You look tired," she said.

"I'm good," he said, and returned to the chair by my knees. The choice didn't need a caption.

They stayed an hour that felt like three. Granny rearranged the items on my side table without asking and declared the arrangement better. Mom read each line of the discharge papers twice and had questions that nurses have heard for decades. She asked them anyway. Charlie answered the ones he could and wrote down what he could not.

When the soup had been ladled and the praise offered and the Tupperware labeled with painter's tape, the women I came from stood at the door with their bags and their orders.

"Call if the room spins," Mom said.

"Call if you need a stern talking-to," Granny said. "He can call, too."

"I will," he said, dead serious.

When they left, the loft exhaled. I sank deeper into the cushions. He covered my feet again and angled the pillow without making a thing of it.

"You know," I mused, "most men would have fled the second my grandmother told them to hydrate."

He grinned. "I didn't come from cowards."

"Where did you come from?"

He took a breath and looked at the window. "A kitchen table with half-finished homework. A mother who taught the girl, who I'd fall in love with one day, how to read. A house that didn't mind noise."

The headache pulsed again. I closed my eyes and waited for it to pass. It did. When I opened them he was watching me like people watch small animals they are trying not to scare. I reached over and found his hand. His thumb traced once along my knuckle, slow and unthinking. The smallest touch, but my pulse found it anyway.

"Stay tonight," I said. "The couch folds out, and I own more than one pillow. You can call the inn tomorrow."

"Okay," he said, like he had already decided and was grateful I had said it first.

Evening slipped in easy. The world outside dimmed to the gray color of a dove's back. He made toast and scrambled eggs and cut an apple with that small precision I had come to love. We ate on the couch because the table felt formal. He set the pills in my palm without looking at the clock. He had already placed the clock where he could see it if he needed to.

Later, Abby called to hear my voice. He handed me the phone and then found the end of the room where he could pretend not to listen while listening. When I said I felt brave and scared at the same time, his shoulders lowered a fraction like the line fit something he had been holding.

When the sky turned full dark, the town did what towns do. One car door. A dog. Footsteps on the stairs above and then silent. In the thin middle of that silence he opened the couch and shook out the second set of sheets like he had lived here all along.

"Do you want the lamp on?" he asked.

"Off," I said. "But leave the kitchen light. It feels like someone is awake."

He nodded. He changed in the bathroom with the door half-closed and the fan off so the sound wouldn't find my skull. He came back in a T-shirt and sweats that made him look like the kind of man who could fix a sink and read a map.

I slept in pieces. The body does that after hospitals. I woke to the sound of rain we had not asked for. I woke to the heat behind my eyes that had nothing to do with fever and everything to do with relief. Once I woke to the old dream of falling, the one that always ends a second before the ground. My breath spiked. The room shifted light to dark and back again.

He was in the chair beside me, not in the bed he had made. Awake. Profile quiet in the glow from the kitchen.

"Go back to sleep," he said, voice low. "I'm not going anywhere."

I let the words wash through and felt each one find a place. Not a performance. Not a promise flung into a night he didn't plan to keep. A simple line said by a man who had finally decided to learn a new way to live.

"Tell me something true," I murmured, eyes half-shut.

He was quiet long enough that I heard the rain choose a new rhythm. "I changed my next month," he said. "I asked for ground. I took it. Lisbon can miss me. Tokyo can find another seat. I want to see what staying looks like when it isn't an accident."

I turned my face to the back of the couch so he would not see the way that landed. "You'll hate it sometimes."

"I expect to."

"You'll love it sometimes."

"I already do."

The heater clicked. The loft held. Somewhere in the building a pipe sighed and went still. I drifted and woke and drifted again. Each time I surfaced, he was there in the chair. An outline I could trust. A pulse within me.

Just before dawn I felt the edge of sleep thin and knew I would slide through if someone told me the way. I lifted my hand, the one without tape, and found his wrist. He covered my fingers with his palm.

"Rest," he said.

I did.

Morning came not bright but honest. The window wore a pale wash. The headache had stepped back a pace. The air smelled like rain and coffee. He was at the stove with my kettle, barefoot, quiet, as if the floor asked for it. He glanced over, saw my eyes open, and smiled like the day had not started until I decided it had.

"Toast?" he asked.

"Please."

He brought me half a slice and a small glass of water, then sat where he had been all night.

"Today," he said, "we walk to the end of the hallway and back. Tomorrow, we'll make it to the porch. We can be ambitious on Wednesday and conquer the mailbox."

"Ambitious," I echoed.

"We do the things that build a life." He reached for my hand. "We practice them until they are the only way we know."

The after had arrived. Not bright. Not loud. Just steady. The shape of what comes next was still soft, but it was here, and it was ours to choose. I ate toast like it was an assignment I wanted to pass. He watched the window like it had news for him. The clock forgot to hurry. The kettle cooled. Somewhere in the square a delivery truck backed up and then stopped backing. The day went on.

He stayed.

CHAPTER 35
The Place We Landed

The drive out to the farmhouse felt different this time. The air had changed—the kind of late spring warmth that smells faintly of rain before it falls. The window was down, the wind threading through my hair. Charlie's hand rested on my thigh, his thumb tracing an idle pattern against the fabric. No rush. No airport waiting at the end. Just the long curve of road, the promise of quiet, and him beside me.

"You sure you're ready for this much excitement?" he teased as we turned off the main road.

"Define excitement," I said.

He smiled, the kind of smile that catches in your chest. "You'll see."

The house came into view the way light breaks through trees —sudden and sure. The white siding gleamed against the green. The porch swing moved in the breeze, and a row of potted herbs lined the steps—basil, thyme, lavender. The blue shutters looked freshly painted. The place looked like someone had started imagining a life here and decided to stay.

When we stepped out of the truck, the smell of lilac and cut grass folded around us. I stood for a second, just taking it in.

"I love it. Still looks like a postcard," I said again, softer this time.

He brushed a strand of hair behind my ear. "Not anymore. I live in something real."

Inside, the air held warmth, not silence. The red routes on the map above his desk had been replaced with something else—a photo of the two of us at the fall festival, my hair caught in the wind, his arm around me.

"You've been busy," I said.

"I wanted to get the place ready."

"For what?"

He smiled. "For staying."

He took my hand, led me through the kitchen to a back room I hadn't seen before. It smelled faintly of sawdust and new paint. Sunlight spilled across two desks pushed side by side, both neat but already a little lived-in. My notebook sat open on one. On the other—blueprints, a laptop, a half-empty mug.

"You made us an office?" I asked, half laughing, half crying.

He shrugged, eyes steady on mine. "You said you needed space to work. I figured we both did. The kind where we can hear each other typing."

I traced the edge of the desk. "You hate offices."

"I hate leaving you in them."

Something in me broke open. All the months of distance, the ache of waiting, the fear that love couldn't survive the empty spaces—it all gave way. I turned, and he was already watching me like I was the only thing in the room.

"I don't know what I did to deserve you," I whispered.

"You showed up," he said. "And then you stayed."

He kissed me then—soft at first, then deeper, a slow kind of hunger that carried gratitude with it. His hands found my face, my hair, my back, like he needed to memorize what he'd almost lost. I melted into him, every wall I'd built falling quiet.

When we finally broke apart, his forehead stayed against mine.

"You have no idea," he said, voice low, rough, "how long I've been in love with you."

I smiled against his lips. "I think I do."

He laughed, the sound quiet and raw, and reached into his pocket. "I have something for you."

The box was small, worn velvet. He handed it to me without ceremony. Inside, nestled against the lining, lay his silver pilot's wings. The same ones I'd seen pinned to his jacket.

"Charlie..."

"I told them I was done flying. I gave my notice last week. They offered ground duty, but I told them I'd already found it." He watched me carefully. "I thought about throwing these in the lake. Then I thought about what you'd say."

"What would I say?"

"Maybe they were worth keeping. To remember who I was. And who I chose to be instead."

I ran my thumb along the worn edge of the wings, feeling the groove where metal had softened from years of touch. "You're sure?"

"I've never been more sure of anything. You're the only horizon I'll ever need."

I laughed through tears. "You're lucky I'm too tired to top that line."

He grinned. "I've been saving it for months."

He closed the box and placed it on the desk between us. Then he took my hand and led me outside. The light was sliding into gold, soft and forgiving. The porch swing creaked as we sat. Across the yard, fireflies started flickering in the grass.

He leaned back, arm draped around my shoulders. I tucked my legs under me and rested my head against his chest. His heartbeat was slow, steady, the rhythm of a man who had stopped running.

"What are you thinking?" I asked.

"That I used to chase sunsets for a living," he said. "And now they come to me."

I turned toward him, brushing my lips against his jaw. "You're getting poetic in your old age."

"I've got a good muse."

He kissed me again, slower this time. The kind of kiss that says *this is home now*. The porch light hummed. The night deepened. Somewhere, a whippoorwill started calling, low and mournful, like it was singing for everything we'd survived.

"I love you," I said quietly.

He pressed his mouth to my temple. "I know. I'll spend the rest of my life earning it."

The crickets swelled. The sky dimmed to that bruised shade between blue and black. The farmhouse glowed behind us—light in every window, no shadows left.

He pulled me closer, whispering, "You make the world stop spinning."

I smiled, tracing a finger along his wrist. "Then let's keep it for awhile."

And we did.

The wind shifted through the trees, carrying the faint sound of water from the creek beyond the hill. I thought of all the places he'd seen, all the skies he'd left behind. And now here he was, barefoot on his own porch, loving me like it was the only flight that ever mattered.

For the first time, I didn't look up when a plane crossed the sky.

He didn't either.

We already knew where home was.

CHAPTER 36
May Fair

By late May, Tunbridge had turned into a watercolor. Time had done what it always does—it moved whether we noticed or not. But for once, I had been paying attention.

When I pushed open the door, I heard it before I saw him.

A low, unhurried strum.

A chord held long enough to feel like breath.

Then another—warmer, certain, familiar in the way only something meant for you can be.

Charlie was sitting on the porch steps, guitar balanced on his knee, fingers coaxing sound out of the strings like he was waking the morning itself. The sunrise caught the edge of his jaw, turning it to gold. He didn't turn when I stepped closer. He didn't need to.

"You're up early," he said softly. His voice carried the warmth of the guitar's last note.

"I heard you."

I tugged his T-shirt lower on my thigh, the cotton still warm from his skin.

"I always hear you."

He finally looked up then—and something in his eyes softened so deeply I had to steady a hand on the railing.

"I practiced a song for you," he said.

"For me?" I whispered.

"For whoever comes out wearing my shirt looking like that," he murmured, the corner of his mouth lifting.

Then he shifted the guitar, thumb brushing the strings once, twice—testing the rhythm the way he tested runways, feeling the wind, the lift, the space between.

And he began to play.

Not perfectly. But honestly.

Like each note had waited months for this exact morning.

When he started to sing, my heart folded in on itself so quietly I almost missed it.

It wasn't a trendy song.

He chose something older, timeless, something tender: "To Make You Feel My Love." The old Garth version.

The kind of song that sounds like a vow whispered into someone's collar.

His voice wasn't polished. But it was real. Raw. And achingly sincere.

The porch, the sunrise, the smell of pine—everything blurred.

I sank down onto the step beside him, knees brushing his.

He didn't stop playing. He leaned just slightly into me, like my presence filled in the last missing chord.

He reached the final verse, the one that always felt like a confession.

His voice grew quieter. More certain.

Something in me loosened and broke at the same time. Heat climbed behind my eyes before I could stop it. A tear slipped down, quick and traitorous, and I pressed the heel of my hand to my cheek like I could catch it before he noticed. My breath stuttered—one of those small, involuntary inhales you hope no one hears. I felt full and hollow in the same heartbeat, overwhelmed by the gentleness of it, the certainty, the way he sang like every word had been waiting for a place to land. My chest tightened, not with fear this time, but with something softer. More true.

When the last note drifted into the morning air, he set the guitar aside like it was something fragile.

"I love our life."

He took my hand, threading our fingers as if he'd been waiting years to do it.

I didn't have words—not ones big enough.

So I leaned in, touched my forehead to his, and whispered the truth that fit. "I love you."

His breath hitched; his hand tightened around mine.

The guitar lay silent beside us. The sun rose higher. The world warmed.

And for the first time, morning felt like something we had chosen together.

The air smelled like honeysuckle and fried dough, and the whole town had spilled out onto the square for the annual May Fair.

White tents lined Main Street, their edges fluttering against the bright sky. The lake sparkled just beyond the square, catching sunlight like laughter.

Charlie's hand found mine as we stepped through the gate. "You okay?"

"Better than okay." I smiled.

Dixie waved us over from behind the Rusty Skillet booth, her apron dusted with flour, her hair piled into its usual effortless knot. "If it isn't my favorite power couple!" she hollered. "Rose, grab a biscuit before they're gone. And you—" she pointed a wooden spoon at Charlie "—you look ten years younger now that you're not chasing planes."

He grinned. "Guess peace is good for my complexion."

Laughter rippled through the crowd. Ute breezed by in a cream linen dress and oversized sunglasses, balancing a tray of lavender iced teas like she was hosting a Hamptons brunch instead of a small-town fair. "Darling," she said, kissing my cheek. "Your campaign for Dixie's rebrand was brilliant."

"Thanks," I beamed. "Amazing what a few updates can do, right?"

"Thank heavens you came along, is all I have to say," Dixie called over her shoulder.

Near the stage, Emerson and Sam sat on a blanket with their little twins—sticky-fingered, sun-warmed, and happy. Alice knelt beside a row of potted wildflowers, teaching her twins, Lucy and Jack, how to braid stems into crowns while Johnny and Hutch manned the fire department's dunk tank, both already soaked and laughing.

"Best turnout I ever remember," Charlie said, taking it all in. "Feels different this time."

"It is," I said. "You're here."

Across the way, Granny stood near the raffle table with Arnold from Drucker's, a man with a hearing aid and a grin like summer. The band struck up a slow tune—"Georgia on My Mind"—and before I could blink, Arnold was leading her to the dance floor. She swatted his arm, laughing, but she didn't let go.

"Your Granny's got moves," Charlie murmured.

"She always did," I said. "She just needed the right dance partner."

Grant appeared then, hair windblown, lemonade in hand, looking half out of place in a town that refused to rush. Elizabeth was beside him, her smile easy, her tone teasing. "You know," she said, "Charlie used to think slowing down meant failing. Turns out it's the best thing he ever did."

Grant looked at her, half amused. "Are you suggesting something?"

"Maybe," she said, and took a sip of his lemonade.

Mom and Dad found us near the gazebo, Mom's arm linked through his. "Your marketing firm's making waves," Dad said, voice steady with pride. "Saw that article in the Tunbridge Journal. Said you helped half the square refresh their businesses."

"She's modest about it," Charlie added. "But I've watched her work. She gives this town its heartbeat."

I felt my throat tighten. "I just helped it see what was already here."

By dusk, the fair sparkled in strings of light. Fireflies drifted above the grass, and music spilled from the bandstand. The crowd thinned to the familiar—the people who'd always belonged, whether they knew it or not.

Charlie pulled me toward the lake path, away from the noise. The water glowed pink and gold, the air warm against our skin.

"Do you realize," I said, "everyone is here? My family, your family, half the town."

He smiled. "And none of them tried to talk me back into flying."

"They wouldn't dare."

He brushed his thumb along my jaw. "They like you," he said.

"They *love* you," I corrected.

I leaned in just enough for his breath to find mine. It wasn't a kiss made for fireworks—just the kind you keep replaying in your mind later, when the world is still.

After we enjoyed the view for a little while, we walked back to see Granny and Arnold dancing again, slow and easy. Emerson and Sam packed up the kids, waving goodbye. Alice handed me a lipstick red carnation from her stall, bright and golden, its stem wrapped in twine. Johnny tipped his head at us.

Charlie tucked the flower behind my ear. "Looks right at home."

The music was soft, echoing across the lake. As the fair wound down, the air still hummed with the warmth of a day that had gone exactly right.

Charlie leaned close. "Ready to head home?"

"Yeah," I said, slipping my hand into his. "Let's go watch the sunset from the porch."

We walked toward the truck under the last of the fair lights, the night humming around us like something alive. Somewhere behind us, the music faded.

We drove home with the windows cracked and the scent of honeysuckle trailing behind us.

The farmhouse waited on the hill, porch light glowing like it knew our names.

When he laced his fingers through mine again, it wasn't a promise.

It was the proof.

For the first time, love wasn't a leap.

It was the landing.

Epilogue

I didn't know where we were going.
    Only that Charlie woke me before dawn with a quiet smile, touched my shoulder as if waking me were an act of reverence, and said, "Pack for two weeks. Pack something warm. And something beautiful. We can buy the rest."

There was no fear in me anymore when he said things like that. Just a steady pull in my chest, the kind that told me I was stepping toward something that had been waiting for us long before we knew how to name it.

We flew to Lisbon first.

But this time, he didn't walk through the airport with the posture of someone half-living in another world. He wasn't scanning departure boards, or calculating wind speeds, or listening for engine notes the way pilots often do long after they've stepped off the flight deck.

He held my hand.

He laughed when turbulence nudged the plane, not because he was used to it—he always was—but because I squeezed his fingers a little too hard.

"You're safe," he murmured. "You're with me."

The words weren't reassurance.

They were devotion.

Lisbon greeted us with sunlight brushing the city awake. Terracotta roofs glowing. Laundry dancing from iron balconies. A thousand windows catching morning like pieces of glass. He brought me to a miradouro overlooking the river, the same place he had once described to me in soft, almost embarrassed tones—the first place he ever felt the world open.

"I used to come here alone," he said, his voice low, thoughtful. "I would watch the ships and imagine the lives inside every window."

"And now?" I whispered.

"Now I look at you," he said. "And the world feels... answered."

We wandered the old hills, climbing streets that curled like ribbon. Tram bells chimed from below. The air smelled of espresso and oranges. At a small café tucked between two alleys, he ordered pastries in perfect Portuguese, then brushed sugar from my lip with the gentlest touch.

We danced that night in a tiny tavern made of stone and candlelight, where Fado singers poured their souls into the room. Charlie held me as though the music had been written solely to bring us here. When the final note faded, neither of us spoke. Some moments ask for silence.

From Lisbon, he took me to Paris.

Not with fanfare. Not with grand announcements.

He simply said, "You should see the city that taught the world how to love."

Paris glowed in a soft, pearled rain. We crossed bridges that held centuries of promises, walked narrow streets where the cobblestones were polished by a thousand romances before ours, and shared a crepe beneath an umbrella that kept slipping to one side. He laughed when I scolded him for letting the rain hit my shoulders. I laughed when he admitted he liked me better in the rain.

At Montmartre, wind tangled my hair as we looked out across

the rooftops. He stood behind me, arms around my waist, his breath warm against my jaw.

"Rose," he murmured, "there are a hundred cities I have loved. But nothing has ever felt like this."

I knew what he meant.

The city was beautiful.

But the way he looked at me made it unforgettable.

From Paris, he carried me north.

To Edinburgh.

The city rose like something carved from storybooks—old stone, ancient spires, a sky that moved in wild, beautiful moods. He brought me to a tiny shop of rare books where dust smelled like honey and time. He lifted a first edition from the shelf as though it held the world, and said, "You should have things that last."

We climbed the Royal Mile hand in hand, stopping often because he couldn't help reading every historical plaque and I couldn't help watching the way he spoke—quiet, certain, as though knowledge was a kind of tenderness.

At night, we sat in a small pub with low beams and a fire that crackled like laughter. Rain streaked the windows, softening the edges of the world. He watched me as though memorizing the moment, storing it somewhere permanent.

And on our last evening, he woke me before sunrise.

"We're going," he whispered.

"Where?"

"You'll see."

He guided me up Calton Hill, the city still sleeping below us. Dawn gathered slowly, brushing the sky in colors that looked painted by hand. The wind was sharp enough to sting, but he wrapped his jacket around my shoulders, hands lingering on my arms.

Then he pulled a folded map from his coat pocket.

The paper was soft from years of travel.

Dozens of circles dotted its edges—Tokyo, Barcelona, Dubai, Montreal, cities I'd only heard about in his stories.

"These," he said quietly, "are all the places I ran to."

He unfolded a second map.

Blank.

Except for one circle.

Tunbridge.

Something inside me trembled.

"Every time I left," he said, voice unsteady, "I thought I was chasing freedom. But the truth was simpler. I was afraid of landing anywhere that could break my heart."

The wind caught at the edges of the map, snapping it softly like a heartbeat.

"Then you happened," he whispered. "And I realized the thing I was running from was the life I wanted most."

His hands shook once—only once—before he reached into his pocket and pulled out a small velvet box.

He didn't kneel.

He stepped closer.

Held my face in both hands.

And kissed me gently, like the question had already been answered.

Then he opened the box.

Not quickly.

Not dramatically.

But with the reverence of someone offering a vow.

Inside lay a simple, elegant ring—gold brushed to a soft glow. Something timeless. Something meant to be worn.

"You are the only place," he said, "where the sky finally feels like home."

My breath broke. Tears blurred the horizon.

"Rose," he whispered, touching his forehead to mine, "will you marry me? Will you build a life with me where I land because I choose to, not because the world forces me down? Will you be the person I come home to for the rest of my days?"

The sunrise crested behind him, setting the whole city shimmering.

"Yes," I breathed. "Yes."

He exhaled like a man freed from gravity. He slid the ring onto my finger, kissed my hand, my cheek, my mouth, each touch saying *thank you* in a language older than words.

We stood together as Edinburgh woke, the light spilling across the hills, the city blooming beneath us.

And for the first time in his life—

he wasn't looking toward the sky.

He was looking at me.

Together, we walked down the hill, the map fluttering between us—the old life behind him, the new one bright and waiting.

And as we stepped into the morning, his hand in mine, I understood something with a clarity that felt like breath after a storm:

Some love stories don't change who you are.

They bring you home.

The End

Continue the Tunbridge Series

Want more Tunbridge right now?
Start *Until You Found Us.*

Until You Found Us

Jack punched a kid.

Not hard enough to break skin or get expelled, but enough for his teacher to call me, her voice tight and hesitant, unsure how to explain the words she didn't want to repeat.

"Another boy said... something. About his father."

I didn't need details. I could already see my son's small fists curling in defense of a man he had never met—a man who walked out the moment I told him I was pregnant.

I told her I'd talk to him. My voice was even. Practiced. The kind of calm you learn when you have no one to fall apart with.

The ache settled behind my ribs the moment the house went quiet—after the rush of breakfast, the hunt for socks, the chase to school drop-off—and stayed until bedtime, when I finally exhaled and let it wrap around me like an old, familiar coat.

I was in my shop, staring at a half-made bouquet that wouldn't arrange itself. The marigolds were wilted. The sunflowers drooped, heads bowed like they knew something I didn't.

I wanted to cry, but didn't.

Jack was six. So was Lucy. All softness and storm, still learning what to do with big feelings. And that day, Jack used his hands instead of words.

I told him that wasn't okay, then held him until the shaking stopped.

"I just didn't like what he said, Mama," he whispered into my shirt.

"I know, Bug." I kissed the crown of his head. "But we don't fight with our hands. We fight with truth. And you already know yours."

But did I?

Some days I felt strong. Other days I felt like I was holding up an entire world with arms never built to carry that much.

The bell jingled at the front of the store. My heart tightened, but it was just Mrs. Gibbs from church. She wanted three centerpieces for the ladies' luncheon, all in fall colors.

"Nothing too sad," she said, eyeing the drooping sunflowers.

I nodded, forcing a smile.

When she left, I sank onto the stool behind the counter, tea gone cold beside me. It was October, but Georgia hadn't gotten the memo. The air was thick and humid, clinging to everything like regret.

In two hours, I'd pick up the twins and pretend I wasn't worn thin. I'd make dinner, read *Goodnight Moon* for the thousandth time, and tuck them in with the same prayer I whispered every night.

"Let them feel loved. Let me be enough."

I believed He was listening. Even when I didn't feel it. So I said it anyway. Every night. Because love like that doesn't go unnoticed.

The bell above the door jangled again. Probably the newspaper delivery kid.

I didn't move.

If it had been another customer, I would have smiled. I would have helped. I would have strung together soft words and floral filler like always. But for one more minute, I stayed still.

Because when I moved, I had to pretend everything was fine again.

There was a half-eaten granola bar in my purse. The kind Lucy liked with the yogurt coating that melted into sticky fingerprints. I pulled it out and nibbled the edge, thinking about the centerpieces I still needed to finish and the bills I hadn't paid.

My thumb traced the worn edge of a photo in my wallet—Jack and Lucy, frosting-covered, grinning with gap-toothed pride on their fourth birthday. Just the three of us. A store-bought cake, a few balloons from the dollar store, and the world's loudest bubble machine I later regretted buying.

But they were happy.

And I held it together.

"Mama, look at my teeth!" Lucy squealed, shoving cake in her mouth.

"Beautiful, Lulu."

It was a good day. But even the good ones were laced with a thread of missing. Of what-ifs. I never wanted perfect. I just wanted someone in the trench with me. Someone to high-five at bedtime when all five books were read and both kids were asleep. Someone who would have looked at me and said, *You did good today.*

I twisted the Always Ring on my thumb. Not from a marriage —just a promise I made to myself, eight months pregnant and panicking, desperate for something solid. I'd found it at a pawn shop. A plain band no one else would have looked twice at.

But to me, it meant: keep going.

I wore it when I needed to remember I still belonged to something.

The bell rang again, followed by a voice I knew.

"Alice?"

I blinked, then stood. It was Emily—my younger sister. Twenty-seven and already ten steps ahead of where I'd been at that age. No kids. No dead-end relationship. A corporate job she pretended to love, and a boyfriend with a five-year plan.

"Hey," I said.

"You okay?" Her eyes scanned me. She'd always been reading too much.

"Yeah. Just tired."

She raised an eyebrow. "Jack's teacher told me."

I froze. "You talked to Jack's teacher?"

"Well, she didn't actually tell me. She's friends with Maryanne, who's friends with Tiff, whose kid is in Jack's class."

Of course.

Small towns had been efficient like that.

Emily's expression had softened. "You're doing your best. He's a good kid."

I had nodded, swallowing the lump in my throat. "He just... he's already getting labeled. And he doesn't even know why."

"You can't control what people say."

"No, but I wish I could protect him from hearing it."

Emily had sat on the counter like she had in high school, kicking one heel softly against the cabinets. "You ever think about telling them?"

"About him?"

"Yeah."

"I don't even know what I'd say."

Emily had been quiet. Then she had said the thing I hated admitting. "Maybe they don't need a story. Maybe they just need a dad."

I didn't respond.

Because she wasn't wrong.

After she left, I finished two of the centerpieces and started the third, losing myself in the rhythm of stem-snipping and color pairing. Maroon chrysanthemums, deep orange lilies, accents of silver dollar eucalyptus. I forgot my exhaustion for a minute. Flowers didn't lie. They were quiet, honest things. They just bloomed and faded on their own time.

I checked the clock again. Pickup was soon.

I locked the shop and got in the car, buckling the empty back seats before I remembered I was alone. I did that sometimes. Out of habit. Out of hope.

The school was a ten-minute drive. I pulled into the car line just as the kids spilled out in their haphazard row of backpacks and jelly-stained shirts.

Lucy saw me first. She waved like I had been gone for days. Jack was more reserved, walking slowly, his face serious.

He climbed in, silent.

"Hey, Bug," I said gently.

"Hi."

Lucy chattered the whole way home about leaf rubbings and story time and how she wanted to be a pumpkin for Halloween but a fairy at the same time.

When we pulled into the driveway, Jack lingered in his seat.

"Jack?" I said.

He looked up. "I don't care what that boy said. I'm not sad about not having a dad. I have you."

The ache behind my ribs bloomed, sharp and beautiful.

"I'm not sad either," I whispered.

But it wasn't true.

Some nights, I still dreamed of someone knocking on the door. Someone who hadn't left. Someone who knelt down and said, "I'm here now. Let me carry some of this."

But Jack was watching me, and I didn't say it out loud. Because what I had was real. Messy. Half-broken. But real.

And then the doorbell rang.

I wasn't expecting anyone.

CONTINUE READING *UNTIL YOU FOUND US*
ON AMAZON

Thank You

Thank you for spending time with Rose and Charlie.

If this story touched you, I would be so grateful for a quick review on Amazon and Goodreads. Even a few words makes an enormous difference.

Thank you—I truly appreciate you.

Elle

About the Author

ELLE CHRISTOPHER writes emotional, character-driven small-town romances set in the heart of Georgia. Her stories blend deep intimacy, Southern charm, and the kind of love that feels both tender and real. She lives outside Atlanta with her five children, a few opinionated cats, and far too many antique books. When she's not writing, she's drinking iced tea, hunting for vintage hardcovers, or dreaming up the next love story in Tunbridge.

Elle would love to connect with you.

- Instagram: @elle_christopher
- Join her Facebook Reader Group: EllesFrontPorch

You can find all of these links, subscribe to Elle's newsletter, get signed editions, and much more at www.ellechristopher.com.

Discussion Questions

1. Rose measures success by achievement when the story begins. How does her definition of success change by the end of the novel?

2. Charlie lives a life shaped by movement and distance. What do you think he's really running from, and when do you first see him begin to slow down?

3. The accident becomes a turning point for Rose. Do you think she would have returned to Tunbridge without it? Why or why not?

4. How does the small-town setting of Tunbridge influence Rose and Charlie's relationship in ways a city never could?

5. Both Rose and Charlie struggle with vulnerability in different ways. Whose journey felt more difficult to you, and why?

6. The story explores the tension between ambition and belonging. Where do you see that tension most clearly in Rose's choices?

7. Faith and grace are quiet threads in this novel rather than overt themes. Where did you notice grace at work in the story?

8. Charlie fears being anchored to one place, while Rose fears

losing herself again. How do these opposing fears shape their connection?

9. The title *The Light at Grace Hill* carries symbolic weight. What does "light" represent for Rose? For Charlie?

10. By the end of the novel, both characters choose a different kind of life than they once imagined. Did their ending feel earned to you? Why or why not?

Acknowledgements

To my greatest blessings in life, the five lights of my world. You are the reason I keep creating, keep trying, and keep believing there is more beauty ahead. You are the wind beneath all of this. Your laughter, your strength, and your fierce belief in me are the heartbeat behind every page. Everything I build, every story I release into the world, carries a piece of you. Thank you for giving me purpose, courage, and a love that keeps me reaching for more.

To my mom, thank you for the quiet ways you've supported this dream.

To Sophie, my impeccable editor. You didn't just refine this manuscript. You expanded it. Deepened it. Challenged me to risk more on the page and in myself. You strengthened the spine of this story in ways most readers will never see but will absolutely feel. Working with you is one of the greatest honors of my writing life. Thank you for believing in this book, and in the writer behind it.

To Michele, thank you will never feel big enough. You walked through every chapter with me, more than once, catching what I missed and loving these characters with a depth that humbled me. Your devotion to this story is a gift I will carry forever.

To Ragini, whose insight and intuition helped this story find its pulse. Thank you for reading with such care and sharing your wisdom and insights.

To my beloved early readers—Jen, Heidi, Katey, Michelle, Noelle, Ashley, and Kelsey—thank you for giving your hearts, perspective, and your time so generously. I am so grateful to have you on this you on this journey with me.

To all of the wonderful women who show up for me day after day—the ones who cheer, message, encourage, and remind me why I write in the first place. You are the quiet force behind my books. Thank you for cheering loudly, loving generously, and reminding me that the heart of this work is connection.

And to every reader who touches these pages. Thank you for letting my words into your world. You make all of this possible.

Made in the USA
Coppell, TX
13 February 2026

72022863R00204